SAVAGE
1986–2011

Other books by Nathaniel G. Moore

Bowlbrawl (Conundrum Press)
Pastels Are Pretty Much the Polar Opposite of Chalk (DC Books)
Let's Pretend We Never Met (Pedlar Press)
Wrong Bar (Tightrope Books)

NATHANIEL G. MOORE

SAVAGE

———

1986-2011

Anvil Press | 2013

Anvil Press gratefully acknowledges the support of the Government of Canada through the Canada Book Fund, the Canada Council for the Arts, and the Province of British Columbia through the British Columbia Arts Council.

Library and Archives Canada Cataloguing in Publication

Moore, Nathaniel G., author

Savage, 1986-2011 / Nathaniel G. Moore.

ISBN 978-1-927380-55-0 (pbk.)

I. Title.

PS8626.O595S29 2013   C813'.6   C2013-904801-4

Cover design by Derek von Essen
Illustrations by Andrea Bennett
Inside cover illustration by Vicki Nerino
Interior design by HeimatHouse
Author photo by Derek Wuenschirs

Anvil Press Publishers
P.O. Box 3008, Main Post Office
Vancouver, B.C. Canada
V6B 3X5
www.anvilpress.com

Printed and bound in Canada

Suffering is one very long moment. We cannot divide it by seasons. We can only record its moods, and chronicle their return. With us time itself does not progress. It revolves. It seems to circle round one centre of pain.

— Oscar Wilde, *De Profundis*

Against this obsession with the real we have created a gigantic apparatus of simulation which allows us to pass to the act "in vitro" (this is true even of procreation). We prefer the exile of the virtual, of which television is the universal mirror, to the catastrophe of the real.

— Jean Baudrillard, *The Gulf War Did Not Take Place*

Randy Savage thinks he represents the light of righteousness. But you know, it takes an awful lot of light to illuminate a dark kingdom.

— Jake "The Snake" Roberts, *WWF Magazine*

Dedicated to

Benji Hayward (1973–1988)
Corey Haim (1971–2010)
and
Spencer Gordon (1984–Present)

Table of Contents

Prologue

You Know You're Right

December 2012

I am hours past a sleep I don't recall finishing—but entered regardless—when, in my queen-sized bed, I tried for a minute to just *relax* and *calm down* and *get on with my life* and other family-crest slogans, when I realized it wouldn't have mattered what year it was of the many I examined (in total, twenty-five: 1986–2011)—and so, I came to the simple conclusion that millions of people have had twenty-five years of family matters to recall at one all-consuming sitting: a big uneatable meal. We all have the ability; nothing unique in forming an interior focus group, now, is there?

Jukebox-fresh, my gut flush to the bar, I vie for the attention of Nancy, her eyes behind her post-ironic Buddy Holly glasses. My drink is empty. I begin to unravel at what I had attempted to understand, to escape from and exorcise, as if writing a lyric redo for the underlying bass and synth beat of a New Order art-house techno gem. *Enjoy each childlike day, of your after-family progress, these slogans of sacrifice, and thank you for the lonely default settings, the banana bread, I was truly being the person I am, pass me another time-bomb can: Family Soda is the one!*

The vodka crested with cranberry undulates; here we are, oh-so-much older, moments anew. I hear the slow-mo citrus and sprinkler sound of an antique family-oriented sitcom theme and its diametric use of rhyme, poetry, perspective, lamenting cliché and the seeds of depression. I down my red drink. My maudlin wasp nest of a brain just gets more Kurt Cobain and River Phoenix from here.

Maybe I was once this innocent child, painting in the kitchen with one of dad's dress shirts on backwards (Mom called it my smock), and she was this incredulous blob of black psychiatric paint— *invasion of the present-tense psyche*—Oh, hey there. Your new girlfriend says you are the best in the world, and you feel the same way. You guys have been babing, babing it up, right? But she has a thing for good-looking people, historically right? (The flashback forecast is a threat of midnight zippers and inaugural orgasms you are not responsible for... always a possibility if you let down your psychic guard. *Player One Up* and *flashing*.)

Nancy's back is to me. I can put the dimmer switch on our banter and concentrate on taming my theatrical unstitching; my ritualistic preoccupation with pain and chaos. *Are you just aren't you just the sweetest most inappropriate maniac and you beat your imaginary wife with ice cream and cake then sniff her sugary limbs all the while getting a big toothache.* Beauty, duty and romance.

"This is a bar not a mental institution," Nancy says, when I make some inference to bleach in a drink she's making.

The Nirvana song I chose comes on, and its Native tribal guitar tears into the bar, soon to be joined by Kurt's ragged, poisonous voice. The small puddle from an ice cube I scooped out of my drink lies awaiting a tap from my finger, the one I broke in gym class playing football in June of 1987.

Here we are among the leather or ether clad, non-entities, our lives on mute, the perennial unemployed as we hear a toothless man's voice, like the derelict from a dystopian time-travelling science fiction film:

"Hey, Nate! It's in the teeth—that's the way they find you, what's that, Nate? What year did you say you think you're in here? *2012?* They don't always send you to the right year, Nate, you see. I'm in the next bar, next door see? *Hurricaines* it's called *right, Nate?* Named after the boxer, isn't that right, Nate? But I tricked them, Nate, I took my teeth out, so they can't find me! I know about you, Nate... *I know your whole story, bud.* Say, did you know something? Section 225.11 of the New York State Athletic Commission clearly states that they don't like any "striking, scratching, gouging, butting or unnecessarily punitive strangleholds," eh, Nate? The commission is there to protect athletes. Too bad they didn't live across the street from you. Could've come and wiped your ass every time you didn't eat your meatloaf or clean your room."

Despite all the investigation, there is still much unrest in the family. *May as well try and enjoy the time we still have on earth.* Well, I feel so much sometimes I guess I just get a bit clouded, a bit off-colour. You know that colour? A trout in a blender or that big dumb fat sparrow hoping around on its twig legs that a part of you wants to crush, and it's plump and juicy, and you want it to dance alive in your semi-closed mouth, then set it free.

Our house (161 Glenvale Boulevard) in north Leaside was built in 1960, and our family of four moved in one crisp weekend in March 1981. During the first week, select relatives visited and photographs were taken of Holly and me discovering the "secret" wood-panel door in the basement beside what would be my eventual bedroom (1985–1994) which led to a small pantry, bunker or bomb shelter under the stairs. The tiny passageway connected to the workshop.

Each and every Sunday we all agreed the roast beef was beautiful; its heart-red and pink cross-section caused Dad to make sex noises in between throat clears. "Oh Diane, orgasm," Dad would groan, rubbing his grey or brown sweater, overacting the pleasure of each sloppy bite with his prop tongue.

The story is disconcerting. It deals with time, madness and a perception of what a family is or isn't. It is a study of desire, of memory, death and re-birth, set in a world coming apart.

Look, I tried the whole straightforward "here is the scene where we were stealing porn, *Variations*, fall of 1988, this is my life" routine... you want to listen to *Savage 1887-1903, Vol. 7*, you got it: it's coming! Jesus is putting on some Band-Aids and making the popcorn.

Excusing myself to Nancy and the bar, I stand up, shaking a fake reporter with my hands. "You're either gonna kill this animal or your gonna cut off its food supply!"

PART I:

SUBSTANCE

(1986–1989)

There will always be a Leaside
With four-way traffic signs
Where sports and scholarships and grit
And youth and age combine

—*True Davidson, first Mayor of East York (1967–1971)*

1)

Bizarre Love Triangle

July 1986

The city was full of glamorously tanned kids on bikes, in hyper-coloured bathing suits, on skateboards, who were having their hair cut, who sweated while mowing the lawn, who fell silent and glazed at the crude video arcades at Bayview and Millwood.

To my left I noticed my shadow with its jagged facsimile, an angular swatch of bony grey that straddled the dilapidated cement.

I waited for the green light before pushing my bike hard off the curb with one big thrust, now fully able to enjoy the breeze, tailing my taller, older sister, Holly, and her best friend, Elizabeth. Holly said sometimes people called her "lanky."

Holly had a birthmark freckle thing over the left side of her upper lip and a windy pile of brown hair that hung down into her eyes, while I had a Playmobil haircut of sitcom quality, parted to the left. Elizabeth was a semi-freckled blonde with blue-green eyes and a hyperactive personality who would occasionally sunbathe and prance, fawn-like in backyards; her legs were long, taut and seasonal.

That summer, Holly got her learner's permit, six months shy of her sixteenth birthday. We sat in the car, driving it up and down in the driveway and once we took the two-tone Oldsmobile tank around the block. Sitting in the car, I watched the keys go from her frayed jean-shorts' pocket to the ignition like she was opening the door to our own private apartment.

The sun had pushed the day into a netherworld of speed, sweat and cool air. The day was a wide, brilliant green and a large, tireless orange; it swelled in crisp miracles.

Taking a left when we got to Bayview and Broadway, we flickered past a hefty waft of hot garbage towards the top of our street, Glenvale Boulevard. "Yee-haw!" I cackled, still pool fresh in my semi-soaked navy blue Ralph Lauren golf shirt, which clung to my sissy torso. We stared across at the great supernova of sun that crested the long stretch of cemetery. I mistook the curb's size and ended up wiping out, right in front of the girls.

"Don't worry; they don't break at that age," Holly joked to Elizabeth. "Come on, Nate, get up, you wimp!"

I sprang up off my hands, dusted off and remounted, ready to continue our Kodak descent, when Holly circled around and stopped me with her front tire.

"Hey," Holly said, nudging her head towards 6 Glenvale, "isn't that where your girlfriend lives? Kerri?"

"That was when I was in grade one, like six million years ago."

"Grade eight Kerri!" Holly laughed. "That's what Nate called her!"

"Oh her!" Elizabeth said. "Blonde with the gel in her hair, tons of eye make-up like a raccoon. I remember her. My mom is friends with her mom."

"Yeah, Nate loved her. He'd walk up the street for blocks behind her after school. I'd always see him tailing her up Broadway."

"She's probably married now," Elizabeth said, rolling her pedal back, balancing on the sidewalk. "Darn, I think I got a sunburn," she rubbed her shoulder and caught my eye on her.

"She'd be about nineteen now," Holly said, blowing her long hair from her face; taking me away from Elizabeth's sunburn. Arms stretched out to the heavens, Holly balanced her bicycle with no hands. She just pivoted the frame with her hips, keeping it steady.

"Now he likes Danielle, a girl in his French Immersion class," Holly said.

"Do not."

Holly began to turn her bike in the direction of our house, then added, "You kept a note from her. You said you smelled it!" We pumped our pedals and breezed down Glenvale; the cicadas harmonized, and the sun, half-asleep now with a threat of rain somewhere beyond the house tops, made the sky wobble in and out of all-blue to tones of white and silver.

*

The three of us had spent the last two hours in salvation at the pool near Yonge and Eglinton. The wet splashing frenzy was still visceral and glistening and clung to my senses.

"Come on, Nate!" Elizabeth said, with a succession of splashing gestures, her one-piece slick black suit shining bright in the sun. I remember pacing myself, my heart racing, taking a scan of the pool, my eyes like a fin across the chlorinated ocean, its wet blue skin hovering over two tranquil black stripes which stretched from the shallow to the deep end. I was fastened to the deck, which was giving off the smell of oiled skin, the sun heating my bare feet starting at the toenail.

"Come on, get in the water. We're bored in here!"

I stood up, felt dizzy and dramatically flopped into the pool's deep end. Heckles from the lifeguards ensued.

"Let's see who can hold their breath the longest!" Holly said.

"OK," I said. "I am undefeated in these parts."

Elizabeth's teeth, her lips parting, water going in and out.

"OK, ready?" she said, mouth burbling in the water.

"One."

. "Two."

"Three."

At thirty-three seconds, Elizabeth and Holly surfaced. Thirty-four, thirty-five, thirty-six. I adjusted my position underwater as the girls attempted to distract me with tickles to throw me off my game or something. I was fighting off a boner. Gone was the wash of cricket noises from the telephone wires. Fifty-nine, one minute, one-oh-one, one-oh-two...

I broke through the water at the one-oh-seven mark. The overcast clouds tightened in the sky. A big fat horsefly circled our little wet camp. My tight grey swim trunks with single blue and yellow stripes seemed invisible. Hands fell over my eyes from behind: Elizabeth's hot breath on my neck, a kiss on the cheek.

Elizabeth spewed a spurt of used pool water on Holly's head.

*

I was half a block behind the girls now, all of us edging towards Hanna Road, when I noticed that the sunlight gave the lower numbered houses a different sheen, and I couldn't fathom how my house was on this same street—how somehow, up here, in the early numbers, life looked completely different.

The sun was a deep orange, filmed in 8 millimetre, played back without sound. I was breathing in slow motion, feeling my lungs burning, my hair now a bit crunchy, in my mouth a faded piece of gumball lodged in my molar, my tongue playing with it. Soon we'd be back to sucking on the homemade popsicles that were on heavy rotation, watching a movie, eating crackers and cheese and dill pickles and maybe we'd order a pizza. We had left the little leeches of leathery Kraft Dinner noodles stuck to the pot from lunch.

The idyllic thought of a tall glass of ice water suddenly flatlined as a chorus of honks interrupted the speedy finish home. A dented grey pickup truck slowed down as we came to Sutherland Avenue's stop sign.

"Well, well, well!" a thick voice said, plucking along with a slow mischievous groan-and-laugh combo. The truck honked twice.

"Lame," Holly muttered, looking at me. "Get lost, Jake."

Jake Cavers, nineteen, red-eyed and bleached blond and freckled, kept catcalling. My stomach knotted up. I looked up and down my street, imagining the infinite statistics attributed to my interactions on this stretch of pavement: the number of times, for example, that I tore my paper-route collection tabs prematurely. Eighteen times? Forty-three? Fifty-two?

Now Jake had a truck. Last summer he was still chasing me bike to bike, trying to kick my legs as I pedalled faster. Andrew had told me that his cousins were close with Jake, and he was totally crazy. I didn't dare say his name. I wanted to bike home fast to our white house that sat like a lone aspirin in a hot stomach.

I stared haplessly into the truck, which had two giant viper decals along the hood. To me, Jake had huge pale arms with bulky biceps, a thick neck, red eyes to match his hair, yellow teeth with a bloody tongue and knuckles full of scabs from constantly pounding on people. From all the speed biking and windy tears, I had no sense of what he even looked like up close; just his horror of a voice yelling, "You're dead, kid!"

I looked to the ground; my heart was beating fast like a crazed clock. The plastic bag with my wet bathing suit inside was wrapped around my handlebar; it hung still, a twisted plastic wasp nest.

"Later, Liz," Jake said and peeled off in a blaze of exhaust and laughter.

"Stupid trash," Elizabeth added, pulling her pedal back with her shoe, adjusting her weight, shifting the handlebars back and forth.

"I think it's gonna rain," I said, looking at our house a half block away. It resembled a toy, the white sidings especially.

"Shall we continue?" Elizabeth suggested, aligning her pedals to a more comfortable starting position.

"Let's," Holly said. "Let's race!"

Soon we'd be inside our house with all the Band-Aids, batteries, condiments and folded denim that lay on exhibition.

"Go!" Elizabeth charged. The girls and I peeled down the street for the short ride to our house as the sun began to set into the concrete's far-off pocket.

I remained dazed for a millisecond before I pushed off and glided my BMX to my driveway past a patch of pink cosmopolitans out-stretched along the side of our neighbour's front lawn.

I felt a comfort once I came to a full stop inside the garage and walked towards the side door.

Saturday, July 26th, 1986

As Dad, Holly and I got off the escalator, deep inside Maple Leaf Gardens' aging belly, I prodded them for the answers. "What section?"

"Red twenty-six."

"Straight that way," the usher said, after examining our stubs through his Coke-bottle glasses. He wore a big fat smile along with a short-sleeved shirt and tie.

"Enjoy the show," the usher said.

As I passed him, I could read his fat face: *You paid for this crap? Grow up, kid. Dragging your father to this shit...*

It was July 28th, and I had been twelve years old for nearly two weeks. As I sauntered behind Holly and Dad, I saw a bevy of teens and dads chattering on escalators and lining up for sugary treats, ready for two hours of feeding on the acidic residue like sweet-sick ants. As we passed a merchandise table, a man handed me a single black-and-white sheet with the rundown of matches.

"What's that?" Holly asked.

"Like a thing for what the matches are."

At home, Dad always exuded a ghastly predisposition, wearing the thin, polyester-cotton-blend tea-coloured pajamas with black socks, fogging his way through the grim early morning routine. It was strange to see him surrounded by extras and wrestling fans in Maple Leaf Gardens. Every morning I saw him, Dad appeared only half-lit; on mute, a stale, predawn musk tricking from his mouth, a mouth full of grown-man realities: failed mouthwash, under-brushed teeth, overlooked food particles. His senses honed in on the substantial, a fresh veneer, hoping coffee would place him elsewhere—if only mentally. This was our Dad; always, first thing, first light, with the rising morning air and the house yawning alive and his first cigarette to set the mood. But I forget about all those tiny corporeal details of my then forty-five-year-old father David, because all I cared about was that those tickets he bought meant we'd be at Maple Leaf Gardens, Red Section, West Gate, by eight o'clock. Each ticket costing $14.00 ($12.73 + RST $1.27 = $14.00), plus snacks and TTC costs. On the way up, I noticed the prices for seats: we had the second-best tickets available next to gold! WWF Maple Leaf Wrestling Live!

Overhead, a crackled voice unspooled from the Gardens' dirty quadrants; a booming, invisible bull roar charged through the building's ghastly innards: *"Welcome, everyone, to Maple Leaf Wrestling, presented by the World Wrestling Federation."*

The voice was tinny; it continued: *"Ladies and gentlemen, souvenir programs and other WWF merchandise are available at the concession stands. Don't forget to pick up the latest merchandise from all your favourite WWF wrestling stars."*

In our cold seats, Dad cleared his throat and peered out into the crowd that slowly filled the Gardens. He asked Holly if she was cold, if she wanted a hot dog, and "ask your brother…"

I fidgeted with my shoelaces; my legs were cold. I stared at the empty wrestling ring, how the colour of the canvas was lighter than my own homemade ring, the ring that had been through so many battles already—real[1] and fake.

"Is there a program?" Dad asked. I showed my father the single page. Dad nodded as Holly took the page from me.

"Just like church, right?" Holly joked, passing Dad the fight card I

---

1. In June, the ring had to be reinforced after an incident with Dad where he hit his foot on my homemade wrestling ring, then in his usual spooling rage, snapped and crashed his size 9 black-sock foot through the meek tangerine box, the wood as flimsy as skin. The toy blew up like a fake prop coming undone at the perfect Moment. After the attack, I had to reinforce the ring's floor with pieces of wood about two inches thick, until the material could be stretched over it again. Bringing the ring back to the living room, I said loudly, "Now it's foot proof."

had let drop onto my knee. I heard what Holly said and looked at my sister. Dad seemed to like the joke and had a smirk on his face until it returned to his standard stiff offering. Still, the mention of church freaked me out because of the whole Jesus thing[2].

"That was funny," I whispered.

Holly's hair tampered with the Garden's dark mystery. She put her hair in a ponytail and tried to hide a yawn. The garden howled with gusts of cold-air reverb.

I had goosebumps. I looked at my sister's legs as she rubbed them, her pale limbs poking through the denim curtain of her fraying jean shorts.

Holly was talking to Dad. She looked down at my month-old blue Converse canvas shoes dangling, not quite hitting the ground, then at the creased program in my lap.

Dad sat dumfounded, his face void of erratic enthusiasm or query. When he did stand, it was at around 5' 9" in total; his greying beard with hints of red in it surrounded his roundish face. He was thin but sometimes bloated in the summer from his usual 170 pounds, depending on his diet and activity. Mom was 5' 2", with a body type that lacked definition. She got perms twice a year which would grow out

---

2. One night a few weeks earlier in the month, Dad woke up in the middle of the night and ran down two flights of stairs to wake me up and yell at me for not apologizing for messing up his workshop. Mom screamed behind him in her pink-and-white nightgown, and I peed a little in my pants. That weekend I took the large crucifix he had given me and hammered a nail into Jesus's heart and threw it from the basement doorway onto the kitchen floor at my Dad's feet. He said, "You're not hurting me when you do that," like Jesus was now in real agony.

and resemble a bit of an afro. I called her hairstyle "meatball" for some reason. Her large nose and coal eyes dominated her face. Mom spoke with a high, metallic twang which made some of our friends ask Holly and I if we were from the South.

Dad muttered something to Holly and got up, blowing his nose loudly as he rose. As he blew his nose in the familiar four-burst chime, Holly and I moved our heads to the beat. He disappeared into the cavernous static.

Holly kicked my foot.

"So, you want Ricky Steamboat to win 'cause of your newt? You know, your lizard, your dragon you have in your room? Didn't you call him Ricky? Is that—"

"No, not because of that, duh," I said, cutting her off. "I think he'll win the belt from Macho Man tonight."

"You think so?" Holly scratched her knee, the tiny hairs on her arms and legs standing up among sparse freckles. "Mom said she found your newt on the floor. Did it get out?"

"It always does. I had to put some records on the top of the tank."

"Oh."

"But yeah," I said to Holly, "I think Steamboat is gonna win because he's a lot quicker. I think he's got better stamina. He's wicked." I had just seen a bloody match on television between former Intercontinental Champion Tito Santana and the current champion Macho Man but missed some of it because Dad wanted me to put my bike away properly in the garage. I tried to tape it but couldn't find an empty tape in time.

The heads of two devout Savage fans in the row in front of us turned around.

"No way, man. Macho's gonna kill 'em. Steamboat's a wimp, ohhh yeeaahh!"

I could smell their Right Guard, they were older, bigger. They were chewing on candy, stuffing their braced faces with a lacquer of sugar nectars and other bright, noisy foods. Holly sniffed the air in disgust at them, disgust for the way their concession-bought candy had caked along their ugly braced teeth.

I wanted nothing to do with them. One boy continued at a lower volume. "Macho Madness all the way," the other declared before both turned to face the empty ring.

"Ohhhhhh yyyyyyeeeeaaaahhhh!" one boy said, nodding and manoeuvring his hands in manic finger gestures.

I heard one of the boys tell his friend in a low rumble, "Stupid kid likes that fag Steamboat."

I swung my legs. I liked Savage OK, but he had won the Intercontinental title in February by reaching into his yellow trunks and pulling out a piece of steel, hitting Tito Santana in the head with it when the referee wasn't looking. I didn't trust him.

"So, it's a title match though? That could happen?" Holly asked. "Who's better?"

"Well..." I said, a bit quieter, still feeling goosebumps. This was like the times on the couch on rainy days, watching videos we'd borrow from the library, when the rain and the movies and the thunder rolled over the house—a few cans of diet cola, a few handfuls of candy, watermelon—and how we'd tug on the Saturday-morning couch blanket until some boundary-smashing question would send me into a fit of shame: "Do you jerk off?...Yet?...You will. *All* guys do...But you're not a guy."

And now here, my birthday gift: the wrestling match.

"Do you have their dollies?" Holly asked.

"You mean *action figures*? Yes. I have both. I want Bundy though, can't find him anywhere."

"So who is going to win? Ricky or Randy?"

"I think Ricky is faster, but the Macho Man is tricky, and stronger. And smarter—maybe."

Holly pulled out a small emery board.

"Who else is fighting?"

"JYD is versing King Kong Bundy," I said. I was sniffing the program, holding the page under my nose as if it were a fence to peer over.

"You mean *versus*."

"Yeah."

"JYD? Oh wait—Junkyard God, right?" Holly said.

"Not 'God'—'Dog.'"

"That's what I meant," Holly said, a decapitated string of red licorice dangled limp in her hand.

"Who do you think will win that one?" She now had the program on her lap and was digging into a small stash of candy in her bag.

She pointed at Bundy's name. I scratched my chin. I looked into the arena's crevices; the sparse audience looked tiny and distant.

"Well? Bundy or Bow-wow?"

I thought about it: Bundy had been furious since losing the cage match to Hulk Hogan in April at *Wrestlemania 2*, but Junkyard Dog was friends with Hulk and wouldn't want to let the Hulkster down.

"The God! Bow-wow-wow!" I howled, stirring with excitement. "The God Dog damn it Dog!"

Holly tilted her neck back and offered me a piece of gum. "What time is it?"

She rubbed both hands over her knees.

"Eight-fifteen," I said, noticing the ring attendants fussing with a turnbuckle.

"Where's Dad?" I wondered, reluctant to turn my neck to look where I imagined Dad might emerge and burst into the ring in some ridiculous gardening costume.

"Washroom," Holly answered, nodding toward the nearest exit. "Or maybe he went to the ring."

"That would be amazing."

"I'm a bit hungry. Where's the popcorn geek?"

"Did you talk to Grammy? She called yesterday."

"No, no one told me," Holly said, pulling her gum out in a long strip and sticking it under her seat.

"Whaddyathink Mom's doing?" I asked.

"Dunno. Talking to herself? Folding your underwear?"

"Gross."

Holly was laughing.

"Mom's probably vacuuming her farts," she said, howling even louder as an announcer stepped into the ring.

Dad returned to his seat as the house lights went down.

"OK, show time, Nate!" Holly said, squeezing my forearm. Standing up partially, I ground my feet into the Gardens' unkempt skin.

*

"Goodnight Nate," Mom said, closing my basement bedroom door. "Glad you guys had a good time tonight."

The eerie and galactic light waned to a thin slit. *"Shoooooooooooooo-woooooooooooooooooo-waaaaaaah-kkkkkkkkkkkkkkkk,"* I said in a low murmur, dubbing a spaceship door closing. "Sweet dreams," I said.

"You too," Mom said. This specific two-word phrase, *you too*, was the hook I always waited for, that exchange, the back and forth.

As I lay there, I remembered some of my Mom's jokes from earlier in the school year when I was sick a lot. She took me for blood tests because no one knew what was wrong with me. She joked that the doctor would use a foot pump to take my blood and that I'd have to start paying rent at his office. I just got so nervous going to school and dreaded the thought of doing presentations. The work was piling up, and I faked illness for about a month straight.

Sleeping in the basement for a year now, the enamelled luxury of my own concrete washing sink and access to the workshop gave me a sense of bounty. The floor was partially covered in an oval-shaped maroon rug; the floor was tiled and cool, especially in the summer. Calculating the dimensions of the floor tiles (10" x 2¼"), often cleaned with bleach and water, the grit sopped up with a cornflower-blue dishtowel...these tiles helped ledger my world.

My paper route that summer had been filled with terrifying news of a girl my age lured out of her house to have her photograph taken at Varsity Stadium. Her body was found a couple of days later. Thirty-two times I saw her face as I carried papers up driveways and quietly tucked them into screen doors or milk boxes.

You too...

Soon I would be asleep, counting flying elbow drops instead of sheep.

*

The remaining days of summer filled themselves with sun-glazed hours, bike riding or ghosting in the basement listening to the radio. When at home, Dad skulked and trotted with Tyrannosaurus procedure. It had been a tough summer, especially when weeks earlier Dad broke my hockey stick in two over his knee right in front of me! Just for leaving it in the driveway.

I looked at the broken Sher-Wood stick. I had bought it at a garage sale for a dollar. I was being careful in how I picked it up; perhaps it could be fastened back together somehow. I had this piece of paper that I wrote all these things down on, and how I loved them. *Sher-Wood hockey stick. Orange Corvette Hot Wheels*. If I lost something, I'd write it down on this faded four-fold piece of paper. There were dozens of entries haphazardly queued on the page: everything from broken toys to dates Grammy had visited, to lost movie-ticket stubs, to items of clothing.

A few days later, I saw the hockey stick pieces stuffed like body

parts into the sides of our iron garbage can resting at the curb, awaiting extinction. I imagined how I would fix it with a plastic blade shaft
and some screws. This reconstructive surgery hung enormous in my
psyche as I tried to calm myself with distraction and fantasy.

2)

Temptation

Thursday, September 29th, 1988

The first three weeks of grade nine were like watching a grade-school photograph get aged for some missing-person article. Grade nine was all the torture and terror I'd seen in panty-raiding, locker-stuffing teen sex comedies over the decade.

I noticed many students at Leaside were people I hadn't spoken to since grade five. (I'd left Northlea in 1985 for Cosburn's Late French Immersion program for grade six through eight). Now, colliding in pseudo-recognition, in that strange divide between rudeness and reality, I felt myself wishing everyone were authentically strangers, beyond any clinging semblance of familiarity.

Save for Andrew, it seemed I would spend the next four years stone-faced, passing these equally denim-clad teens in laid-back oblivion. Not exactly what I thought would happen.

"My cousin told me Jake Cavers was at this party on Saturday and pushed all these tables over," Andrew said, unlocking his bike near the tennis court's tall fence. The sun was all over his face.

"Why?"

"He was partying," Andrew said, pulling his bike from the fence to the sidewalk.

"Where's your bike?"

"My chain is fucked up."

"Later," he shouted, turning his head from me as he peeled out of Leaside High's sprawling school property. "I'll call you later about the cottage!"

The rest of the day was gobbled by sun and daydreaming: me gliding around on my blue-and-yellow Norco 18-speed mountain bike, tucking my neck as I'd edge into Glenbrae at the last minute or swerve and circle around my block via Broadway, left on Laird to Glenvale. These Moments were the best: the rest of the day was mine—alone in the house until at least 5:30 p.m. Holly usually went over to Elizabeth's straight from school to do who knows what—smudge their lips on samples they took from the cosmetics counter or work on school assignments, practice their French, smoke weed. Holly had cornered me in the hallway just as 9th period was letting out. "Why so gloomy today? You're all head down, dead-boy sad!"

I said nothing. Fuck her, I didn't feel gloomy—just waiting to hear about the cottage on both ends, if Mom would let me and if I was in fact invited for sure.

Holly sped up behind a bomb of blonde and red manes and disappeared down the stairwell.

Now, under the late-afternoon sun, I sprint-walked for as long as I could manage, trying to distance myself from any neighbour recognition. I didn't talk to them or their children in class, and wasn't going to speak to them out in the wilderness of our common real estate. Andrew was the only person I wanted to talk to, or *could* talk to, in all honesty. He was rapidly becoming my entire universe.

*

The distribution of anxiety in our house had a four-pronged filtering system; occasionally we all suffered at the exact same time. The emotional magnetic fields twitched like a polygraph test needle—tarnishing a once-clean parchment, ledgering the erratic levels.

The cellar's stairwell cupboard swelled pregnant with two cases of beer, and sometimes four bottles were withdrawn in a night; Dad luxuriating in his post-meatloaf appetite, a little supply and demand in the works. Regardless of inventory, I grew accustomed to the chain-like clanking of empties stacked on the stairs, trophies of disgrace hugging the top step, each brown bottle an ugly tooth in wait. Why couldn't he put the empties back in the case? *Why?* I blasted each bottle with my eyes—at odds with their ugly brown presence.

Placing my school bag on the bed, I scanned my bedroom, noticing subtle changes in the décor. I powered up my stereo, the turntable instantly starting its laborious whirl.

The phone rang.

"So, you're coming to the cottage this weekend? YES or NO? I need to know now...we're leaving at 4:30 tomorrow."

I paused, aware how Andrew's voice was lowering, mine still squeaked a bit. "Um..."

I saw a scrap of paper: Mom had written, *"ANDREW COTTAGE?"* Taking this as a positive indication, I shouted, "Oh yeah!"

"Cool."

"You guys pickin' me up?"

"No, you gotta come here." Andrew said, adding with a chuckle, "Bring money this time, and pack a swimsuit..."

As Andrew continued to laugh, I thought of his house. It was just the way my mind worked, visually branding each person I know with solid shape, like the way an animal or baby becomes familiar with objects; the chocolate-stained banisters and the tiles of kitchen with the cartoon water-blue mesmerized me, the regal authenticity compared to the weak tones my house was done up in: lazy soft pink, pale scuffed mustard, boring off-white.

"I'll do a wash tonight." I said, returning to the conversation.

"Egg-wash!" Andrew blurted out with reverb into my ear. "Ha-Ha-Ha!"

"I hate that, I don't know what it means but I hate it."

"*Whatcha-gonna-do* about it?" Andrew said.

"I'm gonna take it to the max, yeah! You're goin' straight to the danger zone, dig it?!" I said in my lamest, strained, tonsil-dragged voice. I had let the phone cord twirl around my leg and was now trying to kick myself free.

"Get over it. We're *not* wrestling. Besides, you know who'd win." Andrew said.

"Well, are we going go-karting?"

"Yeah, probably. We can go out on the water too, on Saturday."

"That sounds cool," I said. I was about to ask Andrew about how much the go-karts cost when I heard a faucet running upstairs.

The alarm clock on my dresser glowered in green digital numbers. I heard three footsteps, the refrigerator opening...*more noises.*

It was Thursday afternoon; nothing special about Thursday afternoon registered. A lawnmower cut out.

"Hold on," I said. "I gotta go. There's a burglar in the house."

"What?" Andrew said.

"And they're hungry," I whispered, adding, "Someone's in the kitchen. I'll call you back later," and put the receiver down. The stereo was still record-spinning.

I guess normally I wouldn't have been concerned, but this interruption was undeniably eerie, even with the sunlight creeping in all warm through my window in thick tributaries.

Stricken with a slight fear, I slid my door open with one toe, catching the door in my hand so it wouldn't hit the bookshelf and make a sound. I prowled delicately until I reached the first step and planted a light left foot.

Breaths barely there, I pulled myself up, three steps at a time, having to take one step back at the very top. *Who was in the house with me?*

This was it: I clutched the doorframe and pulled myself into the kitchen, voice clasped—I tripped over a small pumpkin—my awkwardness in full bloom for my assailant to witness.

I threw my head back, locking eyes on the intruder.

"Are you OK?"

"Well, that all depends," I said, smiling at Elizabeth. I took a deep breath as sort of a reality checkpoint.

"So, what's new?" Elizabeth said, taking a big gulp of water.

I balked. "Why are you here?" I asked, wearing a nervous smirk, trying to look as though I didn't care, as if I could control who came and went in the house.

"Well…" Elizabeth began, pausing, refilling her cup with something from the refrigerator.

I wanted her to move in. "Your sister and I have plans."

Everything about Elizabeth drew me into a frenzy I couldn't comprehend. She was a wilderness I prowled near and paced in; my shadow was an animal stretching out and howling beside me.

Underlying her cottony curves was a deliberate love of scented lip gloss. Moving her tongue around in her mouth, behind her teeth, I saw her calculating gestures, pursing her lips, a brief grinding of teeth, her jaw adjusting.

"Your sister and I have plans, you see, and she lives here," Elizabeth said with a chuckle.

I could smell her hair, maybe shampoo and sweat and perfume. A definite alchemic taboo filled the kitchen in a swell funk.

The electronic beats from the basement ricocheted around us.

"Cool song," Elizabeth said, slowly moving her hips back and forth.

"You like New Order?"

"Yeah."

Elizabeth leaned to one side, listening. My index finger crept up over my lip. I looked at her, then the door, then back.

Like a select handful of tight denim-clad high school girls, Elizabeth now rivalled all my hand-me-down porno magazines, especially when she wore tight jeans (or what I'd type into my Commodore 64 about the variety of grade nine girls I'd survey throughout my horny week: "Jen Steede wore the tightest jeans I've ever seen today...or Selene Wilkinson, my god, the fade on her back pockets!"

Seeing Elizabeth drinking tap water in the kitchen startled me. I counted down from five in my head...I got to three—

I repeated the count to myself, watching her refilling a glass of water.

"What are you doing here? Is my sister even home?" That was good, I thought. Or did I already say that? Was it a question or a statement?

Her lip balm filled the air between us.

"I guess I'm early. The front door was open. We're supposed to carve pumpkins together."

"Oh." I didn't know what to say, how to breathe, hold my arms, circulate blood. "You like Leaside?"

"I guess so," I could feel myself becoming hot, heated, my head filling with concern and doubt that perhaps I would become physically brittle at any second. I was swooning.

"You OK?"

"OK, yeah, well, continue pouring water or whatever you're doing." I was slow to turn back, to head down to the dungeon, knowing this was a mistake in any rough draft of a romantic battle plan.

The sticky, wet afternoon in my throat and the light, cool September air through the side screen door; even though I was just experiencing it, my memory was tonguing away at each spongy sulcus for the most

NEW
ORDER
—
SUBSTANCE
1987

atomized trace of the older blonde sipping from a cup I'd used a thousand times.

I left the kitchen in a flush, heart racing, and found myself back in my basement lair, wondering how I had left things. Did I say goodbye to her? No time to wonder. Calm down and breathe. Put on some more music? I moved the needle back to the beginning of New Order's *Substance*, side A.

The percussion of each step from upstairs hiccupped through my low bedroom ceiling. She was getting closer; I could feel it. I turned around and saw my bedroom door open and felt my stomach producing premature butterflies, and soon, swooning.

Now she was here, in my room, staring intently in my direction, part of a pulse that connected us, tethered her to my desire.

"Hey," she said. "What are you doing?" My plastic cup was hovering near her lips.

"Nothing."

The television hissed as I connected my VCR. "I'm just trying to… "

I glanced at my guerrilla VCR and TV set up. My clothing was piled over my homemade wrestling ring and other assorted regression tools.

She was scanning my bedroom with her wolfish green eyes.

"What?" Elizabeth said, raking her hair from the left and twisting it, putting the massive blonde wave into a makeshift ponytail. The scent of my room and its heating plastics, solvents and paints mincing with her general teen odour was something. I did my part by fastening the model glue lid and putting the lids on the small glass paint containers.

"Your room is really full of, um, objects," she said.

"Yeah, well, I built it from a kit."

A casual scan of the room would reveal to Elizabeth that I surrounded myself with lonely sports heroes, zeros, *TV Guide* covers that featured the latest teen prime-time drama stars, a Jawa jigsaw puzzle mounted on a piece of plywood and three long, nearly empty shelves, painted navy blue to match my bedroom walls.

"Can you keep me company?"

"OK." I wanted to keep her.

She cut through the air dust, past the bookcase, her sneakers grazing a pile of my underwear.

The model bits blurred under the fluorescent lighting, the glue burning my senses, my windows shut. I felt on pause.

Elizabeth picked up a jam jar from my shelf filled with oil and dyed-blue water, an ornament I'd made from watching a science show on television. (The host told you to choose any food colouring you wanted to mix with the water. It was supposed to be educational: floating history of oil and water to impress onlookers.) She threw me a quizzical look.

"Your room is cool," she said.

I worried I'd left a drawer open or that an inviting closet door would unfurl a crisp porno stash with celluloid faces smiling and folded into one another, giving me imagined hugs, their pulpy, perfumed lips running up and down my body. I could feel the room getting smaller.

"Thanks. The kit was real easy to assemble. It was practically inflatable."

"Ha-ha, you're crazy."

She stood beside my cozy one-seater, facing my bed. I moved a hockey jersey from the seat. "What movie are you gonna watch?"

"Lethal Weapon."

"Haven't seen it," Elizabeth said, looking directly at me, comically bugging her eyes. I was pacing, twirling on my heel, staggering in front of my Mom-made bed.

"Sit down," Elizabeth said, accelerating my willingness to comply. "Come on, I know you can."

Catching her gaze, I felt a vacuum dry out my innards as my eyes brushed the contours of glossy-faced celebrities pinned up on my wall.

She laughed Momentarily, and then stopped full-throttle.

I wanted to say something funny but balked.

"Why are you guys even carving pumpkins? Isn't that something two-year-olds do?"

"Well, goof, it's for a party we're going to tomorrow. Early Halloween."

I twiddled with some plastic bits from a model set. I tightened the glue cap, which appeared haphazardly askew, leaking slowly.

I wiped the residue off on my pants. I couldn't look directly at her face. I had to shake out my eyes, adjust on the fly, her likeness flush against my callow retinas, and I began to choke, needing to throw my eyes at the little bit of sky that came in through the basement window.

I wondered when my sister would get home, if my mom would help me with the laundry I needed to do before the cottage tomorrow night and if she would bother me about my homework and how I really wanted to go for a bike ride but my chain was busted and how it wouldn't be worth fixing right now anyway as I was going to be gone all weekend and plus, I might be able to fix it with pliers; *Andrew knows how.* Each breath I now took contained traces of Elizabeth. I was parched and wanted some of her drink.

A pulse rippled through my temples, soft electrodes in my head. Elizabeth sat in my chair.

"Come on," she said, and patted a small patch of chair cushion beside her. "I'll make room."

The scent of model glue was humming in my nose. I could see my bottle-cap collection mounted on a piece of wood amongst my minutia. Dad had told me how to do it, how to mount it, with tacks, carpet tacks. *Was I telling Elizabeth this?* Bottle caps culled from a thousand bike rides, park excursions with Andrew and convenience store trash surveillance.

The glue's waft was strong, daubs of it hardening on my desk next to plastic bits. I lowered myself down beside her on the chair.

She half-kissed me, somewhere on my face, whispering in my left ear, "Good boy."

Some nights the light got in, a bit of joy crawled underneath the broadloom and I captured the stowaway vignettes of simple cracker-and-cheese bliss with clenched eyes and calm-breathing techniques; I reconstructed harmless domestic scenes of comfort and healing inside my plastic mind. A swirl of original sensations succeeded one another—herbal tea, the thoughtful crunch of toast, followed by the slow crackle of a fireplace on an autumn evening, sometime soon.

3)

True Faith

Friday, September 30th, 1988

B y 10th period, everyone was talking about Ben Johnson[3]. Some were doing imitations, complete with his accent: "I didn't take no stereos!"

Yesterday, on the back of a 4" x 6" white index card, blue with an ink drawing of the letters "M" and "P," I had scrawled "First week of school is almost done...I'm waiting for the stupid class to end so I can get home and then sleep, because tomorrow is the countdown, tomorrow it

---

3. The newspapers that appeared throughout the week had exhausted us with the words "steroids" and "gold medal" ad nauseam as the summer of 1988 officially dried up and vanished into a colossal anxiety chamber. They gave me the wake-up call to grave realism. The bold shame that catapulted Johnson into the media reverberated through lockers, gym class and stairwell. The iconic image of national failure and disappointment was etched immortal. For all intents and purposes, my run "on top" was over. My alleged heroes, with whom I had secret and sycophantic ties, were also winding down. George Michael's *Faith* album had run its bubblegum course. "Kissing A Fool" peaked at #5 in the US as the last single from the *Faith* album.

all starts because *ooohhhhhh yeeeaaahhhhhhhhhh!* We are going to the cottage, one more time, because *SummerSlam* was just the beginning *oooohhhhhhh yeeeeaahhhhhhh!* Nothing will stop the Mega Powers. We'll go on and on and on. It's ah, real emotional type situation yeah! Andrew and I are the Mega Powers, just like Savage and Hogan, nothing's gonna stop the Mega Powers—yeah!"

Now, with a mouthful of hot sun, and some in the eyes, I headed east on Eglinton Avenue. I heard a rustling behind me, whirled around. It was Andrew, who had caught up with me.

"Hey," Andrew said with his familiar cocky, raised-head tilt.

School had released us both, and the last embers of warm weather were a bounty to relish. Walking home together, I saw our shadows morphing into each other. It resembled a crude city skyline drawn by over-juiced preschoolers: tall and bulky (Andrew) and me (short and scrawny), our outlines crisp and fearless on the asphalt.

"We should grab a magazine before we go up."

"You mean like a porno?"

"Yeah," Andrew said in a huff, looking straight ahead, whistling a few notes of an indiscernible song.

"Sure." I said, a piston of excitement now chugging in my system. I adjusted the straps on my backpack.

"That store?" Andrew said, pointing to Laird Convenience, smack in between the floor shop and the bank on the corner.

"Yeah."

"OK. But wait, how?" Andrew asked. "*I'm* not buying it."

"Why not? They'll think you're eighteen."

"Naw, they'll ask for ID," Andrew said. "Tried it a while ago."

I could sense where Andrew was going with this: we were going to steal the magazine. I knew the store well, a good choice: lots of dark spots, bad lighting, slow, elderly clerk. I began to envision the ruse.

I imitated the gesture with manic hand twists and poses, drawing out the plan in the air before us.

"So you go to the back, pull out the chocolate milk but hold it so it's not visible, whether it's like a half-litre or whatever, 'kay?"

"Then what?"

I took Andrew through the Moment, demonstrating with acuity everyone's role.

"Then he'll ask you what size it is. And you say, *'I don't know; where does it say the size?'* OK?" I explained.

"OK."

"Then I'll snatch the mag when he's helping you, you pay for the milk, I wait beside you, we leave and bang—"

In the crusty convenience store, it all went down just how I planned: Andrew walked to the back of the store, opening the milk fridge. The clerk moved his attention to Andrew, who proceeded in asking the price a couple of times. "How much?"

I moved rapidly with the magazine, placing it halfway down my pants, heart beating large in my chest. I turned around and sidled up to Andrew, who was now buying the milk.

The experiment was a success. We left the store with the pornography and milk and headed home.

"See you in a bit. Don't forget your swimming suit."

"Yup," I said, touching the contours of the pocket-size copy of *Variations* I had under my shirt, down my pants.

I was excited at the thought I'd be away for the weekend.

*

Andrew sat shotgun. Me in the backseat. Andrew's older brother Philip (age nineteen) drove. Also in the car, Sandra, a short blonde phys-ed kind of girl Philip was dating (also nineteen). We drove the 131.5 kilometres, for two hours, with a planned arrival just after six in the evening with pit stops.

"Turn on the radio or something," Andrew said, looking at his brother.

"Shut up," Philip said, putting a mix tape into the car stereo. "Don't give me no lip, boy!" he said in his best slave-trader voice.

The tape contained the infamous "Monkey" remix, a joke Andrew had played on me months earlier, when he had fooled me into thinking he and Philip had remixed George Michael's summer hit song "Monkey." To me, the remix was incredible; it sounded totally different from the LP version, with added beats, repetition of words and a ton of realistic monkey noises.

"You guys should send it to the radio," Philip said, glancing back, imitating me while I fidgeted in the backseat. "DUH! Can't believe you thought we did that!"

Andrew was squealing with laughter. The drive was smooth and restful. I had been up there before over the summer.

"What radio?" Sandra asked.

"Oh, genius over here thought we made the remix of "Monkey" and said we should send it to the radio!" Philip howled. Andrew joined him in the howling.

Sandra sniggered a bit, but threw me a look that teetered on sympathy or what I hoped was slight intrigue. "He fell for it, that's for sure," Phillip said.

After the first rest stop, which, for me, consisted of peeing and buying a can of Sprite, I leaned in from the backseat and put a cassette into the car stereo.

"What is it?" Andrew asked, glaring into the backseat.

"That tape we made two years ago," I confessed, red in the face.

"Oh God."

The tape began with Andrew's near-teen voice announcing a match between me and another boy named Eric.

"Our main event has turned into something not suitable for children, ladies and gentlemen…Oh my God, Eric is in the ring waiting for Nate, who I think might have gone backstage to receive medical attention…wait, what's this…he has come back with OH

MY GOD! I can't believe this, he's got a saw blade[4] ... Nate is juggling with a saw blade ... and he's gone again ... so while we wait for him to return, let's go talk to the man who has taken several blows NO! They're back at it! They seem to be calling wrestlers in from all over the world to try and stop this ... they say they'll be here tomorrow morning?! What the heck, where are these people?"

"Ding ding ding!" I screamed on the tape.

"What 'ding ding ding'?" Andrew injected, "This is like four hours later, all the wrestlers have gone home ..." Eric and I laugh hysterically, more exhausted giggles on the tape ensue.

"That was funny." I laughed, back in real time, in 1988, the back-seat, watching Andrew's arm move towards the car stereo. Sandra was falling asleep.

"It's so dumb." Andrew said, hitting eject.

The familiar road sign in cold blue letters came into plush focus: *WELCOME TO BALM BEACH.*

"You sleeping in the cabin or the cottage?" Philip asked Andrew, neither turning their heads as they spoke.

"Haven't decided yet," Andrew said. "Depends."

Phillip changed lanes. "What are you homos going to do all weekend anyways?"

We arrived at the cottage just after six and had a bit of running around to do before the sun expired completely—checking the cabins and bedrooms for proper linen as well as putting away the groceries.

---

4. The saw blade was from Dad's workshop. I admired Andrew's ability to do play-by-play on the fly. At one point, I got overheated and announced that I needed some water, and the match stopped. I checked to see if my electric heater was on. It was, and I immediately turned it down and left my room for a glass of water. Listening to the tape, I heard Eric say to Andrew, "It's your turn." "No way," Andrew said, in what I can clearly state was the only Moment of physical fear I ever witnessed, even though I was in the other room, probably looking for a chainsaw. "He'll beat me." Eric, gasping for air, insisted, "Well, you're going in anyway."

We goofed around in the early evening air, lighting the odd fire-cracker. I tossed a sparkler into the lake and got scolded by Philip for my environmental infringement.

The sun was barely lit now. Down at the beach, Andrew talked about Sandra's body when his brother was out of earshot.

"Did you see her tits?"

Aside from our recent haul at Laird Convenience and abstract pornographic opportunities via Andrew's father's collection, Sandra was the only real-life girl we'd seen all year up close wearing next-to-nothing. Sometimes Andrew would show me her underwear in the laundry hamper, so we could imagine the extra flesh the magazines never offered. Sometimes he told me to steal Holly's underwear, which pushed me into an anxious frenzy, always having to come up with an excuse as to why I couldn't get them.

I took several eyefuls of Sandra's ripe skin. She took the towel from around her waist, revealing hips and legs, sopping wet. I was careless with my glances.

"You can look but you can't touch," Philip said, catching my obvious stare. "I see you staring at my girlfriend."

I felt my dick shrink.

"Yeah, what are you looking at, fag?" added Sandra, her blonde bangs covering her eyes.

"Nothing," I muttered.

Andrew paddled frantically in a canoe, slicing through the lake, his dog Brandy swimming near him. The early evening was being sliced in all directions, and I felt invisible, scrawny, digging in the dirt. Sandra toweled around in the water and on land, glancing coldly at me every once in a while, but I just stared straight ahead to Andrew in the canoe. The sun was wrinkling mute in the overcast sky. Sandra took Philip's hand and walked past me, up the sandy hill back to the cottage. I played with the foamy wrapper of a short bottle of black cherry seltzer, the remnants of its metallic taste still bubbling on my tongue.

I never spoke of girls to Andrew in a candid way. I did, however, start a journal of lists and meticulous scenarios involving some of the girls in my grade nine class, including Selene, Jennifer and Melissa. Sometimes I showed Andrew these entries on my computer.

I allowed Andrew to conjure up fantasy girls for the both of us, more scenarios or options. These activities played into our recreation so stealthily it seemed natural.

We returned to the cold cabin and its dark musty contours. Once the door was shut, curtains drawn, we became like soap in each other's hands.

Soft and strange time together, in public, time alone, together, unchained and scented. I couldn't help but memorize the contours of Andrew's growth.

Now there were no borders.

Andrew was inside the main cottage. It was past midnight, and I was wandering around outside by myself, forty feet from the cottage, when Philip and Sandra practically cornered me in the dark. They'd been down by the beach. I noticed the beer bottles in their hands. Sandra looked at me and asked me if I wanted one.

"No," I said quietly. She took a sip and let out a laugh, "So you're just going to sit out here alone?"

Andrew said he had a few beers with Philip sometimes, but I didn't believe him. I guess I was wrong. "Andrew's having one, come on," Sandra said. Philip took a sip from his beer. "Forget him; come on," he said, luring Sandra back into the house with a mischievous expression.

The porno stashed. The chocolate milk circulating, we went to bed.

In the middle of the night, Andrew spoke into the darkness, "Shut the window," in a startling dark slur. "Raining out...coming in."

I crept along the cold carpet, shut the window tightly and returned to bed.

Go-karting[5] in the morning would take us away from each other's erections. The drive to the track was short and full of waffling sunlight;

wimpy grey clouds had formed on the horizon, and pleasant raindrops tickled the dash, only to be sopped up by the perennial sunshine.

"Pick you up in a bit," Philip said, and drove away, leaving us near the ticket gate.

"Ready to lose, boy?" Andrew let out a loud bolt of laughter, making actions with his hands like he held the ruckus of lightning and thunder in a holster beside his long legs.

"I'll destroy you out there," I said. "It is my destiny."

Now on the race course, we were all chin straps, gas pedals, sharp turns and breaks. Andrew was chewing on a plastic straw. He punctured the top of his plastic soda lid.

I had never go-karted before, but felt it was important to dramatically declare my superiority.

We gunned our engines and whipped out of the start position. I pulled ahead for a while, trying my best to outdrive Andrew.

"Just like Beggar's Canyon back home," I screamed.

"You're goin' down, boy!" Andrew shouted, now tailgating, riding me hard.

On the third lap I could feel Andrew on my back tire. "Stop it!" I screamed backwards. Andrew cackled madly. I felt Andrew's tires on my back, took the turn but poured on the gas, winding up on a hill.

"Fuck!" I shouted. My car's engine wouldn't stop; there was no reverse. "Asshole!"

I climbed out of my car and embarrassingly walked back to the starting point. The attendant looked perplexed as I emerged from the track in my helmet.

"Something happened to my car," I bashfully told the man who had sold me the laps. "It went up the hill."

---

5. "Half a mile of smooth asphalt track, 25 fast, safe karts that really move ... half a mile from the Bay west of Perkinsfield. Balm Beach Go Karts has been a part of summer activities in Balm Beach on beautiful Georgian Bay for years."

Andrew finished his laps alone and approached me while I was nervously pacing around the ticket counter. "What happened?"

"Whatyamean what happened? You clipped me from behind, and I went up the goddamn hill!"

"Did not. You're just a terrible driver," Andrew scoffed, all tough.

"You're a fucking asshole."

Andrew bought another four laps. I was black flagged, not allowed back on the track. I watched Andrew whip around the track from beside a set of vending machines, just out of the sun's glare, grinning like a big dumb clown the whole time.

*

Before dinner, we messed around by the unlit beach, whipping rocks while candy and cola rotted our stomachs. Clouds covered the sky, used like swabs for the eventual mess. In a dip in the sand, Andrew told me to jump. I did, and dozens of birds, nesting in a series of holes, flew from the holes. He howled his reserved-for-special-pranks "Hee-Hee-Hee-Hoo!" laugh. The birds' sudden ascent from nowhere terrified me.

We headed back to the main cottage, dripping from spastic dashes into the cold water. I paced in the living room, watching Andrew's brother unload groceries in the kitchen.

"You wanna go?" Andrew said, flexing his muscles, putting down a stale life jacket and a set of paddles in the mudroom. He glared at me through the screen door, pointing and gesturing with conviction. "Sure!" I shouted back. "You're in the danger zone now!"

Andrew stepped into the living room, where I was sitting on the couch.

"Hold on," I said, "I have to put on the song."

"What song?" Philip asked, walking into the living room from the kitchen. "You need a song to fight?"

"Hulk Hogan's song, 'Real American'," I said.

"You think it'll make you stronger or something?" Philip laughed.

"He *does*," Andrew said, shaking his head.

Andrew began to fall on me, putting all his weight over my back; we landed in a loud heap on the living room floor. The music blared, and I began to shake my arms. "Give up, you can't beat me."

"Gaylords," Philip said, staring at the spectacle. Sandra was in the shower. Philip shook a large glass container of pasta in the air. "You want spaghetti for dinner?"

"Burgers," Andrew said, his face a bit red, his voice winded.

"Yeah, burgers," I chimed in.

"How many?" Philip asked. I shrugged.

From the floor with my feet, I tried to trip Andrew, but he just stepped over me.

"Look," Andrew said, looking down at me. "I'll let you elbow drop me; it *won't* hurt one bit."

"You sure?"

"Yeah. Go for it."

"It's a Mega Powerexperience[6], yeah!"

Andrew lay down, and I stood over him, raised my elbow and pointed to the imaginary crowd. "You sure?"

"Just do it."

I dropped down, my armpit landing across Andrew's neck, my elbow landing on the corner of Andrew's left shoulder.

"See, nothing. I told you. Even if you had the chance, you could *never* beat me."

---

6. In late 1987 WWF storylines, Randy Savage and Hulk Hogan had formed a hyperbolic union of ego, body and soul called the Mega Powers: Macho Madness and Hulkamania coming together to overcome all odds. Though I had partially outgrown my affection for wrestling, Randy Savage's mid-1988 WWF title win and highly enchanting interactions with Hulk Hogan set things up for a dive right into celluloid altitudes and sugary excitement, glancing at glossy photos of Hogan and Savage at the corner store while loading up on overprocessed supplies. One night Andrew carried his black-and-white television set over so we could watch the three-hour VHS of *Wrestlemania IV* which I had rented.

Back in our cabin, Andrew laughed so hard he spilt cola over his white shirt.

"Shit." Noting my gaze on him, Andrew comically smiled and began to tango with a broom. He felt his face. "I probably need to shave soon." His skin felt soft and hot in the dark.

Our young bodies shadowed by night and quiet, blond and brown pubic patches. Softening eyes lowering over each other's skin, as mouths tingled with excitement, anticipating the slow familiar scent rise from our underwear. In the cabin, we were alone. "They're down at the beach." This was our distinct world.

That night at midnight we blasted Salt-n-Pepa's song "Push It" over and over again, rewinding it on the ghetto blaster we had in the cabin.

"Crank it!" Andrew shouted, dancing and laughing in the middle of the night. *Ah, push it Ah, push it Oooh, baby, baby Baby, baby Oooh, baby, baby Baby, baby.*

Andrew had suggested these secret acts two months earlier, in summer's heat camp, during video horror rentals when goalie-masked killer Jason Voorhees was stabbing camp counsellors in bikinis and tiny panties; Andrew stuck a knife in the pizza box, paused the movie on some breasts. He pawed at me, then returned to the film, the freeze-frame, slow-motion scope of Jason Voorhees breaking through a closet door with a machete. Un-paused. The terrified breasts were moving again, running for their lives.

Then another time a few days later, we had camped out in the backyard in a musty tent, drinking grape soda, tingling with acrid heat, taking turns with each other's erections, fumbling and tugging in the dark, the taste of candy, sweat and pre-cum.

The treasures of that night were spoken in code: "Grab a Kleenex."

Afterwards I coiled into sleep.

*

The morning sun lagged. Awake and fumbling and squeezing before the bright sphere rose, before it shot out of the earth's mouth bright and orange and electric, we groaned and jerked. Before the sun shot up into blue-denim sky, before either of us could be quarantined from our own self-love.

When the sun finally burst in, Andrew pulled the curtains together. He was changing. I closed the door. "Lock it." As it closed, I stepped forward into the cabin; the thick carpet muted the action. "Locked?"

"Yeah," I said meekly.

Andrew approached me from behind; I could feel his eyes on me, his hands lowering, pulling me from behind into his chest and leaning over.

"Grab it," he said.

Andrew was wearing his usual weekend-pervert jogging pants. "Push the beds together," he said, motioning with his shaggy blonde hair for me to start rearranging the cabin's interior.

Andrew began to talk about a girl's tits—a specific pair—from school. He approached me. "Did you see Sandra on the beach?" Andrew ran his hand across my back.

Masturbate. Sometimes Andrew just said the word. I could hear it in my head, invisibly charging through the cabin, implying the activity was forthcoming. The word was so casual, as if it were a band's name, a flavour of drink or a simplistic ritual or gesture. Andrew was standing now, in his underwear and T-shirt.

"Look at her tits," Andrew said, cupping my balls, making certain I was on a hot page.

"Just think of that, or Sandra's swimsuit."

The word felt like a utensil that Andrew put into my mouth and made me chew on, hard and cold at first. He was standing right behind me now, his hand clasping my neck.

"Did you see her nipples poking out?" My hockey jersey was full of heat; the routine pressure of his touch was becoming a necessity inside my heart which I pawed at regularly.

"I guess."

Our clothes landed together in a heap, and I imagined their zippers fought like chain mail and swords, metallic teeth briefly grazing each other's fibers.

Andrew hovered around: the faint scent of gum and fountain pop. He pulled and twisted my head and neck into his—this was our skin together.

Andrew leaned down on me, his weight too much on my shoulders.

Our aromas only. Andrew exhaled—touched it. The elastic of my briefs pulled up, fresh air all over.

"Take it out."

I trailed off, wondering what Philip and Sandra were doing in the cottage: maybe waiting for a VHS rental to rewind, considering popcorn, considering turning off the lights and having sex, making hot chocolate, collecting wood for a fire.

Perhaps they would discuss dinner options. What would the boys like? The video rewound. Someone going, "What else did we rent? What are they doing out there?"

Andrew's blue eyes were now checked and wet with a reflective glaze from the heat.

"Now me," he said, his heavy wet breath spreading across my meek biceps.

My name stenciled in my clothing was illegible from this distance. Erections in swimwear liner. As the touching continued, I clenched my eyes and saw a reel of our collective experience: hockey sticks dragged and scrapped against the cement in my driveway.

The parked car hung like a polished cavity along the stony road, slick and jewelled in the brief rain from last night, surrounded by green and reddening leaves.

A rinse of sunlight through the pale curtains.

*

On Sunday morning we dressed and rushed to the breakfast table; I ate some cereal.

Andrew was rummaging for something in the hallway, moving around on the deck outside. "Where are you going?"

No answer. I followed him. He turned around, and as he rotated his body towards me, it revealed he was now holding a gun.

"Oh my God!" I shouted.

"What?" Andrew said. "It's an air rifle, pellet gun."

"Where'd ya get that?"

"From the shed," Andrew said, blowing across the top of it. "We've had it for years."

Andrew was up for another mêlée in the living room. I lunged forward, trying to escape him through the left, then the right, eyeing a nearby chair I could grab, wedge between us. Andrew was a wall moving forward. To him it was a game; he put his head hand on my head, made car noises, now adjusting his grip to my ears.

We finished another bowl of cereal and went outside with the gun. "Let's climb up there, on the roof and check it out." We climbed a large steel antenna that grew from the ground beside the cottage.

He helped me off the antenna and onto the roof.

"Up here, right at the top, it's the best view. We can see birds or squirrels."

Andrew pointed the worn pellet gun at my face.

"Don't point that gun at me."

Andrew took a few shots through the snug trees. "Let's get down. I can't see anything."

We climbed down and moved through the forest that surrounded our cabin, walking deeper into the green.

"Close your eyes."

"Why?"

"Just do it."

Andrew got on the cottage's roof as I walked up the sandy hill.

Andrew was careful, climbing a steel antenna pole, pulling himself up on the shingles. The pellet gun was on a strap across his chest.

"A great big surprise!" Andrew shouted. "Turn around."

I heard a noise and felt a prick on my ass—a piercing prick on my left cheek.

Then, a laugh.

Tears were in my eyes. "For fuck's sake!" I rubbed my ass to see if the thing was lodged in there. "I can't believe you shot me!" I pulled my pants down to reveal the red welt across a cheek. "Let's see," Andrew said. He began to laugh, then held it in.

"You fuckin' jerk!" I screamed in a wimpy high-toned sound. I couldn't help it. Andrew and I walked back to the cottage.

The setting sun turned the beige hues grey like ash. Andrew charged at me, twisting my wrist into an arm bar. We were wrestling again. I tried to reverse it; he pushed his chin into the back of my spine, upper neck, his mouth moved towards my left ear, "Swing low, sweet cherry isle..." he boomed, as if trying to change the subject.

Back in the cabin, archives of *Playboy* memories churned in our skulls, a thousand watts of pink and dark pink lighting up our veins and skin as we lay our heads down on clean pillowcases, the sheets snaking with greedy showgirls in tired lingerie.

I often remembered how it used to be without the touching, before the strange unification of our naked bodies entered into a system of familiarity and alchemy.

Toboggan runs, secret midnight firecracker sessions, Commodore 64 marathons, bicycle-grease errands. And the hobbies: comic book conventions, remote-control cars, and how Andrew came over to help build his hobby car from the set I bought with him just after my birthday and how we picked the car out together: *Striker*. I left the side door open for Andrew, who built the car in my bedroom one night when my family and I went out for dinner. Then the two of us built a miniature racing course in the church's backyard and raced our cars while drinking up the hot pornographic lakes of our imagination. We tried jerking off in the pews inside the church once, but it was too strange with all the ghastly stain-glass. We laughed about that for a while.

*

It was nearing noon on Sunday. The sun grew higher and hotter. A day full of teen-toothed gum chewing, paddles in the water and cereal remnants in my molars.

Steam rose from the paddle.

"Let's go out further," Andrew said. The canoe carved through the lake for hours, the heat crashed down to our cores and hunger grew in our expanding stomachs.

"Get in the water." Andrew said sharply, pointing his paddle at my nose.

"Why?"

"Just do it."

I got in the water. Andrew followed, sliding into the water with me.

"Take off your trunks." Andrew said. I balked, looking into Andrew's eyes, this time not squinting at all. I was about ten months younger than Andrew, but in the same grade. Andrew started school a year late. His mother died of an aneurysm when he was five. I knew everything about Andrew, or so I thought.

"Might as well do it. I guess they can't see us." I said.

"I'll do it," Andrew said, and submerged, squeezing me and taking my trunks down. He began to tug on my dick. His mouth took it in. He broke through the water.

"How does that feel?" Andrew asked, eyes closed.

"OK I guess." I spat water out. I was surprised by the confidence in his voice, how natural it felt. This was what we did now.

Andrew pulled me in; his hands were like mad fish on bait, glistening under water. I took a deep breath rising up; his head disappeared under water until I felt his mouth envelope my dick. Less than a minute later, he broke through the water, gasping, eyes closed and wet, catching the tail end of a body spasm.

"Are you done?"

I finished moaning.

"Now you do me." Andrew said, mouth half full of water.

The sun continued its indiscriminate pursuit of our bodies, moles, crevices and lines to be. The red boat hit shallow water and Andrew dragged it across the damp sand.

We drank dull lemonade and showered.

After it was over, I packed up my things and went to the cottage for breakfast. We were leaving today, at some point. Returning to the city. The sun-sprayed cabin was vacated, beds once pushed together now separated, the evidence rearranged, curtains tied, door locked again.

"What time are we leaving?" I asked Andrew through the screen door of the cottage.

"Not sure."

Today would be another scorcher of pooled youth resources[7].

---

7. The summer of 1988 was now a month-old memory, slow to evaporate, and as the Mega Powers, we really had done it all: bike rides, play fighting as a team with local kids our age, sailing, fireworks, go-karts, shopping in Yorkville, swimming at the neighbours' pool complete with its perverted jet, and "reading" the finest pages of pornography, including the off-season classic, *Playboy Girls of Winter,* which featured girls in cabins with beams of winter sunlight telling time in between and across their legs, on their backsides and swathed across their breasts. Video games too—loads of them, *Summer Games, Winter Games, Ghosts 'n Goblins, California Games,* and some wrestling game where you could either be the white-trunk-clad Ricky's Fighters or the black-trunked Strong & Bad. The dropkicks were especially funny, with the player suddenly in a horizontal position, heading towards their opponent with plenty of time to take a look at the crowd. Andrew would often imitate the experience of waiting to execute the dropkick, putting his feet up in the air, leaning back in his chair and leisurely waving to the crowd.

4)

Round & Round

August–September 1989

When Mom was very small, living in Kew Beach in East Toronto, some neighbourhood kids stole her skipping rope. It was a ruse, a conspiracy which in turn became a legendary set-up I replayed over and over again in my head. As a child, the story was told to me only once, but it had a huge impact on me in understanding anything about the woman who my friends said "floated" in her giant pink tea cozy of a housecoat and had a haircut in the shape of Darth Vader's iconic black helmet[8].

For me, the skipping-rope fable was a signal post; told to me after my own run-in with deception as the 1980s opened up. It was sweet revenge some forty years later when a group of camp bullies took it upon themselves to steal my chocolate milkshake at lunch. This was

---

8. "I think I still have a photo you gave me of your mom standing with her back to the camera in front of the washing machine," my friend told me recently. "And yeah, she had that same hairdo, the triangle bob, black or dark brown. I remember I never saw her feet; she was a bit of a ghost. If your mom was prime minister, no one would ever fuck with Canada ever again."

when we lived on Roehampton Avenue, that period in photographs when I wore glasses (June 1978–May 1980). Mom came to pick me up and asked me about my day, and I told her that someone stole my chocolate milkshake. The drink came in a can and it was not regular fare for me. I was looking forward to it at lunch and maybe I had drawn attention to it when I unpacked my food. I knew the culprits but was helpless to confront them. Mom didn't feel this way at all, however, and proceeded to chew them out in the most ambitious toxic rant I'd ever heard up to that point. (Mom doesn't remember this happening, but it was a life lesson, a triumph; she was making up for lost skipping ropes one shaggy-haired kid at a time, and to me it was a rare act of heroics I have permanently archived.)

The docile sparkplug that would change the course of history and be added to our caustic family flag next to the rolling pin, beer bottle, jar of goose grease, pack of Craven "A" cigarettes and fish-tank bubbler, lay in wait inside our light-blue Buick's tired engine.

The morning was unscripted, tired and passed in tedious ritual as the cereal bowls, mugs, juice glasses and separate refrigerator-door seal breaches echoed in crude symphony.

Mom was antsy and full of tasks. "I have to go to the library at some point today. Do you want to go?"

We were almost finished emptying the dishwasher. "And if you have any clothes for the Salvation Army drop box," she added. "Holly's coming back tonight from camping." I wandered into the den and turned on the television.

Dad was outside, kneading the earth on his knees, his gut rubbing against the open earth; he put a mug to his lip every couple of minutes until his coffee became cold and he tossed the remainder into the garden behind him. The morning had escalated into an impromptu invasion as Dad mapped out his soil-turning conquest.

I could see him in action through the drapes as he tried to make the menacing zucchini sprawl see it his way—its green prickling tentacles and leaves had pronounced themselves vivid past the lawn's original border.

Something had to be done: Dad's way, non-stop, toiling and chewing off his Saturday inch by inch. I never saw any photos of Dad with anyone other than family members; it was great when Dad had new friends, I imagined saying, but he never did that; he didn't know how or develop the need. He read newspapers, played cards, picked weeds and wore plaid shirts on the weekends. I never saw him on the phone talking to anyone for any personal reason unrelated to family topics. Did he know people? Did he see people on the street when walking, or was it blank?

Through the window, I could see Dad's veiled outline stretched large as he came in and out of frame through the curtained window. Mom had joined him now and was gesturing like crazy. I opened the window a bit so I could hear them, just a crack. She stopped with her hands and turned away.

Dad didn't look up. Mom pleaded. "Would you stop it!" Mom growled, cawed, standing behind Dad's dig stance.

I turned the television off.

"David! Stop digging! Stop it!"

My nose was at the window, heart kicking into a rapid-beating frenzy.

Mom repeated, "Stop it!"

"It's my garden!" Dad snapped back, on his knees, his red plaid shirt a big round rectangle of sweat and sun and digging.

The cicadas were holding their notes; their song came to a halt. Inside I could feel my stomach lubricating in a layer of pre-vomit. I sprinted back into the kitchen, jumping over the open dishwasher door Mom had abandoned, running into my shoes as I blasted to the side door. I burst through high noon's Saturday heat, seeing Mom's perm and the sunlight moving through it creating a temporary golden orb. She turned around, nose red, eyes watering.

"He won't stop digging!" she cried. "Would you stop it David!"

These seconds were without sensation; it took forever to reach him, to be beside his dirt shoulder and smell his specific atmosphere.

"Stop it!" I shouted.

He was taking off his red shirt, revealing a yellow mountain of cotton T-shirt and a pair of dirty brown cords. "Stop digging up the fucking backyard, you psycho!"

Dad didn't budge. "Both of you get inside."

He wanted to keep digging. Mom kept screaming. "We will if you just stop!"

"Get inside!"

I pulled at my father's shoulder. Dad pushed me away. "Diane, get inside!"

I returned to the frazzle, now pulling him from his garden crime scene into the driveway near a pile of wood.

"Stop it, you asshole!" Dad shouted at me.

"*You* stop it!" I shouted back. He shoved me. I shoved back, causing him to fall into the woodpile, spilling a few logs.

Dad regained his composure, and with the weed pick in his hand, swung at me.

"Asshole!" He shouted.

I felt sick: hostile triggers and signifiers went off inside me—lighters flicking, the scent of bright-yellow beer and the gross suds filling me up from toe to head, the rage of a lawn gutted, brutally turned over, final.

The language was barbed as we struggled, clenching hands and fists while Mom screamed like a banshee.

Upon passing the driveway, one might have assumed a competitive road-hockey game was going on, but no hockey sticks or

nets were in play; they lay dormant in the garage. Dad was holding Mom by the arms.

"Stop it David!"

Gusting down the hot driveway to the front door, swinging it open and pouring my eyes over the kitchen for something—anything…

…I spotted a wooden tea tray. Returning at full speed to the driveway, I saw Dad trying to shove Mom inside. I was about thirty feet away, standing in front of our car.

"Get inside!" Dad shouted, glaring at me.

"You're scaring me, David!" Mom screamed. I ran at Dad, hitting him over the back with the wooden tray.

TWACK!

The funk of cigarette smoke alchemizing with his crap cologne hung in the air that separated us. I stared deeply into Dad's steel-wool eyes.

"Just get inside!" Dad shouted as I dropped the tray.

"Nate!" Mom screamed.

"Diane, inside!" Dad barked. "Call the police!"

"You're insane!" I shouted. "When they get here, I'm gonna make sure they lock you up forever!"

"Diane, call the police!" He was behind the screen door now.

"You're such a fucking piece of crap!" I said, staring into his glazed grey eyes.

I moved towards the screen door to pull it open. Dad slammed the side door shut in my face, and I heard the lock click, digesting my family inside.

I stood in the driveway alone, the wooden tea tray at my feet, the sun now fully outstretched in the cloudless sky.

Across the street in a bright deluge, several neighbours were huddled in their best late-morning wear.

I dropped out of sense, out of sync from it all, and began shouting with ribbons of tears streaming from my hot face.

"Call the police; he's insane! He's going to kill her!"

I watched my house from down the street. Dad came outside and was standing in front of the car. "What's he doing now?!" I shouted. Even more neighbours were gathering beside me.

The show-stealing antics were rewarded in kind: two police cruisers showed up, just as Dad was fidgeting with the car's engine.

"What's he doing now?" I asked hysterically, looking at my father playing with the car's guts.

The police moved up the driveway, one officer taking Mom to a police car, the other, as far as I could see, talking with Dad beside the car. Dad closed the hood.

I disembarked from the group of local spectators and crossed the street towards Mom.

"What's going on?" I said, sidling up to Mom as she lit a cigarette. She dabbed it out after three tiny puffs.

"They need a statement from me," Mom said. "This is so embarrassing."

I looked at our house now, feeling as if a sinkhole had risen up and formed. In it we would now—*all of us*—slide towards a new-fangled dent in the property schematics, a dismal abyss in wait.

The officer had finished speaking to Dad. He nodded and walked towards Mom and the other officer, passing a few neighbours who had frozen along the way.

"What?" Mom said, her voice rising as she continued, "They're letting him go!?" She was marvelling at the police officer standing next to her, face in a twist of creases and astonishment.

"He's putting the spark plug back in," Mom said, sobbing. "He took it out so we couldn't leave!" she cried, snot dripping from her nose.

I stepped back from the police car and watched as Dad finished operating on the car's engine.

Fucking asshole, I thought, watching Dad drive away. "He's going to cool off at his folks' place," the officer told Mom. "He said in Kingston, right?"

Mom was dripping with wet and mucus. She nodded shamefully, not making any eye contact. "We just need to take your statement, Mrs. Moore."

Slowly the gaggle of neighbours and onlookers thinned out, and we returned to our domestic shell.

"You want to call one of your friends?" Mom asked, blowing her nose with Herculean pomp. She tossed her cigarettes in the trash.

Later in the afternoon, Andrew came over with a baseball bat. Mom served us lemonade on the front porch; her eyes were now dry and open, awaiting another soft deluge. Telling Andrew what had happened both excited and shamed me, as if sharing the malicious porch gossip would provide fodder for the future judgment and ridicule I knew my best friend was capable of propagating. We rented two movies and ordered a pizza. Mom, Holly and I engaged in a silence with occasional facial recognitions in key comedy points. Otherwise, we were hypnotized for several hours wearing flatline expressions.

Dad returned the next day, said nothing to anyone about the incident, quietly milled about the house, avoiding chaos, carpet shocks, raised tones or eye contact.

"Hello, Nate," he said as if nothing had transpired. It was the absolute most terrified I'd ever been.

Within the high noon showdown, we both flinched, and my fantasy uncoiled, spoiling a reel of seamless smiles. Each toothy grin killed forever.

*

At school, I submitted to the boys and their phys-ed steak arms, glistening in dark hairs, and new deodorant, their skin scabbing in places, from battles from sex, from falling down new and drunk. These growing and grizzly fourteen- and fifteen-year-old boys would pick me up vertically, my head under their pits, my feet way up above their own heads, then they fell back on a gym mat. It was called a suplex. I stood five-and-a-half feet, weighed 118 pounds. When I had a bad headache from anxiety or illness, Mom suggested an Aspirin intervention while I sought to believe in the gods of synchronicity, not logic.

Weeks passed, and I thought this one rip in the psychic fabric was a one-off thing that wouldn't repeat itself or linger, but it wasn't the case. By mid-September, the after-school special-type treatment was in full effect and unravelling in bounty.

It was nearing four in the afternoon, a time of relishing the pre-dinner vortex, I thought, walking up the front steps. Despite the glare from the warm sun, I felt a deep coldness washing over me.

I opened the screen door, and Mom emerged in a cloud of cotton, backed by the distinct chugging of the dishwasher, racing through silverware. I knew something was up when she greeted me at the door with a crooked grin Scotch-taped across her pink face.

"Oh, hi, Nate, glad you're home," Mom said, in a calm but definite voice, slowly turning her body to the living room. Her movement in the hallway was its usual, spectral shift, with the creases in her forehead coming together in a linear fashion.

"Come on, now," she said, rushing me to de-backpack and unshoe myself, waving me in towards the familiar set of pink couches. I imagined a camera crew in the living room, doing light readings, setting up boom microphones over the coffee table. *Something was up.*

"Why are you home so early from work?" I said, moving lethargically into the living room behind her.

"I wanted to just, now, this is Mary, she is a counsellor, and she's here to talk to you."

"Talk to me?"

"About you know, how you're feeling, and you know…"

I moved cautiously into the living room where a woman sat on the couch holding a pad of paper in her lap.

"Hello, Nathan, my name is Mary Greene from Child Services," she said, not getting up.

"What do you want? What is this going to accomplish? He's not even here!" I said. "He's the problem ... "

"We want to hear your side of things," Mary said. "Talk about everything." She had fierce red hair pinned back, wore glasses. I didn't like how she kept putting her pen in her mouth. "How you are feeling today," she said in a clear, demure voice, matter-of-factly.

Mom stood nervously in the hallway, looking in on us. "Nate, just put your bag down. Do you want some tea?"

"Don't you see it doesn't matter what I say? The police come, and he lies."

"Just relax, Nate," Mom said. "We just want to talk about things. About your violence."

"Are things OK at school?"

"School is fine. It's here, at home, my father, he wants to fucking kill me!"

Your violence. Never *his* violence. The words flew in miserable arrangements. I was now parched. "You're making it out to be all my fault, aren't you? That's why she's here. That's what this shit is about. Listen, this is not a one-sided thing where I just attack him out of, like, no reason."

Mom spoke up. "We want to figure out what is bothering you. She's here to help you."

"Are you insane? Figure out what is wrong? He comes home drunk or angry, bursts into my room in the middle of the night to finish a fight we had like a week before. Then, if the police come, they threaten to bring in the Children's Aid. On top of all this, I have school. He's making his drunken problems my problems. It's not my fault. It *can't* be all my fault!"

"Nate," Mom said, snorting away, her voice accruing in pitch, her nose red from embarrassment, from helplessness. "We just want to know why you are, you know, acting up all the time. You seem so angry and we want to know what's bothering you."

I stood up in front of the both of them, trembling and snorting, blowing my nose as Mary, the family's new narrator, jotted and nodded.

Biographer. Morgue clerk.

"When did these incidents with your father start?" Mary asked, Momentarily taking the pen from her mouth and putting it to paper. I watched the pen. I wanted to spit on the floor. Instead, I started to cry louder, mouth wider, wetter, spit everywhere inside my jaw.

"Well, it's fine when Nate's at work, or David is at work, but when they're both at home..." Mom's nose was glowing now, red and raw; her eyes watered, mouth gobbled in wet slop. "We can't function," she said in a liquid voice.

And the muscles on television worked out and posed in my sleeping head, malnourished and altruistic, rusting in my blank head, where I hid against a tide of fluff and laundry noise, hid from human timeshare, where dressers barricaded my knobless bedroom door, where my stuffed-toy lion and giraffe still remained intact, on which I practiced, picking on their weak spots, rehearsing body slams and atomic drops against their weakest counterstrikes until the giraffe's neck tore off completely. Mom had put a silk handkerchief around its vulnerable neck, but still it leaned to the right, permanently injured. These taxidermy toys had been with me since day one.

Mary looked at her watch, then at me. "Where do you work, Nate?"

I *knew* she knew. The grocery store, where I pawed at tabloid photos of Marla Maples during my fifteen-minute breaks. I wanted to lie; I wanted to say brain surgeon or bounty hunter. I said nothing.

"Nate, please cooperate with her," Mom said. "She's trying to help you."

"I don't understand, I don't know why this investigation is a...why that asshole isn't here being grilled for being such a horrible...asshole person."

"I have to assess the situation to see if a formal report needs to be made, to you know, other departments."

"Why can't he move out? Why does he have to be here? It's like prison with him here," I said, gobs of spit pooling in my mouth. I began to cry louder. "It's total hell."

Mom's nose was dripping, and her face was twisting into a contortion, an odd grimace. One day, I knew I would detect this facial stance on my own skin. Mom posed the question: "But why do you get so violent, Nate?"

The counsellor looked at me, then at Mom, whose eyes were teeming with juice.

"I just remember it wasn't always like this, remember when I used to take you to the library? Remember—"

"OK, let's play remember. Remember when he came into my room a few months ago and threw all my shit around, and I pushed him, and he looked at me and said, 'YOU THINK YOU'RE HURTING ME?'"

The promo I cut was charged with more honesty and sadness than I thought was possible. I hated every word, every little molecule that made up the world I lived in.

"What starts the fighting?" Mary asked, adjusting her position on the couch.

"What starts the fighting?" I asked. "Fuck."

"Nate, please, she's here to help."

"Help what? Help how? Help me move my furniture against the door so he doesn't attack me in the middle of the night?"

"Just take your time," Mary said, shifting her position. I detected a pocket of perfume hitting the atmosphere. "What would you like to do?" *Welcome to the family,* I thought.

"About what?"

"You and your father."

"I don't know. It's so hard with him; he's a bully who lies to everyone. We have a long history of hating each other. He treats me like I'm his little brother, he mocks me, he acts differently when no one else is around. The police side with him; wanna know why? 'Cause he fucking owns us? This house? Pays taxes, right?"

Mary and Mom looked at one another. Then Mary glanced at her piece of paper. Mom to the carpet.

"This one time, we had a fight, and I shouted at him about how I was so sick of his bullying, his like, how he treats us, and how I wanted to sue him for everything he's got, and he just looked at me and said: 'YOU WOULDN'T HAVE A LEG TO STAND ON.' Then the cops come, and he's like all calm and a fucking totally different person."

I continued bawling, snatching a tissue from the box Mom had in her lap.

"Nate, you're father would *never* say that."

"He did!" I screamed. "No one believes me. What am I supposed to do when no one believes a single word I say?" I shrilled. "Then he tells them, sitting on that couch right there where you are sitting, he tells the cops that he can handle me in a fight, but is worried for my sister and my mom. He's so Dr. Jekyll, and no one is doing anything about it; it's like the goddamn *Twilight Zone*."

"Why do you think your father reacts this way?"

"He's worried about the future," Mom inserted[9]. "We're all—"

"Weeks pass with nothing, and then one night, he starts in on me. And what are you going to do about it? Write down stuff where in the end, I'll be the bad guy. Why? Why am I the star?"

"We can't go on like this," Mom moaned, blowing her snotty nose, her voice gurgling in moisture. "It's so awful."

---

9. A few years later, while dealing with various family histories and my ongoing emotional problems and the negotiations with various doctors and hospitals, Mom would tell me that when I was still a baby, the three of us went to counselling in regard to Dad's past, involving his own father (my grandfather) and the church. The details were always spectral and vague, but something happened to someone in the church group. There was an accident. And Dad was extremely upset. Though candid, the takeaway was always that this was something we were never to discuss or bring up or inquire about—ever.

My eyes were now stinging. "What are you saying? That, ah, he, feels like he hasn't made his point? That I don't get it? That I need to be told my behavior isn't good? Well, I don't appreciate *his* fucking behavior, but that's not what this is about, is it? No! It's about me, the bad guy Nate. His point is clear; it's been made, and I have videotaped my weed-pick cuts on my legs from our last battle to prove it."

This went on for a few more minutes until Mary announced she had another appointment. She spoke to Mom alone at the front door.

My legs felt cold on the pink sofa. I got up and went to my room and lay two cans of diet soda and a box of crackers on my bed. Shoes on, eyes closed, feeling weaker than the plastic straw in my mouth. I looked through a notepad until I came to several pages full of dates and erratic checkmarks: plans and escape routes.

The last date was August 21st:

Sweaty as hell. Went to Consumers Distributing but they didn't have the joystick I wanted. Called Andrew, and we went for a bike ride, played road hockey with for like six million hours. Well, more like three. Then we watched a special about the making of Batman.

The Phantom Cousin[10] *(1990)*

sixteen: anxious, fidgeting alone;
white noise of sixty-five-thousand fans;
popcorn in my sneaker treads.
My ninety dollar *Wrestlemania VI* ticket;
Toronto SkyDome saved from Dominion
Grocery shifts where a handful of twenty-year
old girl cashiers roll their eyes and one
changed once in front of me. I saw her
panty-crotch rayon or something—It's just Nate—
and her friend guffawed in terror at the undressing
(a guffaw that made it all the better to jerk off
to on my breaks in the washroom,
imagining things went further than they ever did,
ever would, for all the universe that's worth.)

---

10. On the way to the snack bar, I ran into some classmates at *Wrestlemania VI*. They were watching it for free in one of their dad's SkyBoxes. I said I was there with my cousin.

PART II:

SAVAGE

(1991–1996)

5)

Blue Monday

March–April 1991

The edge of afternoon was full of activity. I relished that sprawl of time before dinner—the end of daylight and beginning of evening frost and black. *Ventilation*. The notion presented itself to me as the only relief from the toxins creeping into my sinuses. I was putting the finishing touches on my special effects laboratory: a galaxy of stars in space on a large particle board, salvaged from a train set I never used.

The large, simple loop of track was set up as a surprise for Christmas morning. The board now served a larger purpose: outer space. It took several more laborious swishes to completely nullify the textured grey particleboard into solid black.

I picked up the spray paint bottle and shook it vigorously, taking a deep breath as a jet of black mist blew across the basement onto the board.

Again. *Ventilation*.

But which window? The one in my room or one in the workshop basement? Or maybe the side door? Either way there would be questions from above: *Nate, what are you doing down there? YOU BETTER NOT BE GETTING PAINT ALL—*

I propped open two basement windows letting in cold winter air that disrupted sawdust. It covered most of my sleeve before settling on the floor.

In my highly choreographed basement lair, in which I pantomimed the grand creator role, I hammered, painted and affixed. My after-school ritual of transforming the unkempt space into something fantastic occupied my every spare minute.

Over the past few months, plastic models, makeshift spaceship gears and mechanical innards were accumulating over the basement awaiting a mission, exaggerating my galactic fantasy camp.

I had the school camera booked for the upcoming weekend when, in addition to a class project for English, I would shoot segments of my VHS sci-fi films, all part of my fictional escape plan.

Dad was fettered to the kitchen phone, his head craned down, knocking back coffee and saying "I see," in an ongoing imitation of reality, furiously crossing out phone numbers and adding new ones, cribbing impossible notes. He was trying to locate any type of insurance job, the sector he'd worked in for nearly fifteen years—*I can start immediately . . .*

All I had left to add were the stars, which I did with white spray paint and liquid paper.

With a *wooooshhhhhhhhh* from the can, a light white mist hit the black space void. I coughed, my eyes tearing up. I put my nose under my T-shirt collar and moved the basement door back and forth to move the fumes, trying to avoid the chemical daze.

"Looking good!" I said to myself, as if addressing a film crew of sixty.

Now I was hungry and dizzy. I came up from the basement as quietly as I could, still not completely used to him being home so early.

At the top of the stairs, I watched the backs of Dad's legs: his brown socks gaining a film of dust along his pivoting heel, his pant cuffs dipping into the surface of Sadie's wet food.

As I crossed the threshold of our off-yellow kitchen (its sour orb of egg-yellow a constant theme, running from wallpaper to tile to fridge colour), my eyes towered up along Dad's form. He began rubbing his moustache as if it caused him great agitation; his index finger furiously moved through the orange and brown hairs, perhaps to extract a genie wish. I grabbed a plate and glass from the cupboard.

When Dad spoke into the phone, his voice sounded as if his throat was swallowing him, each word barely breaking from within a vacuumed tone as he nervously pinpointed his vocational purpose. "Environmental risk and insurance, yes for twelve years . . . the complexities of pollution risk explained thoroughly to clients, yes, to make . . . exactly . . . informed decisions. I streamlined the underwriting process . . . four years or so . . . Environmental liabilities consulting . . . sure . . . on site . . . well, virtually any aspect of a manufacturing and distribution, especially those companies which may find . . . what was that? Yes, I worked on policy terms and premiums for almost fifteen years. Cleanup coverage? Yes, I was a specialist on those for I would say . . . the last four years or so. Yes, you may . . . I see . . . if nothing comes up, sure, yes. As soon as possible, that would be appreciated. Yes, 7355. Yes, the only phone number . . . that's correct."

I had my head inside the refrigerator, unscrewed a jar of kosher dill pickles, snagged one, let it drip out all wriggling wet, grabbed a cheese slice, unwrapped it, slapped it onto a bagel, prodded at a gooey slice of ham all rubbery from its plastic garrison while Dad's thin voice said, "Good day," and the receiver returned to the cradle. *Throat clearing and the hmmph and sigh and the pivoting of his heel.*

"Hello," Dad said.

I looked down at the colourful shock of ingredients balanced in between my fingers (mustard, mayo, pickle, tomato, ham) as I squeezed the sandwich together. Mustard painted my hand.

"Having a snack?" Dad asked, walking slowly towards me.

I nodded and looked at the half-chewed green pickle, the kind Dad had given us in our stockings just four months ago; the brand's logo could have been sewn onto our family crest, if we had one. The pickle was our thing; a product that united us, with cheese and cracker dust falling across our pajamas.

"That was my headhunter. So we'll see what he comes up with."

My stomach tingled in uneasy waves. My sinuses still battling toxins, I dropped the bread and ham collision on a small plate. The pickle bite was lodged in my dry throat and my eyes were watering again.

I swallowed hard, turned my neck towards Dad.

"That sounds good," I said.

What would happen? Our whole life, my room, the backyard, Holly's stuff, my stuff, our bikes, where would we live, would we have to move, put things into storage, live in the woods? I had, on a few occasions, ventured out on long walks in the snow, sat in the dark, even once with Holly when we were pissed off, tired of the yelling, and fantasized, for a millisecond at least, of living out the rest of our days in the icy blue nothing. *That was years ago.*

I looked down at my hands...black bits of paint illuminated by the margarine in a strange shellac. *All those years ago.*

"How was school?"

"S'OK."

"I'm going out for a while," Dad said, snorting as he passed me. He shuffled in the hallway with his coat and hat, taking a cigarette from his pocket and putting it in his mouth, anticipating nicotine. The creak from the front hall closet was jingle-like in its familiarity. "I started to defrost the spaghetti sauce," he said. "It's on the counter."

"OK."

"See you soon," Dad said, a minor winter howl sneaking inside for a second, only to be snipped off by the door closing.

I stepped towards the front door to see Dad smoking and backing

out; our weird two-tone grey second-hand Oldsmobile had trails of exhaust billowing a temporary cloud onto the street. Mom would be home
from Community Care East York, where she worked Mondays in a
basement office, mostly filing and faxing and calling the elderly and
their immediate families.

   I fished around in my corduroy pockets, remembering the clipping
I had cut out from a newspaper at the school library. Last night was
Wrestlemania VII, and the results were published in Monday's paper.
I pulled it out and read as I chewed my creation.

Hulk Wins 3rd WWF Title! Plus, Warrior Ends
Randy's Career! More on S15.

*Despite delivering five big top-rope elbow drops on the Warrior, Macho
King is no more, as The Ultimate Warrior bested Randy Savage in their
career-ending confrontation at Wrestlemania VII last night in Los
Angeles. In other big matches, The Hart Foundation (Bret "Hitman"
Hart and Jim "The Anvil" Neidhart) lost the WWF tag-team belts to
The Nasty Boys, managed by Jimmy Hart, and Hulk Hogan became a
three-time WWF Champion when he defeated Sergeant Slaughter (with
his advisor Colonel Mustafa, an Iraqi military personality who was
rumoured to be a close confidant of Saddam Hussein) in a bloody
encounter in which Slaughter got a hefty dose of justice at the hands of
Hogan...*

*

It was Friday evening. After some miserable meatloaf, boiled green
beans and a soft-core salad (iceberg lettuce, choke-cut carrots, frayed
celery and dressing-drenched raisins), I was in my bedroom watching
Holly do laundry. She was back from university in Kingston for the
weekend. When she came to the pantry in the basement stairwell to
sneak beers, I poked my head out.

"I didn't know you were coming back *this* weekend." I said.

"Yeah, last-minute thing," Holly said, blowing her bangs from her eyes, putting the beers into her laundry basket.

"I have to do a multimedia thing tomorrow for English. Like film it with some guys from class. On the play *Death of a Sales Guy*."

"*Man*," Holly said, dragging her still-warm laundry into my room.

"Yeah, *Man*. These guys from class are coming over."

"Andrew?"[11]

"No, he's not in my class."

"Don't tell Dad," she said, putting a bottle of beer into the laundry basket. "What time are they coming?"

"Noon."

Holly was balling socks. "This laundry is a futile abyss."

"Maybe you could be in it, like the video we gotta do, help us out?"

"No way. Going shopping; can't."

*

"I'm going to punch that little bitch in the tits next time I see her!" Holly shouted on the phone. I shook my head and torpedoed down the stairs to my room. I had no time to spare; those idiots from school would be over in less than two hours to work on our English assignment.

---

11. We had quarreled in January while watching Madonna's *Justify My Love* video, which Andrew had taped. This full version he had taped was a hot property, and he wanted me to see it because it was banned in late 1990 when it was released. He kept putting it on PAUSE/STILL as Madonna undulated in black lace panties. Andrew shut the door to his den and began to prod and poke at my semi-erect penis with one hand as his high-powered VCR slow-motion scanned the shot of Madonna's lace covered behind writhing in black and white. I got up to leave, feeling a strange reluctance to participate. I got up off the couch and stormed out, with Andrew's condescending tone reverberating down the stairs, something about never talking to me again. I walked home feeling angry and somehow relieved. We had just started speaking again weeks later in early March, the incident erased.

I shifted my custodial activities to the basement, attempting to normalize it. Mom chimed in, with her usual mauve sweater, and exhausted, dowel-eyed glare. I was halfway down the stairs.

"Better clean your room!"

To which I retorted, "Those jerks aren't going anywhere near my room!" Then I laughed maniacally. "They will never see my laboratory, my master plans, my secret hidden ... "

"All right, fine," Mom growled. "Help me unload the dishwasher!"

I knew finding material to add realism to the video project wouldn't be hard; props were in abundance; excess wood, metal and plastic objects were everywhere. *Mops, lumber, pipes.*

From where I stood, I could see that my bedroom door was ajar. I had moved my geeky sci-fi props from the main basement into my room (wooden guns painted grey and black, model space ships and other odd creations were covered with clothing). The thought of strangers from school sitting on my bed, asking me questions about my choice in décor or requesting an explanation after giving me a *what the hell is that?* twisted-teenaged face in regard to a *Star Wars* prop made me shudder with disgust and terror.

Mom shouted, "What time are they supposed to be here?"

"They're coming at noon, I told you already!" I shouted up the dirty stairwell.

"Do they want food?"

Mom had a thing about food and people coming over, no big deal but really, even the most minor snack getting plus-oned was enough to throw her into a fit; as if another hot dog or peanut-butter sandwich was the equivalent to fixing a rack of lamb followed by a deep-dish seven-cheese lasagna.

"I told them to eat their own food outside in the driveway before coming in."

"Oh, be quiet," Mom said. "Just *answer* the question."

"I don't know; think they probably will have eaten."

"Well, you should have *asked* them," Mom said, shaking her head and vanished in a wash of late-morning noise.

"I can't think of *everything*," I said, appearing with a half-full plastic bag. I shoved it into the kitchen garbage can. "But it's been a big learning experience for all of us."

The boys arrived just after twelve, refusing at first to really speak to or accept any offers of sustenance from Mom. She helped them put their coats away and repeated the offer of a hot drink or sandwich.

"I thought we'd start in the basement; there's way more room."

Politely repeating their refusals for sustenance, they swished their way down to the basement, wall-pawing in astonishment along the way.

"Just let me know if you get hungry," Mom said, with a shake of her head in all directions that at once amused and confused me. She mouthed something as I left the kitchen, but I couldn't decode it in time.

I carefully shepherded them past my bedroom door.

"Uh, is this your room?" Stephen asked.

"No, it's the basement."

"Where is your room?"

"Upstairs."

I lied.

Once the minuscule red REC button went on, the camera was capturing us in all our bad-acting glory, our *ums* and *uhs*, stutters, and *I dunno's* and *oh shits*.

"Uh, can we start over?" Stephen Chaing asked, his braces covered in shiny elastics, bits of dribble pooling along his lips.

"No, just keep going; we'll edit it out," I shouted.

"Where's the script?" Stephen asked.

In class, Stephen used mechanical pencils and chewed on his

eraser. I also remember his very, very bad breath and how his braces kept his mouth constantly agape—a further public cruelty.

I moved the shoot into the next scene. "What act are we on now?"

"Still, ah, act one, I think."

For some reason we decided to narrate the scenes from the play in fake British accents, perhaps taking our cues from Stephen, who began speaking in this slant when we started to shoot news-desk commentary scenes.

"Jesus, if this guy owned a funeral parlor, nobody would die!" I shouted.

"What's that?"

"What's what?"

"That line?"

"From *Wall Street*."

Stephen had headgear and braces, and spat when he talked. He wore a tie and played three different roles. He was nervous, doubtful of my creative ideas, but for the most part, cooperative.

"It's cold down here," Jeremy[12] said.

I scanned the script.

"Hey, I just thought of something! For that scene with Willy and the hose, when he tries to kill himself, we can use the vacuum cleaner!" I beamed. "It's perfect. Those hose parts!"

"I guess," Stephen said. "Uh, you don't have a *normal* hose?"

"What's a normal hose?" I countered. "I don't have a box full of hoses to choose from."

We all paused at the sound of Mom's footsteps on the metal stairs. A pained smile and bright-eyed greeting, as if she were flexing her pupils, took over the basement. All this action previewed her inquisition.

---

12. Jeremy was a nice enough guy. I remember he wore a blue mock turtleneck. He wore Dad's bowler hat in one scene. I hated having them backstage in my real life. Still, we did a good job and got a pretty good mark, though our teacher, Ms. Fertuck, admonished us for being a bit too tongue-in-cheek and comedic.

"How's it going?" she asked as she entered the basement, carrying a tray of food and beverages. "Thought you guys could use a break," Mom said, setting the wooden tea tray down on a small table.

"Yum, radioactive pink water and egg-salad sandwiches," I said. I hated the strong egg smell, but thanked her.

"Let me know if you need anything else," Mom said, leaving the basement, returning to the surface.

The boys nodded, slurped on their drinks, took quiet bites from the soft oozing egg salad on brown bread. "Let's film the rest upstairs in the den. We have a piano; it might look good in the background," I suggested.

"Uh, who says that line again?"

"Which line?" I asked Stephen.

"Ah, the one that goes, 'He's liked but he's not *well* liked.' I think it's Biff, right?"

"I'll check."

We moved the filming upstairs, taking the fireplace and piano as our backdrop.

Stephen was now playing Linda, Willy's wife. He wore an old hat of Mom's from the 1970s, a floppy felt black one with a thin pink ribbon that went all the way around. "Willy, darling, you are the most *hand-somest* man in the world," Stephen said, putting his hand on Jeremy's shoulder.

"Thanks," he said. "Shit, that's not right," Jeremy said.

"Should I keep going or stop it?" Stephen asked, the camera humming along, recording everything.

"Just keep going," I said. "We'll fix it."

At my direction, Jeremy stood by the fireplace, walked over to the piano, paused, then looked off-camera. The camera followed. "Work a lifetime to pay off a house. You finally pay for it, and there is no one to even live in it," Jeremy said, trying his best to remember the line.

Stephen and I looked down at a scrap of paper where we had written in all capital letters: ATTENTION MUST BE PAID!

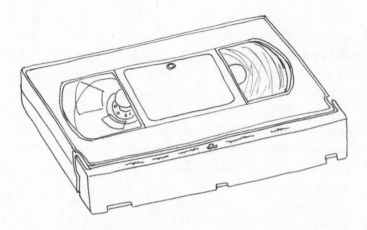

"That's Linda's big line," I said.

Jeremy looked at Stephen. "You were great as my wife."

"OK, so let's do that line, the one about, you know, the one where he says, 'I realized what a ridiculous lie my whole life has been,' OK?"

Soon it was time for the abject hose scene. I intentionally overacted the scene, struggling with the vacuum hose as if it were a live snake. Everyone cracked up.

"You guys OK in here?" Mom asked, poking her head through the door frame.

"Cut," I yelled. "Let's do that again, and Jeremy will try to hide the hose and Stephen you come in and ask what he's doing."

Mom shut her mouth slowly into a flat line. She saw me holding the vacuum hose extension and shook her head. "Just be careful, Nate," she said, disappearing again.

"We're almost done: just the car-washing scene. We can do that with Lego."

"You have Lego?" Stephen asked, his face trussed in judgment.

"Sure." I said. "Why wouldn't I have Lego? Everyone has Lego."

"Oh, Nate, I'm picking up Holly from the subway. I'll be back in half an hour or so."

"OK, thanks for the newsflash."

Setting up three Lego men beside a toy car, Stephen did the final commentary, his sloppy pronouncements the results of egg salad, his severe dental work and forced British accent: "Willy becomes immersed in a daydream. He praises his sons, now younger, who are washing his car. The young Biff, a high school football star, and the young Happy appear. They interact affectionately with their father, who has just returned from a business trip."

Slow fade.

"That's a wrap, boys!" I said. "I'll be right back; hold on a sec."

I ran to the front of the house, knees on the pink couch, peering through the curtains to see if Mom had returned with Holly. The driveway was blank.

The phone rang. I hoped it was Andrew or Holly.

I picked up before the third ring. It was Dad.

"Is your mother there?"

"Nope," I said. "She went to get Hol." I twirled the cord in my fingers, turning them beet red.

I could hear a faint organ playing in the background. It was death, and now I knew that it was true. It was that close. He was *there*. Working.[13]

Dad asked some more questions, his voice remixed in an indiscernible glaze but with the same focus. I just snapped in frustration, "I don't know! Ten minutes ago? OK, I'll tell her, I'm busy, school project—" and hung up.

I scuttled on my sock feet along the tiles, stopping at the cupboards, doors smacking into their frames, quick pours and plopped in some ice cubes, returned with three glasses and a bowl of chips.

---

13. Dad started working at a few funeral homes in late 1990 after several months of secret temp work, the result of his being fired from Aaron Elliot Ltd., a Toronto insurance firm where he had worked as an environmental insurance specialist for the last five years.

Ejecting the videotape from my camcorder, I put the tape into the VCR, hit rewind and sat down on the floor.

The VCR gears whirred.

When it finally stopped, I pressed play. Instantly we began to laugh, watching the inside of my house transform into the Loman household: the bad costumes, the bad acting, the stammers and acne.

"Oh God!" I choked.

Stephen was chomping away as the opening shot played out, his braces overcome by pre-digested potato chips.

Mom was home, her feet across the carpeting, down the hallway.

"You guys OK?" she asked. When her eye scan met me, her eyebrows went up high, along with her voice. "OK?"

"No, we're all dying. Help us," I said. I hit PAUSE on the tape.

"I went to get your sister, and she wasn't there. Did she call?"

"No."

"It's pouring out. Do you boys have umbrellas? I can drive you to the corner when you're ready to go." The boys nodded in slow motion.

"Oh, Mom, Dad called looking for you. He is coming home at seven, he said, with two dead bodies."

She was now upstairs, probably in the master bedroom. We returned to our academic video theatre. Squirming on the couch, I hit PLAY.

"Oh, come on!" Mom yelled. "Don't give me that!"

I shuddered at the shrill reverb.

Stephen stared at me. I blocked them out and listened to the shuffling upstairs and cringed at Mom exhaling dramatically and stomping, "Well, when will you be back?"

I turned the volume up on the television.

Mom's voice tore through the afternoon. "I WAS THERE!"

I could still feel the boys' eyes on me but wasn't going to let them in; it was all business, a class assignment. I focused on the television. I eyed the chips. Took a sip of icy juice. We laughed at our British accents.

"Not bad," Stephen said, reaching for some chips. "I think it's OK, I mean, we gotta edit it."

"I'll edit it," I said.

I wiped some egg salad residue off on my pants. "I think it's great. Fertuck will like it. When are we presenting again?" I asked.

"I think we're third, so probably not 'til uh, Tuesday," Stephen said.

It was nearly five o'clock when Stephen and Jeremy left, having narrowly escaped the prospect of staying for dinner and working into the night. I felt relieved watching them walk down the driveway into tiny rainy blurs.

"They seem nice," Mom said.

"Yeah, they are the best friends a boy could ever ask for."

"Oh, be quiet and set the table."

"I will. I just have to make a phone call."

"Who are you calling?"

"The prime minister," I said, and dialed Andrew's number on the kitchen phone and pulled the cord around into the hallway.

"He's helping me with my assignment." The last four digits of Andrew's number were permanently etched into me, and when Andrew got the number, he told me it was *sixty-four, thirty-six*, and I remembered how he pronounced the two numbers instead of four. I heard him saying those numbers whenever I dialed.

"What are you doing?" I asked, recognizing Andrew's voice when he picked up.

"Nothing. Going out for dinner. Then might play squash."

"Oh," I said. "Squash, huh. You love that now."

"What?"

"Squash. I thought we could play hockey after dinner."

"Naw, too dark," Andrew said.

"Yeah, you're probably right," I said. "Who you playin' squash with?"

"Alex."

"Oh."

"What are you doing?" Andrew asked, half-enthused.

"Just finished my English project, Arthur Miller thing. Salesman. Who's in your group again?"

"Stuart and Cam."

"Oh."

"Hey, is your dad working at the funeral home now?"

"Uh," I stalled, "whaddaymean?" My heart sank. A choke was building around my throat. I remembered the joke Andrew had with his dad, who was round and fat: *So you're going to be around the house?* Emphasizing *around,* as in *mass,* as in elastic, as in—

"My brother says he saw your dad[14] there all weekend."

"I guess so," I said, followed by a shameful sigh.

"You guess so?" Andrew was silent. A car horn sounded off on his end.

"What's that?" I asked, trying to swerve the silent space between us into something else, anything else.

"I gotta go; anyway, talk later," Andrew said, hanging up, the dead dial tone now filling up into my ear.

---

14. I could just imagine my father's interaction at Beverly Funeral Home, quick to laugh at his own jokes, stepping on everyone's silent pauses and excusing himself for cigarette breaks. Dad had method-acting intensity; he treated everyone, no matter what age, in the exact same way. A child's ball would find itself in the path of his car on a family trip, and he'd pull over and get out and begin to lecture the tot. I would begin to panic, heart flooding into my lungs as the parents of the confused youth would come down the driveway onto the street, where Dad would continue his sermon, the same speech: how he was right and they were wrong and that this should not have happened. He loved his voice and sang in the choir. Mom would get nervous whenever a hymn began. Dad sang loud and odd, perhaps out of a necessity to be heard. "I'm doing the harmonies," he would say. When he was young the choir master taught him to sing harmonies, which is fine, but to the general pedestrian world, well, kids in Sunday School would often ask me, "Why does your Dad sing off-key all the time?"

6)

Every Second Counts

Friday, April 17th–Saturday, April 18th, 1992

"My liver is," Holly began, "...full of liver." Her head was a storm of brown hair cracking through the living room and its morning sun. "Good morning, Doctor Silverman, how's the knee?" Holly said, dragging her feet in tiny steps toward the couch. She stared at me with a monstrous smirk.

"What's that from?"

"My mouth, jerk-off," she said, adding, "*Terminator 2: Judgment Day.*"

"Oh right."

"Maybe this afternoon you can get Mom to take you to the store to get the new *Playboy Girls of Fetal Alcohol Syndrome.*"

"No thanks. You're probably in it," I said. "What's your problem?"

"Headache," Holly said.

It was true. I had spent the morning sniffing the usual *Playboy* sheen in my bedroom jockeying my heart rate as I pawed mentally at the

hyper-pink women that delicately paraded themselves, their bodies fingerprinted and creased from our constant exchanges.

Holly picked up a raggedy Penguin paperback of *1984* and began to perform a section. "'With those children,'" she exclaimed, "'that wretched woman must lead a life of terror... Another year, two years,'" Holly continued, dramatically charged now, "'and they would be watching her night and day for symptoms of unorthodoxy...'" Holly wilted onto the couch.

I sprang up. "George Michael has a song like that about two fat children and a drunken man."

"Fuck, I have to finish this essay," Holly said, flapping the paperback.

"I feel crazy today, I want to go outside, and I hate this rain."

"Why?" Holly asked. "You don't like the way it is manifestly attacking?"

"I feel like I'm a bug in a jar."

"Who is it for? All the lonely people..." Holly muttered. I turned off the television.

"Hey punk, I was watching that!"

I was trying to read the instruction manual for my camcorder, intent on doing some dubbing over the weekend.

"I feel like I'm on fire," Holly said.

"You were pretty high last night when you got in, or this morning, whatever," I told her.

"Well, I've been accused of everything," Holly said.

"What did you do last night?" I asked.

"Partied with Liz and some boys."

"Where?"

"Just around. You?"

"Nothing happened to me," I said. "Hey, where's Greyskin?"

Greyskin was the new jab; over the last month or so, Dad's skin appeared to be greying. I mean, it *was* greying. Other family members had endorsed this notion; even at church people were mentioning it to Mom. *David OK, Diane?* Mom would blame the chemicals at his job.

Speculation, but no real proof. I didn't need it or seek it out: Dad *had* grey skin.

"At work I think," Holly said from behind the bathroom door. Flickers of her brown mane ambushed the mirror. I could see just a cropped section of glass from the hall. She flicked the light off and on comically howling, electrocution style.

"Dad is so grey. Am I gonna have it?"

"Grey skin? Do you want grey skin?"

"No."

"Seriously, what's it from? The formaldehyde?"

"I dunno. Mom says he looks awfully uh, ghoulish, I think she said."

"Yeah," I said. "Maybe he fucks the dead bodies."

"Nate! That's fuckin' gross! I have to take a shower, jog and do a bunch of stuff. Let me be. I'll visit you in your cell later."

Ha! *Ghoulish*. Holly even said so. "Hey Hol-o-caust, can-can you-you read-read my story; it's like only four pages long; it's for school," I yelled in long senseless broken staccato up the stairs.

"I guess so," Holly snapped. "Later, Queer-Bait."

*

Mom had her hands on her hips when I trudged inside the house from the grey wet nothing. Long weekends were always especially dull.

I had started taking off my boots when her tinny voice charged at me, full speed.

"Nate, your Hydra died; I found it in the basement when I was doing a wash."

A shiver ran through me as I imagined its horrible tiny skeleton lying on the cold basement floor like a dead anorexic finger, amputated and abandoned.

I had bought a newt during the March break and housed it in our old aquarium. It was the second newt in five years.

"It was just a skeleton," Mom said, shaking her head as she passed me on the basement steps. "They seem to like to escape your room to kill themselves!" Mom laughed.

"Gross," I said.

One night it must have, like its predecessor, scaled the side of its glass home and high-tailed it out of my room, only to end up starving to death on our basement floor.

Mom was full of apples and moved to a static bounce in her step as classical music chortled through a tiny radio. She wore a mauve knit turtleneck with brown slacks. Her hair was a loose perm, falling from its coiled decadence, wash after wash, flattening out at the sides. Her crisp coal eyes targeted nothing in particular until she met my gaze. In her pre-grocery-store military mode, she surveyed the supplies and planned counter-attacks to a variety of operatives, including Sadie's meows, the addition of Holly to the size of the salad, and of course, the gas mileage to take into consideration for various obligatory inner-city jaunts that might present themselves over the weekend. The miserable weather made a screen of rain at every window.

Holly banged around in the shower as I drank up the remainder of my cereal juice. Mom walked out of the kitchen and stood in the hallway. I stopped, frozen with a spoon in my mouth, suspended in my own animation.

"I was just talking to your dad on the phone. He was having his lunch, and it'll be a year ago that he started working part-time at the funeral home," she said, putting down a box of books on the dining-room table. She was good with numbers, personal statistics and morbid anniversaries.

"A year of working with the dead bodies," I said. "That's reason to celebrate."

What was so incredibly ridiculous to me about the whole undertaker routine was that it just *had* to be good ol' Andrew's family funeral home; nope, no other funeral home in town would do. It had been a full year of his family laughing at our poverty and accruing shame.

Sarcastically, I clutched my hands together as if a crop of puppies had appeared in a wicker basket. "Our *very own* undertaker. Can we keep him?!"

Dad was still green but very eager in the mortuary arts; he spoke of it with gusto over meals: stews blown over and the reluctant salads. *Go, Team Death.*

While looking for vacant VHS tape space for one of my morbid surveillance bedroom press conferences, I accidentally stumbled upon the VHS recording of Dad on the evening news. Holly had labelled *"Daddy on The National: January 4, 1990."* As he talked on the phone, the CBC voiceover called him Dave. *"Dave ——, who works for Aaron Elliot Ltd. in Toronto says..."* and Dad's dull voice played out for thirteen seconds in a low-watt treble leaking from underneath his ragged moustache, barely cleared the threshold of sonar wavelength. It was his last few months in the environmental-liability insurance industry, before he got loaded at an office function and told off his boss.

The significance of his one-year anniversary was tenuous, at least to me, simply because I knew that he couldn't be earning that much money part-time and that Uncle Carl was more than likely still handing us cheques every couple of months, *and it was just so incredibly—*

"Do you know what I want?" Holly said, emerging dramatically from the bathroom, chewing on an apple core, hair dripping wet, shaking her lowered head from side to side as she chewed the remainder vigorously. Bits of water from her hair landed on my face.

—tense in a way, unstable. Mom talked out loud to herself in a walking list of errands, acting out conversations with Uncle Carl in which she would ask him for some more money. "See if he can help us out again," was more than a common rehearsal refrain, one she rarely covered up.

"I want..." Holly continued...

"What do you want?" Mom asked, her face paused on a grimace of genuine anticipation.

Holly spoke, her voice now imbuing a soft southern twang. "What I want is a view. I want a window where I can see a tree, or even water. I want to be in a federal institution, far away from Dr. Chilton..."

I laughed. "That's funny," I said, forgetting about the mini shower my sister had just given me.

We had watched *Silence of the Lambs* the last time she was home from school, very late, falling in and out of sleep like two raccoons plump on refuse.

"So what's the deal with Easter dinner, Mom?" Holly asked from behind a wall of wet brown hair, large towel draped over her mane. "Are we going to Grammy's or is she coming here Sunday or what?"

Holly posed these queries with an impatient-sounding voice, one that demonstrated kinetic urgency, waiting for her jogging gear to dry, waiting for Elizabeth to wake up and call.

"I wanted to have dinner Sunday, but your father has to work, so we might do it today at around four o'clock and Grammy *might* come over," Mom said.

"Do we really have to go get her from Plum Island Animal Disease Research Facility?" Holly asked, now frantically drying her hair with the towel.

"I don't know what you are talking about but I don't like it. I'm waiting 'til your Dad phones and I'll know for sure. In the meantime, why don't you finish your laundry; and Nate, you must have home-work to do."

"Wait 'til your father gets home!" Holly said, doing an obnoxious dance. She twirled up the wet frenzy into a towel. I just stood there waiting for Holly to shut up. She was high or something.

"Be a dear, Nate, you wish-washy, prissy sweetheart, and check on my clothes in the dryer. If they're still wet, put them on for another twenty?"

"Is Uncle Carl coming over?" Holly asked Mom.

"If he feels up to it. We might meet him over at Grammy's."

"After my run, I have to do some stuff at the library on Slobodan Milošević and the whole Sarajevo crisis. They're attacking the city with canons. It's really intense. I have to do a fake field report for my world issues class," Holly said, now striding up the stairs.

The phone rang. "Got it!"

*

Andrew and I had been waffling in routine, sometimes road hockey, sometimes pornography. I knew that if I got a ride home with him after school, he'd turn things into one or the other: hockey or...porno watching.

And a part of me got excited at the thought that one of these activities would happen...like perhaps his silver car would sidle up, and he'd slow down and drive me home, my newly dubbed mixed tape jiggling in my pants, the one I stayed up making, hoping to play for him.

Andrew had mentioned how, if I wanted to, I could pirate one of his Dad's pornos we'd watched recently. He knew I liked the one with the woman fucking the navy sergeant, her pink lipstick smeared from the task, her spit fettered to his long hard dick.

On her knees, blouse open, long skirt compromised; she pumped her head while he ran his hands through her honey-blonde hair. Another one on the same clunking tape showed a guy getting a brunette ready with tons of fingers, including hers. (Her hands came from between her legs, entwined with his until all their fingers met inside.)

We had planned out a dub session in the late afternoon. Andrew had assured me we'd have time to dub the whole thing once we took care of our own enjoyment of these hard adults and their acrobatic efforts. I arrived just before three and, with his eye on the front door, Andrew navigated us through the opening credits, the test dub and mouth over his hard dick. After it was my turn to come, and the dub was complete, Andrew drove me home, just in time for dinner, my absence barely detected.

"There you are," Mom said, as I huffed in through the front door. "Your coach called, says there is a practice next Sunday at his place. He wants you to call him."

Traces of smells and odours carved up the dinner hour: the red meat sauce browning and bubbling; the beef smog and faint cigarette stink lingering in the hall closet, muted by our coat fibres; the formaldehyde footprints: domestic ingredients were all caged inside the house.

"I'm going to the liquor store, and then I'll be back," Holly hollered. I didn't answer.

Twenty minutes later I heard the action at the side door, recalling a terrifying evening nearly a year ago, when I had accidentally knocked a full beer bottle from Dad's hand when I energetically burst into the house to find Grammy, who was visiting.

Dad was en route from the pantry when we collided. The next thing I knew he was screaming at me while I was on the basement floor picking up pieces of glass. The shouting attracted Grammy, who sat at the top of the staircase watching Dad admonish me for murdering his bottle of beer.

It was obscene: the energy exuding from Dad's angry sermon was God-like. The ridicule came out in bursts of sawdust and other alchemic symbols that I associated with him at the time. Strapped to an indoor lightning rod in the basement, I absorbed it all.

And when my tiny Grammy took in the show on the top of the stairs, who sat down in protest of her grandson's abuse, Dad lifted her up and carried her thirty feet back to the living room couch and continued his beer eulogy. All I did was come inside my own house, just as Dad was retrieving a beer bottle from the pantry. As the door sprang open, it hit his shoulder, sailing the bottle in the air for what felt like ten minutes, smashing into pieces in front of my bedroom on the cool, tiled floor, staining the drywall and sending Dad into an acidic fit.

Too ugly to recall verbatim, he said something like, "I'll put your face in it," as he pushed my neck down towards the dirty suds, tiles smeared in its foul dreg stench and my snot dripping dangerously close to the putrid-smelling liquid. Dad raged with adrenaline, acting as if I had murdered his unborn child, run over his dog and burned down his house, all on the same day.

When I slinked my head up the stairs, Holly was cleaning her heels with a paper towel at the front door.

"Holy shit! At the LCBO parking lot I successfully navigated sheer black ice, sloped driveway cross-wise, and just now our ice-covered steps in the pitch dark in stilettos without wiping out: the crowd goes wild!"

"Why were you wearing heels?"

"To see if I could manage them tonight. I think we know the answer to that one."

"I think your laundry is done. The machine stopped mumbling."

"It's *so* nuts out there!" Holly said, blowing her hair from her eyes. "I'm freezing."

I looked at the bags beside her stocking feet. "Whatcha get?"

"Some rum for me and Liz, and some garbage snacks. She's in town for the week from Vancouver. Haven't really seen that much of her since Christmas."

"Drunk drivers of Canada."

"Oh, Mom says we're going to see Grammy tomorrow, not today."

"Why?"

"They're having some potluck thing, and Mom is taking over a card or something and then coming back. She said there was only room for one at the potluck last supper. I wasn't really listening."

"Oh."

"I just wish she'd come here for the weekend. I don't understand why it's so political. She can sleep in my room, and I can crash on the couch."

Friday night was a high-energy session for me, filled with oddly lit solo driveway hockey marathons, homework and queuing up what was now a clunky fortress of videotapes; their meticulously noted labels the only way to discern unique content.

I cued up the porn I'd dubbed from Andrew and turned the volume down, watching the blonde-haired woman in the blouse with the bulbous honey bun bob her head up and down on the second generation VHS copy. She appeared to be sucking off a man back from the war, or an airline pilot. The moans and slurps were digitally muffled and garbled by the video degeneration of piracy. I watched his thick dick glisten in and out of her mouth, her large eyes opening and closing. I thought of Andrew and I, our sessions, his torso leaning over me, descending himself and sliding his tongue around my shaft until eventually enveloping my shy dick in his hot mouth as I closed my eyes and rolled my head back until a familiar chorus rang through my entire body.

*

Late Saturday morning, Holly was telling me about her new boyfriend, Steve, when the videotape in the VCR began to make a garbled ruckus. Steve had a car and was sort of hysterical and really smart, but most of the time they fought about *everything*. "He's a year older than me and thinks he knows *how the world really works*, he tells me, and all this other garbage—but he can't even change a flat tire or fix my shelves, or spell Michigan."

I blurted out, "Who cares about spelling Michigan?"

"I care, dickless!" Holly laughed.

The VCR motored past the glitch and jumped back into frame. It was a popular film about a dead rock star. The bearded lead actor twisted the cap off a bottle of alcohol and took a noisy swig.

"You can die from just about anything," Holly said. "My humanities class has shown me this, you know, that collective deaths of a group of people or random individual deaths and the way we react as a society and individually, IT'S MIND BLOWING! A town will mourn the death of a small-town football hero but some big-city taxi driver or a family wiped out by a drunk driver or mother of ten in Cambodia gets stabbed, it can be tucked into the back of our psyche forever."

"That's a class?"

"Yeah, I love it."

Holly came in and out of the living room. The telephone, left off the hook, went into a big pulsing headache. "Why is the phone off the hook?"

"I don't know."

"What movie is this?"

"I think it's *The Thing* or *The Blob. The* something." I didn't answer her. She rattled her cup of ice water.

In the film, a bright-eyed wino saw an asteroid. His dog was equally disturbed before the film cut to two varsity boys at a drugstore planning their sexual escapades for the weekend, when into the store walked the local priest.

I hit PLAY. On a tape labelled *Dec. 7, 1991,* I watched a recent rerun of my own life: Sunnybrook Park, the bucolic winter nothing, and me. In the video, I move through the thickets, the twisted thorns and burrs as I took my *GT Sno-Racer* down into the cement path, past the rippling woods on either side.

"Swear to accomplish this task before nightfall!" Holly shouted, pointing her finger at me.

"Huh?"

"Mom wants you to vacuum your room. Do you know if we're eating the midwinter boar for Easter or what?"

"No idea," I said.

"I'm sure there's a big cadaver in the fucking freezer."

"Oh." Holly looked at the television.

"What fresh hell is this we're watching?"

*

By mid-afternoon, Holly had disappeared again, so it was just Mom and me visiting Grammy at Central Park Lodge—a retirement home in Thorncliffe Park, an offshoot neighbourhood in East York, a ten-minute drive north of our house.

The area was a ghettoized suburb comprised largely of stuffy high-rise apartments, a dilapidated mall (Zellers, a bowling alley, shoe repair, custom T-shirt print shop, food court, BiWay, women's and men's fashion, designer footwear, Radio Shack, Pizza Pizza, a large grocery store, beer store, electronics, lotto-and-cigar shop, dentist, optometrist) a feeble library, and a high school recently renamed after a Canadian astronaut, Marc Garneau.

For nearly two years now, Grammy had slept each night in a tiny metal-rimmed bed and puttered around the miserable confines of her walk-in closet-sized room, which was furnished with a crummy desk and dresser, a one-seater chair, and a terrible view of the gaping parking lot seven floors below. Her room was barren, devoid of the rat-packing bounty for which she was known. Even her trademark geraniums, which in her former apartment, could always be seen spread out on display, were never replaced. Instead, two greeting cards and some photographs lay warped on her dresser. She would, on occasion, ask me about the whereabouts of her cassette tapes, which featured recordings of random evenings in her Etobicoke life with my Grampy: playing the piano, having friends over, indiscernible merriment. I told her they were safe, stashed neatly next to my own cassette inventory. I found it depressing that Grammy had been reduced to this miniscule quadrant. Our visits were short-lived, overheated, with nowhere to even hang our big dumb winter coats.

When we got to her room, Uncle Carl was already there, standing by the window.

"Hi Unc," Mom chirped.

Uncle Carl wore a dull grey suit with old and new dandruff caked on his shoulders. A tattered red sweater-vest was worn underneath, while his dress shirt was light blue and accompanied by a crusty clip-on tie. He looked like a vacuum-cleaner salesman from a 1961 episode of *The Twilight Zone*. His hair was slicked back (grey/black), cut extremely short on the sides. Sparse white hairs could still be seen from within his dark, neat coif.

Mom said he dyed his hair with a tonic. "It's what a lot of elderly men do," Mom once told us. "It sometimes doesn't looks very good, but we shouldn't say anything."

"So it's women's hair dye?"

"No, it's a special tonic cream," Mom had told us without getting into any clairvoyant detail. I just filed it under *Mom's War Room Mystery Facts*.

"You're looking fine," Uncle Carl said to Grammy, who lay cork-screwed and twisted in starchy sheets, his dwindling sister-in-law, both aged seventy-four years, who had known each other since the late 1930s. Uncle Carl was my godfather, my "Great" Uncle Carl, the arbiter of my on-call super-VHS glory reel, the controversial camcorder that cost $1,276.56, the one who slipped me twenties, developed my rolls of film from my insatiable documentation of driveway hockey or Han Solo poses, or prop *Star Wars* models or any other evidence of my inability to socialize in normative levels. Through Uncle Carl, I had become a mental tourist, photographing and videotaping the nothing around me.

"Just fine," he said, nodding to her and glancing at me for an endorsement. "It's warming up. Soon you'll be able to go outside for a nice walk," Uncle Carl said, with a denture click, giving Grammy a big diplomatic smile, talking in an elevation of tone, bordering on condescending baby talk.

"Gotta get some fresh air in here," Mom said, beginning her usual tirade of blunt commentary.

"Yes, dear," Grammy said, on her back, head tilted on a slant, as if sunk deep in her thick mattress,

"Yes, Mom," Grammy said, reversing order, reversing roles. As Mom tried to get the window open, she continued, "You've been eating too many bananas, Mom."

"Pardon dear?" Grammy's tiny voice asked.

"Eating too many bananas, I said," Mom repeated, this time louder.

"Gonna get fat," Mom added, finally cranking open the window. "Hot in here." She was chewing her Trident peppermint gum wildly on one side, smashing the tiny piece of malleable sugar-free goo like a factory piston up and down.

We took our coats off.

The nurse came in with a big smile and hellos and a loud narration of her intended actions: "JUST GOING TO CHANGE YOU NOW, THEN TAKE YOU DOWN FOR DINNER SOON, YES, IT'S DINNER TIME, THELMA, IS THIS YOUR GRANDSON SO NICE OF THEM TO COME VISIT NOW ISN'T THAT RIGHT MOM OH SO KIND SO NICE LOOKING SUCH A NICE FAMILY I RECOGNIZE YOU BOTH FROM YOUR PHOTOGRAPHS..."

When we left Grammy's furnace of a room and headed to the elevator, Uncle Carl began his escape route story. I was still filming. An elderly woman approached Mom. I took some shots out the hall window before I spun the camera down the hall when I heard the interaction, trying my best to capture some of it.

"It's so *hot*; you've got to tell them to do something about the heat," she said in a half-voice. You could tell it was a struggle for her to speak.

"OK, I will," Mom said, her gum-chewing now coming to a standstill.

"It's *terribly hot*," the woman said, her voice flinty, bits of the words truculent over mucus slime in the larynx, reaching her hand out towards Mom. She looked as though she was about to fall over. "I'll see what I can do," Mom assured her, as the woman disappeared down the hallway, clutching the rail the whole way.

"I should probably go before it gets too late," Uncle Carl said, as he entered the elevator. "Traffic and such."

"It's not even five yet, though; stay for dinner, why don't you?" Mom said encouragingly. "I'm making a nice pork roast and *patatays*," she concluded, matter-of-factly, as if the meal she had in store for us would bring our scrawny, elderly relative rushing to the table, napkin around his neck, salivating.

Mom's lips were wrenched in a question mark, her eyebrow cocked, sheer eye whites on pause, looking at me with a tinge of anxious concern.

I lowered the video camera, turning the power off and slid the cumbersome machine into my duffle bag. "It's so hot in this place," I said to my uncle, who was once again clicking away inside his mouth, his dentures and his jaw at work in a symphony onto itself. The small reserve of energy that remained in my uncle's day wasn't going to get him through the variables of the ever-tense innards of *good ol' 161 Glenvale Boulevard*.

"Maybe there's a hockey game on," Mom said with a hopeful chirp, now desperately trying to entice him. "David gets back from work at seven, so—"

"No, no, I should get going," Uncle Carl concluded, now looking straight ahead towards the UP/DOWN eyes of the elevator's electronic door.

"I'll be seeing you soon; give me a call sometime."

"You sure?"

"Say hello to Dave for me," he said. "I'll see him next time, I'm sure."

"OK, well, I'll give you a call next week, Unc," Mom said.

Uncle Carl nodded, car keys just rows of glint, indistinct teeth, losing colour in the rainy darkness. Hunched, he vanished into the early evening melancholy.

Mom and I walked to the car. "Gosh, it's still horrible out," she said, quickening her pace through the parking lot. "Holly wants us to pick her up at Yonge and Eglinton."

I nodded. "And when's *Greyskin* coming back?" I struggled for a second with the slickened door handle, my other hand carrying the duffle bag. She now accepted *Greyskin* as my official nickname for my undead undertaker of a father.

"Seven, I think," she said, starting the ignition, my mixed tape automatically continuing to play George Michael's song *Heal the Pain*. We slowed down as we approached the familiar corner of Yonge and Eglinton, trying to sort through the cluster of youths in puffy parkas and neon scarves. Billows of smoke and breath hovered above them.

"There she is," Mom said, slowing down.

Holly waved goodbye to a selection of smoking friends.

"Hey, guys," she said, cheekbones awash with rain, her eel-coloured hair flattened in chaotic ropes against her head.

"Library didn't have what I needed, but I did find some information on Grandfather's Anglican '60s cult and other assorted family witch-craft history," Holly said with a wet snarl.

"Don't start in about that. I had to yell at your aunt and grandfather on more than one occasion that I don't want them to talk about it in front of you guys, especially when you were little. They were obsessed with all that stuff."

"OK, sorry." Holly said. "Oh, I ran into Liz and we went to the record store. Oh, and we're going to a party tonight at ten."

"You need the car?"

"Nope, but you can drop me off. What's for dinner? I'm starving."

"We're having cake and eggs for dinner." I said.

"All right. I'll have mine raw and cracked over my cake." Holly said.

"Me too!" I shouted.

"We're having spaghetti," Mom said, returning us to culinary reality.

"Another recipe from the *No Surprises Cookbook*, hey, Mom?" Holly said with a shit-eating grin, as she fastened her seatbelt and exhaled dramatically.

"Well, the thing is, I don't know when your father is coming home," Mom said. "So it's easy to heat up."

"It's good that he's out of the house, a part of society again, maybe he'll meet a new family," I said in a barbed tone. "I've always thought that he had another family."

"You're a weirdo," Holly said, reaching for the radio knobs.

Mom laughed as we turned east on Broadway, heading towards Mount Pleasant, through to Bayview, Hanna Road, Tanager, Rumsey, Beaufield, to Sutherland to Glenbrae, eventually turning north until we reached Glenvale; our Oldsmobile station wagon acted like a room-temperature-seeking missile as we pulled into the driveway.

"It's hail," Mom said, holding her hands up against the sky.

"I think its sleet, Mom," Holly said, shutting the car door with her butt. I waited for Mom to have the front door open before leaving the car, securing my camera tight in my bag.

*

"You're father's home. Clear the table, Nate; he'll want to eat."

I moved the remnants of dinner and some newspapers Holly had been rifling through for school.

"Hello," Dad said, Mom sprinting in the hallway, status-updating the situation, the blow-by-blow account of the last eight hours.

"I'll read your story tonight, homo," Holly said, passing me in the hallway, her hand covering her mouth as if giving me spy instructions.

Mom opened the oven door, which always sounded like a huge iron drawbridge lowering. She took a plate of hot spaghetti from its dark mouth.

"I was just going to call you at work to see if you'd left," she said, adding, "There's a salad too. You can start with that, then I'll bring your dinner to you, nice and hot."

"Thanks," Dad said, followed by his three to four honking nose blows.

Accompanying Dad was the faint ghostly film of his Craven "A" cigarette stink. Despite the fact that he had quit smoking (or had led many of us to believe as much since the fall), I knew for a fact he was still smoking and would routinely go out for long walks to smoke. Holly said she saw Dad smoking on Eglinton a few times.

Dad directed his comments to Mom in particular as he went through each detail of his day at Beverly Funeral Home: pureeing words and collective opinions of staff on various aspects of this death of a day. In his dull voice, Dad used funeral slang as well now, calling the deceased "stiffs" and shortening the name of the funeral home to "Bev's." He talked with pageantry of each funeral, how the flowers were late and orders mixed up, and what he said to the flower store manager, as politely as he could muster under the circumstances, explaining how the families had spent hundreds of dollars on particular arrangements.

"It was a lovely service," before blowing over a fork full of pasta. "Family came from Vancouver, Washington and even Australia."

"Sounds rough, Dad," Holly said, patting his forearm, "flowers, frost, passports and formaldehyde."

"School going well? Your studies keeping you busy?" Dad asked her, as she headed towards the den.

"My *studies* are fine, Father," Holly said in solemn voice, sneaking me a toothy laugh, sipping on her ice water. (Later laughing with me at how Dad always called them "studies.")

"Exams?"

"No thanks, I'm good," Holly snapped, getting up. "Um, next week," she blurted out from the hallway, TV remote in hand. She flicked the television on, twirling the remote as if it were a gun from the Wild West. "I'm going to watch the boob tube."

Dad finished the last strand of sauce-tangled pasta as the kettle began to boil.

The way I saw it, Holly could tell all the quick-wit jokes in the world she wanted. It was a cameo for her, one she knew wasn't going to play into any larger, drawn-out battle. She was in and out; no longer here for the long haul, the endurance test, and the moods galore that rotated Russian roulette style on a big invisible whim wheel we all took turns spinning, one that hung enormous in my psyche.

7)

In a Lonely Place

Sunday, April 19th, 1992

After my paper route, I took a shower and ate the two pastries (one apple fritter, one dutchie) I had bought with some hot tea. The house was beginning to wake up. I cleaned up the scattered remains of plastic from the newspaper bundles and went outside. Mom began her floating housecoat routine in the kitchen and hallways. She poked her head out the side door, eyes soft with a tired glaze.

"Nate! Did you want some breakfast?"

"No, thanks, I ate stuff."

I shot the tennis ball into the empty net for about an hour. With its subtle motor purring, the video camera witnessed my repetitive driveway pantomime. We were live.

At noon, Holly made her way downstairs, groggy, her eyes barely open. She was holding my story for English class, eyeing me in the den, my hand clutching the VCR remote, a glass of milk in the other. The story I had composed, all four pages of it, consisted of an early evening alien invasion and its effect on some neighbourhood children.

"Morning," she said in a tiny chirp. "Can you make me some tea?"

"Yeah," I said. "Want a waffle? I was gonna have one."

With her hair a tangled web, Holly didn't seem to care, the faint stink of booze still emanating from her.

"I heard you puking this morning."

"Do we have any Tylenol?"

I shrugged, as Holly began scrambling for the antidote. Gulps ensued. She punched the air triumphantly as she chugged a final cup of tap water. "Holy shit."

She plunked down beside me. I passed her a pillow and lowered the volume on the television.

"You drink a ton last night?"

"Shhhh."

After a few sips of tea and a big bite of waffle, Holly shook my story up in the air.

"Your story makes no sense. The alien thing? A bunch of kids on the street see a light in the sky, and then a man comes out of his house and says to the kids, 'YOU MUST NOT TELL ANYONE WHAT YOU SAW!'"

"Makes perfect sense to me."

"Weird. Is it supposed to be Dad?"

"No, just, like, some dad."

"Are you going to hand it in like that?"

"Dunno. Why?"

"How much is it worth? Do you have Fertuck?"

"You make it sound like a disease. Yeah, she's my teacher. She's *always* my teacher for English, like, every year."

"And it's for how much?"

"Like five percent or something."

"Well, fuck, then—who cares!"

"Not me!"

"Did Fertuck ever tell you that the gymnasium is described in the opening of *The Handmaid's Tale*?"

"No."

"It's true. It's the gym, that's what the teachers at Leaside say. I'm sure they'll tell you all about it. She went there."

"Who?"

"Atwood."

"To Leaside?"

"Yeah," Holly began to nod in a trance, her mouth now half full of a syrupy waffle clump.

"Freddie Mercury tribute concert is on MuchMusic today."

"George is in it too."

"Really?"

"And Guns N' Roses and Elton John. Pretty weird combo."

*

The afternoon passed in a blitz of television signals, the grazing of homework and assorted personal VHS inventory. I lulled in my room. I watched the footage I'd shot six months earlier up at Andrew's cottage, where we played Frisbee on the beach, the wind blowing the res disc back to him every time he attempted to throw it to me. Another segment showed Andrew telling his brother the story of how I got black-flagged go-karting because of my bad driving.

My hands were crushing my cheeks. I stared at my feet lumps under my fading blue comforter. I gulped water and wiped a premature tear. I put on music, looking at the back cover of a tired hand-me-down *Playboy*. I slid it under my bed. I felt sick, like a cold had colonized in my throat. I had just heard half a garbled answering machine message from an accountant and feared the worst. My gut reaction was the house would be sold and that we were broke. Holly poked her head into my room as a thousand unknowns pinballed around inside.

"Just doing some more laundry."

I didn't look up.

"What's wrong?"

"You think Dad's OK? I mean, do you think we're going to be OK?"

"What do you mean?"

I drew my knees into my chest. "Like, are we going to have to sell the house?"

"I don't think we're going to sell the house anytime soon," Holly said, shaking out a pillowcase.

"Sometimes I want to live in the park."

Holly spun around on my bare bedroom floor, hands full of balled socks.

She sat on my bed. She put her feet in the freshly dried laundry.

"Remember when we ran away?"

"Yeah. Those were the days. I think of that, about sleeping in the park and having lots of blankets. Not having to spend money."

"Come on, park boy; let's go watch something upstairs. Get out of your dungeon for a bit."

I heard the electric tingle of the heater that ran along the southern wall of my room and the churning dryer. Grabbing an empty mug, I headed to the surface. The kitchen sink had the remnants of some-one's chicken pot pie, all soggy flakes with floating peas in a gross sink swamp. I turned on the tap and unclogged the drain, running my hands under the clean current. A half-empty glass of fruit punch also sat in the sink's bog. As the stream poured through and I loosened the obstructions near the plug, I watched the runs of blood red trickle weak and pink in the glass, becoming near invisible in the stream.

"Shit!"

"What happened?"

"Just the water; it's hot." I shook my hands, noticing Holly take something from the refrigerator. "I'll be right there," I said.

I joined Holly on the couch. She was flipping through the channels.

"Hol, it's so weird, Dad working for Andrew's dad's company, the funeral parlour."

"Yeah, I guess."

"Like how many funeral homes are there in this city anyway?"

"Dunno, not that many, I guess," Holly said, folding a faded yellow T-shirt and placing it gently in the pink laundry basket. "Why?"

"Never mind."

"Speaking of that, you, ah, seen my Nirvana yellow happy-face tee?"

"Huh? No idea where your shirt is. I haven't seen it, but Mom might have put it in my drawer."

The house smelled like a hostile chemical warzone; a dense sick-cat smell that hung like invisible fungus. The musk of death perfumes, elixirs, and an invisible powder that I imagined the funeral men swallowed in Styrofoam cups each morning instead of staff room coffee— a disgusting drink that would keep them solemn, calm and respectful around the continuous barrage of stiffs they had to carry, drain, manicure, deliver and hoist.

"Oh, Dad's dentist called this afternoon, can you tell him, in case I'm not here? I think he's sleeping upstairs," Holly said.

"Just write it down. *Hey, Deadman, call your teeth master. Love, Repo Man,*" I said.

"Dad bought all these new undertaker clothes like special pants and a jacket and ties," Holly said. "He did a fashion show for me last night."

"Rigor Mortis Man fashion show. Maybe he takes the teeth of the dead and has them..."

"Nate, that's so gross!"

Digging in the couch, I found half a cherry-bomb dud under a cushion. Once, playing with Andrew, one had gone off in my hand and felt like a knife had been jammed in and out of my palm for several minutes.

I poked Holly's toes.

"Quit it."

For the last few weekends, Saturdays were the same predictable scene: me calling Andrew, and his brother or father being polite as they informed me he was out playing squash or driving around the city in his new car.

"My roommate drives me nuts; she is so fucking loud when she eats apples. Sounds like bones breaking in her mouth."

"Gross."

"I love her, but just didn't know she ate food like a prehistoric monster."

When she wasn't looking I had hit PLAY on the remote. The VCR began to cue up an image in a netherworld of previously recorded and

recorded-over material. As it cleared up completely, it revealed four
tanned men inside a ring, ricocheting into one another. The announcer's
starchy voice explained the action: "Once again, here, the pendulum
has shifted and is now in favour of the champions..."

"Let's watch *Die Hard*," Holly said. "Not this, *please*."

I hit EJECT.

*

The phone rang. It was Andrew.

The night's detour took the form of an early evening drive to the
parking lot of the CNIB, where we fumbled in the cold. We didn't discuss the hockey game, our family's grim activities or school assignments. We took turns in the dark, pumping and sucking like we had
done dozens of times like we were on a nature program like this was
how it all went. My eyes were half-cocked and watching the dark road
for any passers-by or cars or cyclists, elderly couples strolling towards
the crest of Bayview Avenue and the cemetery that lined the long
stretch like ancient gray teeth hidden under the cold Leaside moon-
light.

"I'm freezing."

"Hold on," Andrew said, cranking the heat, his fly lowered, shirt
dangling over his public hair and shadowed girth. After the low-lit
fondling, he dropped me off at home.

*

The ham was carved, served and the dishwasher digested the memory
with a long wet hum. A dry apple crumble was lapped up with vanilla
ice cream. Mom and I toiled in the aftermath.

Holly had her backpack at the door; she was all ready and waiting
to be driven to the subway.

"I wish Grammy coulda come. So stupid she has to be in that place, eating toothpaste for dinner," Holly snapped. Mom turned to me, eyeing the open dishwasher.

"Did you get all the dishes from your room?"

"Yes. There were twenty-five different cups and plates."

"I'm going to bring Grammy some ham tomorrow," Mom said. "And some dessert, so don't eat it all."

Holly was all agitated, hand tapping out a treble on the dinning-room table.

"Why don't you just have the guard bring it to Grammy's cell instead? They stopped feeding her or something? Do they make her do the dishes in between her gerbil-wheel exercises? It's like a sweatshop for the undead there. I feel horrible every time I go. It's so gross, I—"

"Don't play woe-is-me all the time," Mom snapped.

"I just don't like that place; it's depressing as hell!" Holly shouted.

"Quit feeling sorry for yourself. It's important to visit. To remember—"

"I'm just glad we didn't run into any of Grammy's gang members."

"What are you talking about?"

"Those toughs who roughed up your donut the last time," Holly said.

"Oh, be quiet."

"Yeah, we don't want to get mugged in the elevator," I said, shaking my head in melodramatic nuisance.

Last week, Mom had returned from visiting Grammy visibly upset. I consoled her as best I could, unable to comprehend the showdown she claimed had taken place. While visiting in the dining room area, a resident who was sitting at their table had put her cigarette out in Mom's éclair, causing Mom to weep when relaying the incident to me with all the emotion of a grieving astronaut's wife.

I thought it was the funniest thing I'd ever heard: a skeletal hand stubbing out a lit cigarette in Mom's unsuspecting dessert, on instant replay, like a crime re-enactment or anti-smoking ad created just for the immediate family.

Dad was on the couch reading the newspaper. I decided to do my homework at the living-room table, a few feet from his traditional couch spot. The discussion about Grammy had ended, and now an independent study was on the agenda as Sadie walked by demanding a catnip fix.

"WOULD YOU JUST TELL ME, FOR GOD'S SAKE?" Mom bellowed, tea towel in hand.

"I TOLD YOU: 8:40!" Holly shouted from upstairs.

In Technicolor brilliance, history was about to be made. As I read my history text, I noticed the house's slowed-down vibe growing into this pink afterglow. How it began: Mom slapped some raw beef into patties, a monthly or weekly ritual depending on the price of beef. She started slapping them together from a big mixing bowl, adding eggs and breadcrumbs. The meat's noise created a loud rhythmic spank.

Sipping his coffee, shuffling newsprint and clearing his throat in boorish symphony, Dad gauged the living room's turbulence. He started making disapproving sounds with his teeth and tongue. At first I thought it was something he was reading, but I could tell he was staring towards the kitchen. The slapping continued.

Dad put down his newspaper blinders and, waiting now for a good series of meat slaps, he pounced, as if on cue, on the seventh or eighth consistent meat slap, from his sofa spot, said with surround-sound: "DIANE PUT YOUR PANTS BACK ON!" then laughed maniacally, proud of his zinger. Newspaper rustle, silence from the kitchen. Dad kept laughing.

I felt a jolt of disgust. Mom answered, half choking on something, water perhaps, "What?"

The air was still in the house; my stomach tightened as I looked over at Dad, the living room now turning into a gauze of orange.

Dad stopped his thunderous laugh track cold to add, "Sounds like you are spanking yourself in there."

My face flushed, insides a bit off-balance, I turned my head and glared at Dad, disgusted by his unmitigated crudeness, his insane delivery of perverse hatred of all things normal and sane. When he caught my gaze I delivered my own bolt of living-room terror: "You know, you're a *real* asshole."

Dad's face paused, caught in the 60-watt accent.

"I *beg* your pardon?" *I beg your pardon?* was Dad's most classic catch phrase, from which I coined what I felt was a massively catchy retort, "Yeah, you *better* beg," fostering the conflict into a certified, plaque-like permanence.

It happened so naturally: Dad rose from the pink sofa, walked the twenty feet towards the dining room table where I sat, took off his belt, undid his pants, turned around and mooned me, spreading his cheeks to show his actual asshole.

Catching a single frame of his anus, I quickly looked away.

"*That's* an asshole!" Dad said, his back to me, holding his cheeks open for a few more seconds, the pose frozen in time like a prehistoric exhibit roped off for all to witness.

At midnight, Holly called long distance from Kingston to let us know she was safe at home, and Mom said, "Call me on Wednesday...I just made hamburger patties for the week, I can mail you a care package or something...no, I won't mail you hamburgers! OK, good night."

As I fell asleep I imagined myself in the throes of wrestling supremacy. My current foes in 1992 were Alex and Andrew, the new duo of squash games and long drives throughout the city buying batteries or whatever the hell electronic equipment Andrew needed to tweak his greedy universe. At first I didn't mind Alex; he even played hockey with Andrew and I a couple of times in my driveway, and we did a video project together for English. But then, both of them just sort of vanished... As I tried to fall asleep, I jostled for position, fingers putting pressure on their trapezes, counter arm-bar with illegal hair-pull: Alex's greasy face sliding off my knuckles, my fists hitting the canvas, the other hand pulled out from under skull like a magic tablecloth. Tripped up, they fall down, and I leap on top of them, shake both their skulls with hands into the mat. Jump up: land the knee across the left jaw. The skull feels it on all sides, from all angles. Flashbulbs went off in a storm of preservatives.

The next morning at school, I couldn't wait to tell Andrew about all the action through the distracting clink noises of our lockers opening and closing. I was relaying the showdown with as much suspense as possible.

"It was so fucked up."

"So what happened?"

"I called him an asshole 'cos he was making some gross joke about my mom spanking herself, and he gets up off the couch, undoes his belt buckle, turns around, pulls down his pants *and* underwear, spreads his ass cheeks and shows me his asshole!"

"Are you serious?" Andrew said, eyes lit up pinball style.

"Yeah, he just mooned me, showed me his butt hole."

"Oh my God! That's hilarious!" Andrew beamed. "*And* disgusting!"

"I know," I laughed, eating the remains of a bran muffin I found in my locker.

"Your family is nuts."

"How was your Easter?" I asked, with a bedeviled smirk fit for a sit-com prince. On the inside, I felt ashamed, and a large bolt of panic tore through me.

Andrew shrugged. "Just had dinner, whatever. My family didn't expose themselves to me," he said, yuk-yuking and shaking his head side to side.

"Well, you know, everyone celebrates holidays differently," I said, adjusting my backpack and wiping some muffin crumbs off on my light-blue pants.

8)

World In Motion

August 1992

O ver the weekend, bored out of our minds, Holly and I filmed the inside of our boring house and threw a bunch of dirty towels down the stairs, drowned the backyard and made muddy rivers and documented the whole thing to show Mom. We cleaned up the towels but the muddy grooves were still pronounced in various depressions throughout the garden. When Mom got home and saw what we had done (both on video and in person), she flipped out and shouted down to me from the kitchen, my camera capturing it all during yet another bedroom press conference: 'I'M GOING TO RUIN YOUR LIFE, KID, BECAUSE YOU RUINED MINE!"

Despite getting my driver's licence at summer school, applying for a job at Jumbo Video and listening to a lot of Doors music, the summer was an uneventful loner fest.

As the summer dissipated, I was logging more and more silent hours under the watchful robotic eye of my camcorder. I imagined Andrew's silver Camaro sharking through the neighbourhood. It would only be a matter of time before we'd meet again. School was weeks away, our last year of high school.

I kept my unhealthy fantasy warfare workload set on high; between Andrew and my father, I had my work cut out for me delivering taunt videos for my growing infestations and insecurities:

And as for you, David, you and your evil moustache that contains all your powers, well, the way its colour has become diluted with beer suds and those embalming bleaches you groom it with, yeah, well, you can't keep that sick thing on your face much longer! The same fire you breathe, you shall burn by! You are in the danger zone! [I caressed some of the tools in the workshop.]

One day we will be freed, like when Jesus returned from the video store. Oh yes, David, on that day, with your still-alive moustache in my hand, ready to be glued to the cross, vengeance shall be my Valentine! Ohhhh Yeeeeaaaahhhh!

I walked towards the camera and hit STOP.

As for Andrew, since we had stalled over the summer and not really hung out, I figured I'd challenge him to a showdown, just to see, between friends, who was the better man.

On a whim, I called him up to see what he was doing.

"You get your schedule yet?"

"No," I said, coiling the phone cord around my fingers. "I can't remember what I signed up for."

"What'd you do this weekend?"

"Wrote a play about my Dad's moustache," I said, trying not to laugh too loudly or get all hyper and hyena.

"What? You're insane."

"I'm joking. But I hate it. Mostly because he slurps from it, like it's a wet paint brush. And I think it's possessed by Satan."

"Anyway," Andrew said, changing the subject, "you doing anything?"

The husky scent of ground-beef remainder percolated in the kitchen, where the phone hung on a wall, imprisoned.

"Not really," I said.

"Can you get the car?"

"Doubt it," I said, wishing that I *could* take the car, drive Andrew around and listen to a mixed tape I'd been working on. Husky ground-beef particles were soaking in the sink with fluorescent liquid soap. I dangled from the phone cord, exasperated, clinging to the door frame.

"But don't you have your licence now?"

"That doesn't mean much around here," I said, staring blankly into the living room.

"Is your dad at work?" Andrew asked.

"Nope; on call," I said, looking at Dad sitting comatose with a newspaper shield. "I'll call you back when my life changes."

"Cool," Andrew said, now unable to control his laughter. "Later."

I sensed this final year of school would determine everything be-tween Andrew and me, and in my guts I feared the worst. He had this air to him, as if to say to me, somewhere in the halls at school: *So, that's what you're wearing, that's what you like, that's what you're going to think about all year.*

9)

Everything's Gone Green

Friday, September 18th, 1992

I n the couch cushions, I found a sheet of lined paper with what I concluded were Pearl Jam song lyrics written in Holly's loopy handwriting, something about having a beautiful life and being a part of the sky. I folded it up and put it in my pocket. This year would be different: I had promised myself that I would not lose, that I would win at something.

I had a strong desire to be popular and not wind up alone each and every Friday and Saturday night, tiptoeing around my parents. I wanted to be seen.

Earlier in the day, I left a note for Andrew inside his locker. Yesterday, it had been announced that the student-council elections would be taking place soon and that a nomination meeting would be held on Friday—today—after school. I was convinced that Andrew and I should run. All we had to do was show up to the meeting and sign up.

Dearest Mega Power partner Andrew:

So, listen. Here are Some ideas for our presidential campaign:

Send it to the radio day (we make up new remixes of songs and try and get them on air: the whole school sends in hundred of tapes!)
Come to School Naked Day!
Food drive (run over food)
Video dance party with Erica Ehm
Erica Ehm Day
Roof Day (classes on the roof, suntanning, barbecues, concerts, just like The Beatles!)
Wednes-Day

This is the end, my only friend, the end. We should go to the meeting (it's 15 mins.) at 3:20 tonight and see who's runnin'; then we either run or run for the door! Imagine: Don't be sour, vote Mega Powers! Also, I think I'll be playing hockey in the same league as that guy in our Eng. class, Steve, Stevie.

Signed truly,
Nate Savage (co-Mega Power)

*

"Ohhh yeeeah!" I shouted down the sunny third-floor hallway. "Andrew!"

He was wearing his now-trademark green zippered sweatshirt and Boston Red Socks ball cap, blue jeans and tennis shoes, the same combination of attire he had started wearing last spring. He appeared to live in that crusty green thing, lumbering around the halls, his books and Alpine car stereo in one hand. A part of me began to really associate him and his constant rejection of our friendship with the evil forest tone.

A part of me still had hope.

I pointed my finger in the air majestically, then at Andrew.

"What?" Andrew said, glaring quizzically, car keys in his mouth.

"Did you get my note?"

"Yeah, but it made no sense." Andrew said. "So I put it in a pile with the others."

"Did you read the part that went: DON'T BE SOUR, VOTE MEGA POWERS!"

"Kind of hard to miss. What does that even mean?"

"Did you hear the morning announcement yesterday?"

"No," Andrew said, not slowing down his pace.

Inside my own production-studio mind, I was culling up music suitable for montages and spliced my thoughts with campy video shrapnel: cottage go-karts; road hockey; remote-control car racing; a photo still of Andrew and I and another boy from 1983 in front of the church before I went camping on a cub-scout weekend retreat. My recent co-op placement at Rogers Sports made me think in timing and cuts and fades, in voice-overs and sound bites. I was learning new terms like "SWIPE," the button that put text on the screen. Or "FADE-EDITS" from the top left to the lower right, a wash of video, the passage of time and space with crisp toggles and adjustments of frames.

"Mega Powers all the way, oh yeah!"

"We're not running. Are you crazy?"

"Come on, we have a shot."

"No way," Andrew said, dismissing the suggestion.

"So what do you think?" I said. A slight manic tone in my voice cut through the hallway chatter.

"It's stupid."

"I'm playing in the same league as Steve; did he tell you?"

"Yeah, I asked him. He has *no* idea what you're talking about," Andrew said, squinting into the sun, his large head and thick blonde hair, moderate in personal grease, were kept hidden under his aging baseball hat.

"So what do you think?"

"No way."

"Why not?"

"You're totally nuts. No way!"

"We could run!"

"Not."

"The meeting is tonight. We have to go. Just think of it!"

Andrew popped the doors and started to walk up the roadway toward Bayview Avenue. I gave slight chase.

"Where are you going?" Andrew asked.

"I don't know. You have a spare now?"

"Yeah."

"What are you doing this weekend?"

"Squash probably with Alex and Scott."

"What are you doing now?" I asked. I wanted to tell Andrew about *Blade Runner* returning to theatres after ten years. We had seen the original together with Andrew's dad a decade earlier.

"Going home," Andrew said.

"Can I get a ride?"

"I guess so. Don't you have class?"

"No, my co-op placement thing; it's only three days a week. I don't have to go in today."

"I can't believe they let you work on television."

"I mostly just walk around with video tapes and move equipment. It's not like I'm hosting a show in my driveway about road hockey or something."

"I'm sure you'll suggest it."

On the bus rides to and from the television station, I would sketch mythological friendship logos while a haunted, possessive tone filled me with a sense of comfort and belonging. I lived inside the energy of the drawings, until the faint blue-ruled line became filled with clutter and intrigue, the page entirely consumed in my dark etchings and explosive contours.

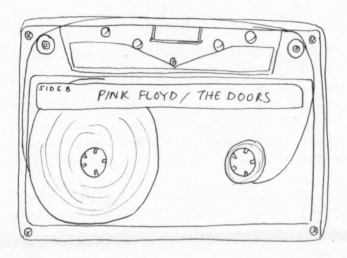

"I got a tape we can listen to."

"No way."

"It's good."

"What's on it?"

"Doors. Simon & Garfunkel. Some New Order, and I also got this cool mixed tape from this guy at my co-op: Pink Floyd, its really—"

"You like all old music, from like a thousand years ago."

"What?"

"It's crap," Andrew said. All week I had been trying to trade CDs with Andrew—U2 for Pearl Jam was my latest offer—even going so far as to borrow from my sister's collection.

"The madness can formidably be felt, all around the world, yeah, I am gonna take it to the limit. No one can stop me!"

"You see, you start to drift into like, I don't know, outer space, and its goodbye Nate. There you go. You're gone: you go into another dimension."

"Wanna play hockey?"

"*Hockey-Hockey!*" Andrew laughed. He had this staccato tone when he said the line, mocking me, reflecting my enthusiasm for playing. "Maybe. But we're not keeping score or anything. I have to pick something up from my dad at work."

"OK."

"Just don't smoke or anything," Andrew said. "You'll get me in trouble."

"I don't smoke," I said, sliding my seatbelt across my chest.

"My dad said you came over the other day and you smelled like smoke."

"It's not me, it's my Dad," I said, shaking his cassette tape.

"Sure," Andrew said. He took his car stereo from his knapsack and placed it carefully into the dashboard.

"I smoked, like, one time," I said.

"Well it must have been that one time. You and your dad smoking, best buddies."

"No way! He stinks. He has grey skin. He's turning into The Undertaker!"

Andrew's silver Camaro chortled along the familiar streets. The radio blared. My cassette jostled inside his pant pocket. He left me in the car and went inside the funeral home. The music continued to pump. I looked at the street from the rearview side mirror. Andrew's form slowly returned to view.

"I might get a sun roof put in," Andrew said.

"Oh, great," I said. "That's good for fishing and stuff."

"Yeah, for *fishing*," Andrew said. He gunned the engine and peeled around the corner.

"So you got your licence, but your Dad won't let you drive the car?"

"No."

"That's dumb," Andrew said. "Does Holly drive?"

"Yeah, but only when she's in town. She doesn't have a car at school."

The trees were wild with sun and wind; fluorescent backpacks, shorts and T-shirts popped in the late-afternoon electricity.

Andrew stopped his car in front of my house. "I got to go home first and get my stick."

"OK," I said. "I'll get the nets out."

"You're in net," Andrew said.

"Urine net, OK." It was my favourite road-hockey joke.

I struggled with the seatbelt. Andrew honked his horn as his car tore down my street towards Laird Drive. I opened the large brown metal door where the hockey nets lay in wait. The smell of grease, dried grass clippings and mildew filled me. I had a quick coughing fit, then dragged the plastic net from the garage's uneven shadows.

As I fished the nets from the garage, I saw my bundle buggy with bits of newsprint and plastic in the bottom fermenting in the garage's dank atmosphere. At seventeen, I felt like the oldest paperboy in history. I looked up at the overcast sky, then to the driveway and prayed the rain would hold off for at least another hour.

10)

Confusion

Thursday, November 26th, 1992

I had asked my supervisor, Steve Spice, if he could tape the WWF's *Survivor Series* event, which was airing on pay-per-view on Thursday night. I was excited about getting the tape from him first thing Friday morning.

I was shocked that morning, walking up to Steve Spice with a bit of trepidation, nervous to get the tape. Giddy even. "Oh, no, I forgot," Steve Spice said, shuffling papers at his desk.

I had been looking forward to watching the event all week. Getting the courage to ask my supervisor to tape it had been a big deal; this omission to tape it was just cruel, humiliating and awkward. I got on the phone with Andrew when I got home that night.

"He didn't tape it," I said on the phone to Andrew.

"Oh, well, call me later or something," Andrew said and hung up.

Earlier, I'd even bragged to Andrew about watching the event live and had tried to lure him into coming to Rogers that night to watch it with me, hoping somehow that Randy Savage's replacement tag-team partner might be a surprise return of Hulk Hogan. Of course, that turned out to be a rumour I had conjured in my own mind. Days before the event, it was announced that "Mr. Perfect" Curt Hennig was Savage's new tag-team partner, replacing the suspended Ultimate Warrior. My backup plan was to watch the taped event sometime that week with Andrew. That, of course, didn't work out either.

Now at home, the early evening was filled with my usual near-silent bedroom activity. I was cuing up tapes on my VCR. Just before dinner, Mom and I visited Grammy at the hospital. She was barely holding on in her giant hospital bed. They told me to take the video camera out of the hospital. I filmed Mom in the elevator; she scowled and waved her hand at me like I was a mosquito. I managed to capture a grim shot of Grammy's hand and a bit of her cheek behind the steel bars of her bed.

Her small body, tangled with tubes and monitoring systems, replaced the humorous vigour I had known her to possess while playing piano or frolicking in the park when we fed the geese. Grammy would call them "dirty birds."

Mom's voice snapped down the stairs from the kitchen.

"Nate, it's for you," she said. "I think it's your supervisor from Rogers."

Scraps of bright neon material had covered my bedroom floor for days. I put off vacuuming for days, and opted instead to pick things up manually, at my leisure.

"Just a sec," I said, lifting the phone. My head was a haze of neon glows, of frayed hope and determination, obsession drove me as I cut jaggedly this nightmarish outfit, a poor man's version of Randy Savage's hyperbolic ring jacket, complete with cowboy fringe and disco glitter.

"Yes, hello?"

"It's Steve Spice. Can you meet me tomorrow at 10 a.m. instead of 8 a.m.? The shoot time has been changed."

"Yeah, that's no problem," I said.

"See you tomorrow."

I gazed down at the remnants of my tailoring project. The fluorescent routine had consumed me for the last month. A late Halloween costume that would never fully materialize in public, its assembly ate up countless hours, including trips to fabric and hardware stores.

Once I had the long segments pinned in position along the inner arm, I had Mom sew things into place, turning a once-simple jean jacket into a bright laughing stock.

Each arm had six eighteen-inch strands that fell to the ground to create a curtain of colours. With glitter paint I wrote the words "MACHO MAN" on the back, added more glitter and covered a garage-sale cowboy hat in orange spray paint. Wearing the hat and jacket, I turned on my video camera and stood in the southeast corner of my bedroom.

I cued up Sir Edward Elgar's *Pomp and Circumstance* on my cassette player, dubbed from Holly's *A Clockwork Orange* soundtrack, did a dramatic twirl in my low-lit bedroom and pointed my finger at the camcorder. In a soft growl of a voice, one that tried to conceal my intent to my buzzing family, who coffee-slurped, newspapered and dish-washed above me, I laid out a challenge to Andrew, to face him one on one, somewhere down the road. It was the usual spiel I'd send him in letters or live talks.

"The Mega Powers will explode! Andrew, I'm gonna getcha! You're in the danger zone, *oooohhh yeeeaaahhh*! Eleven years is a long time, brother, yeah, the Mega Powers, the irresistible force meets the immovable object, and we will finish the score!"

I raced towards the camera, fraying neon streaked at my arms. I was winded, in frenzy, trying to hit the PAUSE button; the neon strips drooped from my arms and got tangled in the armpits of my insane coat.

I shook them free.

Peering into the camera's view piece, I relived recent history: "I'm gonna getcha! You're in the danger zone—"

The eerie taunt clip would appear at the end of a thirty-minute VHS video that featured road-hockey clips mixed with wrestling audio, a few minutes of George Harrison's "All Those Years Ago," and the pivotal chorus in Simon & Garfunkel's "Bridge over Troubled Water." There were also clips of George Michael's "Monkey" and even original audio dubs of Andrew and I from a 1986 audio cassette, play-wrestling in the basement.

NATE: "I'm Macho Man Roddy Piper!"

ANDREW: "Macho Man Roddy Piper?"

NATE: "I'm Macho Man and Roddy Piper, put together..."

ANDREW: "Put together as one...there are people dying..."

Andrew sang, channeling his best recollection of "We Are the World."

The editing I was proudest of was the final shot of Andrew walking to his car some six months earlier, shot from my front porch, with me in the foreground, cleaning up the road-hockey aftermath, as Andrew walked west to Glenbrae Avenue where he had parked his silver Camaro. To me, it all looked unbelievably real. As the shot's simple trajectory played out, an interview clip from George Michael was dubbed in:

It was an incredibly intense four years, you know, um, and I think I lost maybe some of my, uh, perspective during that time I became, uh, very negative about a lot of things which I should have been very grateful for I think I got back that kind of perspective. Also I've had time to remember myself as an individual again as opposed to being part of what was called a phenomenon. And I worked very hard to create that phenomenon, but, um, having created it, it did kind of run away. And it's taken me a while to see where I want to go and what I want to do with the rest of my life. But I'm happy now, I'm much happier than I've been in probably four or five years and I think I'm very balanced at the Moment.

I showed Mom the clip. "Balanced? Good one," she scoffed. I had asked her to watch that particular segment, not fully explaining the context of what I believed to be an epic film. After weeks of editing, re-editing and culling references that only Andrew and I would know, I prepared his package.

"DEATH OF THE MEGA POWERS: 1987–1992" was etched across the front load label in a fat green marker, wrapped in hardware-flyer newsprint.

One of the last clips was Andrew and I in low-fi (and low-lit) resolution racing our remote control cars on the street with jagged lightning beckoning the night. Andrew had left because of the pending rain, but I remained outside, filming the lightning from the safety of the garage, sitting on a discarded couch while the camcorder wheezed in and out of focus, sounding blind and frightened, watching the jagged storm scar the night and lick the houses.

I slipped the VHS anonymously in between Andrew's screen door and front door. I pedalled home, my bike a seamless tool along Broadway Avenue, then Brentcliffe, traversing the slackening rain-wet pavement, my heart pounding, feeling lost, defeated, souring and slithering in the neighbourhood's hostile groves.

*

When I awoke the next morning, I peeked through the thin curtain on my window: a blanket of fresh snow that guarded my basement bedroom windows was now being eaten by an intense morning sun.

Mom snapped down the stairs, "Is Sadie in your room?"

"Maybe she went to the store," I mumbled, coming up the stairs.

The phone rang. I walked past it to the main-floor bathroom.

"When?" I heard Mom ask someone. I was in the bathroom now. It was super early; no one called us this early.

"Well, thank you, yes, we'll call later on, then," she said, hanging up on whomever.

I brushed my teeth. When I stopped running the taps, I could hear Mom sobbing and Dad's distinct treble bouncing in every few seconds. Her nasal ignition turned on and began its familiar gunning sound, water works, bright red.

"Just now, I have to phone Unc," she said.

I walked into the hallway.

"Grammy died this morning," Mom said, her steps slow, looking to the ground, hands wringing, eyes watering, breathing hard.

"When?"

"Just about an hour ago."

A growing abject itinerary followed, which I found curious. My stomach ached with each commandment Dad began to unleash. I got a drink of water from the kitchen, trying to drown out his rant in the process.

"I'd better call Holly," Mom said, biting her nail.

I was amazed by my father's insistence: once he found out about the death and that the cadaver was cold, he went into funeral-planning mode, as if his mother-in-law's death was a scenario drawn from the night-school course material he had been reviewing. He repeated himself, determined that I be one of the pallbearers at the funeral, which by all accounts was now scheduled for sometime next week.

"Hell, no!" I said. "I'm not carrying my dead grandmother's coffin!"

"What did you say?" Dad asked.

"No! It's too weird." I turned the tap on fiercely, watching the stream blast the mustard and ketchup from the plate. The thought of carrying her coffin was grotesque.

"You have to or else we have to pay someone," Dad said.

I poked my head into the living room. Dad raised his eyes to catch my face.

"Then pay someone."

"If he doesn't want to, he doesn't have to," Mom said. "There's still time to think about it, all right?"

Dad stewed on the couch in obvious distress and agitation.

"You don't deserve to go to the funeral," Dad snickered.

"Fuck you," I said. "You're not even related to her!"

"Just calm down," Mom said.

I ran to my room, pulled my bed across my door frame and got dressed for school. I felt tears in my eyes, swelling. I didn't know why I was crying, whether it was anger or fear or sadness or everything swirling in a threaded heap of brutal annoyance lodging itself miserably in my throat. I turned my electric heater off, closed my window and turned off the stereo.

I drew a sketch of my father's severed head boiling in a big translucent witch pot, then a caption: "LOOK SON, IMAGINE FOR A MOMENT THAT I DIDN'T GET A JOB AT A FUNERAL HOME BUT AT AN ICE-CREAM PLANT. THEN I'D BE LECTURING YOU ON HOW TO EAT ICE CREAM, TELLING YOU THE RATE AT WHICH IT MELTS, THE TYPE OF CAKE TO SERVE WITH IT, HOVERING OVER YOU AS YOU ENJOYED DESSERT. BUT I WORK AT A FUNERAL HOME NOW AND KNOW EVERYTHING ABOUT THE DEAD AND SO EVERYONE IN THIS HOUSE MUST ABIDE BY MY CENSUS-CANADA INSIGHT. REMEMBER WHEN I FILLED OUT THOSE FORMS FOR US WITHOUT ASKING YOU GUYS ANYTHING? SAME DEAL! I AM THE OGRE! WASH MY DISHES!"

*

I hit REC on the camcorder and in a retro outfit a little tight and binding from my fall 1987 collection (Polo Ralph Lauren plaid dress shirt, tapered pants and a T-shirt) recorded the following video diary entry in fuzzy low-lit headshot, interview style:

This year no one is going to stop Nate Savage, no way, no how, dig it, yeah! Death by Squash? Hell no, I will squash squash Andrew! It took two of you to destroy me; you and Alex may be best buddies now, driving around eating sandwiches at all hours of the night talking squash and hogwash while I sit here waiting for a title shot, yeah! Well, go to the woods of your world, Andrew Beverly, yeah, and take your buddy Alex with you and slice open his heart and let him slice open yours, and you shall see there will be no blood flow, because from black hearts, no blood can flow! Dig it? And with no blood flow, no bond can form!

[PAUSE.]

"Nate, your inserts are here!" Mom bellowed from the kitchen. Assembly usually took close to an hour, and depending on the weather, I would place a garbage bag over my papers inside the buggy to prevent them from getting soaked.

On these early morning paper-route missions that spanned sixteen blocks, I would pass Andrew's house, imagining him asleep, then waking up, eating breakfast and then being filled with the desire to call me, see what I was doing for the rest of the day. *Maybe a movie ... a game of street hockey.* I left Andrew a note on his car windshield and would follow this gesture up with a phone call.

After my papers were delivered, I jumped back into my bed to warm up, clutching my faded blue comforter, bunching it up towards me. I could hear my parents speaking some mysterious words, words slackened in coffee and toast as they prepared for church. I took refuge in this crack in time, inhabiting the morning sun, listening to them work in the house with tread and routine.

Late in the afternoon that Sunday, I found Andrew at home, apathetic over the phone. I squirmed on my end, unable to speak, and then suddenly needing to say anything, the simplest arrangements of words.

"I just wanted to hang out," I said.

"What's with the note? It's like you're acting like I broke up with you or something."

"No, it's just," I said. "It's just—"

"There were tear marks on it!" Andrew laughed, a scalded brief laugh, followed by a short sigh.

"No, it was the rain," I said, nervous and aching.

"Didn't rain today," Andrew said.

"How'd you know? It was like seven in the morning."

"Yeah, right."

11)

Ceremony

Thursday, December 10th, 1992

Grammy's funeral was on a cold Thursday afternoon. She had died the previous Monday on the seventh at the age of seventy-five.[15]

It was a bright afternoon when I began the twenty-minute snow stomp from school to Beverly Funeral Home, where Dad had, of course, arranged for Grammy's funeral to take place.

Andrew's dad greeted me at the door, offering me his condolences. Dad was somewhere behind the scenes, acting out his dutiful destiny. I spotted Mom and Holly and sat beside them.

After the service, Mom served pie and coffee at our house, telling me, "Grammy's having a good laugh with this weather," pointing to the blizzard that had cropped up. I wasn't exactly sure how her funeral and the blizzard were related.

---

15. "Having grandsons seemed to be one of the happiest times of her life, but her health didn't give her the energy she needed. Thanks for remembering." Note from Mom, December 2012.

While Grammy's death was not a massive shock to anyone, her departure represented a larger significance for sure. I was down one ally, one less person who could sympathize with me or even understand me. After her funeral, we all sat around the living room. I urged everyone to watch the last known footage of Grammy, at which Uncle Carl waved me away, suggesting it wasn't the time. That was it: she was gone. The streets outside were empty. The snow billowed down, and it was cold in the house. The hot gauze of pink from the living-room decor filled my head, as did the foreign perfumes minced with coffee and tea. I kept staring through the slight gap in the front curtain, across the street to the large maple tree's voluminous branches swaying in the wind and snow.

Since her death, whenever I pass those plump red geraniums at a grocery store or in someone's garden, I travel back to the 35mm footage from the late 1970s, and me in my glasses and gay cheeks, my Eskimo hood, running across the street in the minus-eleven December weather, and Uncle Carl lending me the camera to film him getting some more film from his car. *Action sequence!* Eating Chinese food: the foil plates and turtlenecks and cheeks filled with rice and chicken balls. These were silent films, lost dialogues from ancient history.

The geraniums were inside Grammy and Grampy's incubator of an apartment, all year long. Those thick petals, dropping leper-like. That apartment was the land of glossy salmon-coloured hallways, TV dinners and second-hand smoke, blueberry jelly with toast in the morning and *Hee-Haw* every Saturday evening (a terrible country and western sketch comedy and music show), which was on at the same time as CHCH's WWF *Maple Leaf Wrestling*. I would have to flip back and forth pushing the light-brown buttons of the channel changing box, much to the chagrin of my grandparents, who needed their country and western comedic fix.

As the guests left our small gathering of family and friends, Dad carried out his final act. True to his new calling as chief administrator of death and ghouls, Dad went over to our United Church minister, Julia Thomas, and tried to give her a hundred dollars for doing the service. She awkwardly refused.

1992 and all its roller-coaster anxieties with Andrew and Dad was almost over. On my way to school one frozen day, I couldn't help but get lost for a second or two in the faces of the garbagemen, about a week before Christmas break. I just stood there, mouth agape. They asked me what was going on, but I remained silent.

I felt eerie and a bit dead too, as if Grammy's death was a partial passport into my own sense of ... whatever. The garbagemen resembled a cut of brutal roast beef, a tough end, peering from behind a film of morning fog. As I walked south of Sutherland, approaching Broadway, I thought I saw Andrew—just a fleck of pink face peeling by in his silver Camaro through it all, the sun now golden, having chased the depraved and odd fog away as his car glistened pristine and rapid, heading west, shrinking as it zoomed towards Hanna Road.

I had reached this stretch of cement a thousand dull times without meaning. Grammy was dead. The Mega Powers were finished. High school would be over in seven months.

Friday, December 25th–Thursday, December 31st, 1992

I filmed all of us on Christmas morning, on which the housecoat-wearing trio of Holly, Mom and Dad opened gifts, slurped coffee, scratched and yawned. The lamp in the corner, sitting on a table, created a halo of lighting concerns when I would eventually play the video back. Holly can be heard grumbling about wearing a paper bag over her head, and on two occasions, gave the camera the finger.

The hour-long "Christmas Morning 1992" clip ended with Dad

coughing, followed by his hand slamming against the coffee table, Mom handing him an orange and Holly throwing a ball of wrapping paper at the camera.

Videotapes filled with housebound surveillance were now a commonplace time-filling activity, their production growing in frequency since Andrew and I had dissolved our friendship via video tribute in the fall. I found myself consulting the lens on a daily basis before going to bed, the time of the recordings was usually just before midnight.

On New Year's Eve, I was watching television when my parents returned home from an errand around nine o'clock. My father said, "Oh, look: Nate's home." I took it as a jab to my global unpopularity and began to cry, retiring in depressive sobs to my room.

As midnight approached, I set up the video camera in the obscenely pink living room and filmed myself jumping up and down with joy that 1992 was over. Downstairs in my room, I continued my broadcast, vowing that I would not let anyone hurt me in 1993.[16]

---

16. In February 1993, I saw a psychiatrist at Sunnybrook, who asked me if I was attracted to girls and if I had fantasies. I remember him being very hairy and aggressive in nature. In April, at *Wrestlemania IX*, Hulk Hogan returned and won his fifth WWF title. Randy Savage was there but didn't wrestle. In June, I bought an army jacket and had "Vengeance is Mine, Romans 12:19" silkscreened large on the back. When I was picking up the order, a middle-aged man said, "You know, there's a meaning to that." I also had a shirt made with a biblical font that read "Death By Squash." I ignored Andrew, save for my yearbook write-up in which I referenced the death of the Mega Powers 1987–1992. My caption began with "left to the wolves" and only got more emotional from there. No one seemed to notice. I graduated from Leaside with little fanfare, spent the summer arguing about school, stayed at friends for weeks on end and finally got into Glendon College, taking a full course load. In October, I attended commencement and got my diploma. I wore white Doc Marten dress shoes, a pinstriped suit and had dyed my hair insanely blonde.

12)

Fine Time

"Nate, if you would like, you can work wi—*Dad's staccato coughing like thunder in a paper bag interrupted his speech flow and the sentence's subsequent recovery*—with me Sunday. It pays seventy-five dollars, I believe, about two-and-a-half hours of work," he said with his mouth full, eating a toasted sandwich. "Two o'clock."

"I guess," I said.

"They need another pallbearer," Dad said, making a series of little vocal pulses that just skimmed across our nearly fifteen-year-old sand-coloured broadloom.

"You may borrow my overcoat," he told me. "I have an extra tie."

On Sunday morning, I filmed myself getting dressed for the pallbearer gig. I was still recording a low-grumbled VHS diary entry. *Low grumbled* only because I didn't want anyone to hear what I was talking about on video, or because I usually would record late at night as I had perpetual insomnia.

Dad pulled into the parking lot, the familiar signage "Beverly Funeral Home" in white letters, permanent and regal, greeting my gaze from the passenger's seat. The building's grey brick and shutters were painted the same colour as parts of Andrew's house. It was emblazoned in my psyche, nudging me with familiar warmth.

When I walked into the funeral home, I immediately saw Andrew. Andrew was working too. I had no idea he would be there, and I must have looked as shocked as he did when he saw me walk in with Dad.

We didn't say a word to each other. I hadn't talked to him in over a year. I thought: *We were doing a job; this was professional, and this wasn't personal. I was being paid and so was he; this will be over and no one will remember a thing*—but all I could feel was my giant red heart accelerating as if a lead foot was pressing down on it and I was aware, now, that something else controlled all. That it was never ever me.

I can't speak for Andrew, but I was consumed with a huge raw discomfort as we got into the car, as we lifted the casket from the service room to the hearse, as we nodded hello to the priest, as we took instruction from our director, as we moved slow and somber from the car to the gravesite and then back.

As we approached Laird Drive, I asked to be let off; no sense in traveling all the way back to the funeral home, which was on Mount Pleasant, another fifteen minutes east.

"I can get out here," I said, and was pleased when the driver slowed down for me, happy not to be going back with the rest of Team Death.

"I'll see you at home," Dad said. And I got out of the car and walked from the red-light intersection on the northeast corner of Laird and Eglinton, where Andrew and I had bought a thousand freezies, Reese's Peanut Butter Cups and half-litres of chocolate milk to amplify our foul nights of teenage excess.

When the cheque from Beverly Funeral Home came two weeks later, I photocopied it before cashing it, feeling smug, glad that I'd been paid for a portion of our time spent together.

13)

Ruined in a Day

Sunday, February 6th, 1994

Outside, the gusty winter blustered away, and I knew it would soak my pant cuffs and add to my torment. We were going to visit Aunt Rebecca and Uncle Tom in Kingston for dinner. Grandmother and Grandfather were also going to be there. I opted to wear double socks in my clumpy, overheated boots. Mom had packed us both snacks. A riot of colours lay blurred in the twisted plastic-bag cocoon.

"Share these with your father," Mom said. "I need to lie down, and this cold is killing me."

"Just take it easy; don't throw out my room," I said, adding, "I'm serious."

Mom had this consistent habit of throwing things out of my room in sporadic bouts of amnesia or some weird game in which I had to guess which memento she had sacrificed to indifference.

Don't throw out my room was my latest jingle in a series of catch phrases designed as a type of mutiny against the unauthorized purging of things in my bedroom: some minor object or trinket would invariably go missing, snatched up into a an ethereal nothing and now floating in the home in sad purgatory.

We[17] drove in silence with sparse radio traffic reports and one coffee stop. "What time are we supposed to be there?"

"Half past five," Dad said.

Aunt Rebecca and Uncle Tom's house was blanketed in predictable snow, resembling a structure you'd see in a sketch on a gift-shop greeting card. The snow had subsided and for the first time that day, the sun emerged bright and real.

Dinner was still a few minutes away, my Aunt Rebecca[18] informed us. It was our first time at her new house, which was located in a remote wilderness, miles from the highway in Kingston.

After the cold snakes of scarves and hats, coughs and galoshes were removed, I detected the bright, harsh tones of my aunt's middle-of-nowhere country home. The hallway walls were filled up with family

---

17. Dad and I were the only ones willing to go that weekend, when at the 11th hour, my mother got the flu, and of course my sister Holly was studying for exams. (Even though we were about ten minutes from her campus in Kingston, she insisted she couldn't spare the time away from "cramming.")

18. My Aunt Rebecca was the second eldest child next to Dad. She had ears that stuck out like his and mine but had surgery in the early 1980s to pin them back. She married Tom, an architect who enjoyed acting like the useless husband who couldn't get anything right, always laughing at his own domestic shortcomings, whether it was making coffee, setting the table or hanging guests coats. Tom loved to fail and get a rise out of my Aunt. It was their thing. Rebecca had been a nurse for twenty-five years and was now only taking sporadic shifts at the main hospital in Kingston. Though not as religious as her father, or Dad, Rebecca did possess an amazing ability to give sermons on just about any topic. You didn't even have to know the person to visualize their shortcomings. Her succinct sound bites and re-enactments were completely believable, be it something stupid Tom did with his sailboat or a fabulous recipe she had improved on and impressed a room full of boating enthusiasts with one summer afternoon.

photographs. They might as well have been portraits of aliens, I had no idea who most of these people were.

The dining room table was set, all crisp and angelic, long and empty awaiting clutter and population. In the living room, my grandparents were sitting on a couch. A small bevy of snacks had been put out. The way Dad said "veggies" drove me nuts, I found it degrading to them somehow. The house was filling with gravy scents, high-octane red wines and the pithy scent of cranberry sauce minced alchemic with my ghastly cologne, borrowed from Dad's bureau that morning.

"So how was the drive up, Dave?"

"Fine."

The three-hour drive, peppered with traffic, was slow at times, so I put in the only tape that Dad could tolerate, which was the Barenaked Ladies.[19] He would expunge little half-syllables of what I believed was approval that would ping-pong in the car; his effort to loosen perhaps, an emotional muscle. He had the same type of half-cocked interest when I started listen to the Beatles ten years earlier.

Dad sat down and leaned in for a piece of celery, while his sister, my aunt Rebecca, brought him a glass of wine, calling him Dave over and over again and speaking in a tight, loud pitch as she entered the room with her five-foot frame.

I had a miniscule glass of ginger ale with ice and watched Dad take the first sip of his adult beverage, as more relatives appeared in the living room—some still coming, some in the washroom, some still in mid-greeting.

"There you are now," Grandfather said, grinning all holy and slow as a vampire, shifting on the couch, looking a bit uneven in his sweater

---

19. When the album came out and was getting substantial Toronto video and radio play, Andrew used to sing the line from the song "Enid": "I took a beating when you wrote me those letters," as a conversational stilt. At this time, I was writing him notes almost every week.

and priest collar, restricted to the standard threadbare he'd worn for sixty years.

"And school? How is school? University now?"

"School is fine." I didn't know what to say. "And your sister? Mom?"

"Mom is sick, has the flu," I said. That much was certain.

Just like history does, like a flagpole exploring soil, Dad was deep in the conquering.

"If Diane wants the house, if she tries to take it from me, I'll tie her up in court for years," Dad began to say, shifting his weight, half a cracker awkwardly juggling in and out of his jaw.

The vegetables and roast's steam coaxed things: sleeves, sweater collars, rims of eyewear. We had only been in the house for a short while before things got messy, before I balled up into a myriad of clammy symptoms, hands hurting, dry throat, nauseous stomach, thick salty tears aborting, and the swell of a panicked, bull-like breathing pattern.

"I'm in control; she's not going to get the house. I'll keep her tied up in court for years; if she wants to leave me, she'll get nothing," Dad concluded, legs crossed like a talk-show guest, and now awkwardly stuffing that final bit of cracker and cheese into his mouth, as if the piece of food was afraid to enter.

I began to tear uncontrollably. A sickness flamed up in my stomach and dried out my heart.

My embarrassing tears pulled me up from the couch and told me to leave the house, to cry in the snow in the afternoon, and so I put on my jacket and boots and went to the car to smoke a cigarette.

I shuffled into the passenger's seat, smoking sickly, jarred by his callous words. I stared blankly at the scenic house—white and blue tones, simple stone brick base—and smoked and panicked. Things would change, they would surely change, the storyline would swerve and change.

That second, that little Moment, that time trickle: *Dad was all Real Estate, sip of drink, cracker-and-cheese cough.*

My heart was on fire when I saw Dad opening the front door. He was walking towards the car. *What the fuck?!* He opened the driver's side seat and slid in... *I could smell Dad: the worst stink known to mankind.* I felt sick with rage; the cigarette not enough, his words still barbed and bleeding in my throat.

"Thought I'd join you," Dad said, sitting beside me in the car. Was he just going to sit down? I'll never know, because his presence spurned me to leap from the passenger's seat and, like I'd seen so many times on police dramas, *they'd race around to the driver's seat and open the door...*

"How could you say that shit about Mom!" I said with a gusty shout, and pulled him out by his winter-coat collar. "Asshole!" I threw him down on the ground. "You fucking piece of shit!" As he tried to get up, I kicked him twice hard in the stomach; bits of snow exploded around each leg thrust.

The words would get erased. Just me kicking him. That's it.

"YOU FUCKING ASSHOLE!" I blasted with hateful fangs.

The gargantuan winds had subsided. All that remained was a cold and brutal afternoon, the fake sun hanging benign.

I was dead and could no longer breathe. I went back into the house, smelling of half a cigarette and smarting with hate and frosted skin. Dad entered shortly after. I was still taking off my shoes and putting my coat on a hook. He motioned to Aunt Rebecca, coughing, holding his ribs, "I need to lie down." And so he did, on a couch in a spare room.

"It can be difficult with family sometimes," Grandmother offered in a soft, unspooling murmur, unaware of what went down outside, the wintry, abject unravel. I felt sick.

The three-hour drive home loomed ahead. *What would Mom think? What would we tell her? And Holly...*

Why did I agree to drive out here with him?

I was still fuming in silence as I clenched my teeth, sucking up the remaining ginger ale and ice.

"Smells great, Rebecca," Tom offered.

"Tom, why don't you finish setting the table!" Aunt Rebecca shouted. Tom looked at us with an impish smirk, rising from the couch to assist his wife.

Dinner was swelling now. It was time to eat.

To this day, I know that I was right, that I had done the right thing, that Dad had started on a venting rant and that I was right there, watching him monster it up, talking over everyone in his chalky voice.

Dad eventually made it to the dinner table. I said nothing, save for the necessary table responses like, "That's fine," as I watched the dense mashed potatoes cascade from the serving spoon to my plate. My uncle returned the large silver spoon to the hot white mound, and then pulled out a fresh snowball-sized clump of carbohydrates for the next plate.

Dad and I avoided eye contact. Grandfather said grace.

"Amen," everyone repeated. I ate fast.

No one else knew the real, I thought. No one cared about the meaning of things, the way it felt. I just wanted it to be over.

We drove in silence for nearly three hours, back to Toronto. The road was imperfect: cuts and nicks, bumps and snow swells. Reverse. Acceleration.

Besides the cold wind that trickled in and the intense empty highway's infinite darkness, the drive home was put on mute, permanent, save for the sound of lighting and extinguishing cigarettes in the culpable dark.

14)

State of the Nation

Late April 1994

Outside, the telephone poles, trees, parked cars and construction artifacts were bigger to me than before, livelier and raw. Maybe it was because I was about to share these objects with Carie-Jane, or that this frenzy of teary, early adult energy and the extra anxiety of university calculated itself cruelly and panicked me.

"Home from school?"

"Yes, it appears so. We just had to hand in our essays," I said, appreciating the campus was forty minutes from our house.

Friday afternoon just after three. Dad was skulking around the house looking for shoes and socks.

"I have to work at five," Dad said, buttering a piece of toast and washing a tomato. "Probably be on call all weekend too."

I spent the next half-hour in my room hiding any embarrassing signifiers of juvenility that would open up portals of shame, ridicule or emasculation.

I went to the basement stairs to get a pop from the cupboard.

"Have you seen my shoes?" Dad bellowed from the kitchen.

"No. They're probably in the front closet. Mom puts all the shoes there."

"Did you remove them from the closet?"

"Did I *remove*[20] them?"

Dad stared at me now with his cold grey arctic-wolf eyes, his jowls beginning to show under the 60-watt lighting brilliance of our dilapidated kitchen.

"No. I haven't seen your fucking shoes. And if I wasn't here, what would you do? Blame Sadie?"

"Oh, fuck off!"

After a stare down, a back and forth of shouting and more low-syllable count obscenities, Dad came at me, and I felt his hard centre-of-gravity torso push into my shoulder, so I shoved back, pivoting him into the refrigerator, knocking a box of cereal over into Sadie's food dish.

Regaining footing in our sock feet, we both pushed off the unkempt tiles and lunged at one another. I didn't want this one; I didn't want to go through it all. *Not now. You win; you can have this one, asshole . . .*

Dad went for my throat, and I went soft. I just didn't want this, not this time, and went limp as he clamped down. My face teared up, all red inside and out, feeling fucked up and dead, smelling his calloused hands still firmly clasped around my stupid neck. My brain was pissing itself in sadness, and I couldn't decide what had lit the powder keg this time.

---

20. Throughout all the domestic surveillance I'd shot, my Dad made one blurry appearance. The shot was taken from the living room with a basket. I was doing stop motion. My father is blurry brown in the far corner, sitting on the couch. "Then remove the basket, then remove the cat, then remove..." He kept saying "remove" over and over again, and you can hear me say "Would you be quiet, you...removing! ..."

All I could think of was Carie-Jane, finding her on the corner, my new girlfriend of five weeks, the one who had travelled ninety minutes from Scarborough to spend the weekend, or at least a Friday night sleepover with me. *Here.*

It was going to be historic, the first time ever a girl would sleep over.

Running across my front lawn, neck smarting, my throat strangle-fresh, I howled and wolfed down the street.

Holding my side, as I walked jarringly down the street and turned south on Laird, I could still feel the tingle from the scratches, the vice around my throat, how we went back and forth with each other, shouting and pushing, how this was closer, more real, his attack this time straight-on, no passive-aggressive body language, weird defensive turns, none of that. This was a new arsenal, the air being gobbled up by our wild punches, a rough collision and torment.

Dad's hands had left their final resting place on my corpse. The wind pierced my eyes, forcing them even wetter.

Carie-Jane's face was all red and raw.

"Can't go home," I said.

"What happened?" Carrie asked from behind her ski coat, which was zipped up to her nose. "Fought with my Dad, he, oh shit, he just [bawling] tore into me…I don't know…he's pissed at me or something!" I blurted out. "I'm not sure what this could mean, I said, exhaling loudly.

Carie-Jane shoved her hands into her coat pockets. "So now what?"

"Can we go to your place?" I suggested.

"I guess so," she said, shaking her head in disbelief.

"Sorry," I said, "I know it took you forever to get here," adding in between sobs, "I had no idea this would happen."

The traffic noise was suspended in the air as we boarded the bus. She made room for me beside her, offering me the window seat.

"I don't care," I said, rubbing my hands on my pants nervously. My room tidied and anticipating her presence: *dinner, movie, alone—now this, rush hour, commuting nightmare overwhelming, sitting in, replacing what could have been—*

Now we'd travel east for close to two hours, TTC and Scarborough RT included, telling her mom the ordeal in a series of humiliating conversations that lasted all weekend, the fierce recollections of Dad and me in fisticuffs assembled raw and brutal in my sleep.

15)

Procession

August–October 1994

Carie-Jane broke up with me in late April, ending my first major run (six weeks, fourteen days) with a girlfriend. The summer had provided me with few answers: return to school or not? Move in with friends, try to live at home and return for another year at university? I had also started experimenting with cutting myself on the chest with a razor blade I'd found in my father's workshop. I would take the time to burn the blade to disinfect it; somehow, I thought that was necessary. I'd cut several half-inch digs into my chest, watch the blood trickle and lie down topless on the bedroom floor.

Autumn arrived, and I moved in with a new friend named Karen, and began living in the basement at her family's house. Karen was an anorexic redhead with freckles, one year younger than me,

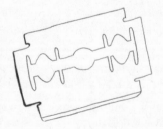

and our sole shared common interest was George Michael. The George Michael bond was enough to accelerate our friendship to a closeness that transcended time and space.

Karen took me to her psychotherapist, named Leslie Morgan, who listened to me moan and wail about my homelessness, uncertainty and rage. I told her money was my only emotional problem. I was starting my second year at Glendon, taking Spanish, French and a couple of other electives and was still new to the world of student loans and administrative blizzards.

I'd been in to talk with Leslie sporadically at Karen's mother's suggestion since, just prior to moving in with Karen, I'd hacked into my forearm with a steak knife and had to drive myself to Sunnybrook Emergency.

The grim steak knife slash ordeal was a jump-cut in my life's edit if there ever was one. I remember feeling a chaos brewing, that something was simply not being said. Would I return to school? Go on welfare? Work retail and find a mysterious apartment? The white void that represented my future lacked any colour, so I had pushed the colour bar with this red tirade. I couldn't discern any reasonable facsimile to a normal life, a beginning, ending. It was hopeless, formless and unconditionally disparate.

I remember showing Mom my cuts, and she did her usual feigning of concern with the bunched up forehead and brow all hound dog. "Put a Band-Aid on it," she said, and floated in her housecoat into the unlit hallway. I went back downstairs, looked again and saw some veins presenting themselves.

I called Karen and told her what I'd done. She came over to find me in my room, and she looked at the bloody facecloth and paper towels accumulating on the bedroom floor as I clasped down on my wound with a fresh towel. It felt like I'd been shot. She cried, "We have to take you to the hospital right now." She sat with visible concern, big-eyed and nervous as I drove us to the emergency room at Sunnybrook.

Two hours later, we were both back in my bedroom, sitting on the small couch that ran across one wall. Her large eyes looked at me; I felt weak and sick, ashamed, undead, really angry and confused. Karen put me to bed and slept on the couch upstairs. She left me a note[21] saying she'd talk to me later, writing it in pencil on a scrap of wallpaper, of all things.

Mom told me later Karen was crying when she woke up. A few days later, I made the move to Karen's place, and with the exception of some minor administrative changes at home (phone messages, a pack of clothing, some books), carried on as if nothing had happened.

*

---

21. Dear Nate,

Ah yes, well, it seems you've REALLY done it now. Was it inevitable? Have I been commissioned to save you? Only you can rescue yourself. You are your own cavalry. Still, I'm the optimists' optimist (or perhaps plain hard-headed) and persist in trying. Everyone's a fool at heart. What's next for you? Can you escape without any severed members? Am I to stay tuned for the next episode? You ought to know now that I can't watch. I don't have an iron gut, and you don't have iron will. Quite a pair we make. I trembled at the hospital. In fact, I felt ill. The answered questions painted a gruesome portrait of some madman I refused to recognize. How far you've strayed from my initial image of you! Your arm looked like a cadaver's limb. And when the doctor reached for the surgical thread, I felt like bursting into tears. It wasn't because of the sight of your blood all over the table and floor; it was because he couldn't suture you where it really hurts. I'm forever grappling with helplessness. Is THIS rock bottom? Please go out and get the best help you can find. You need more than I can give you. Have I failed you? I'm writing this on pages torn out from somewhere and in pencil because it's more immediate, less permanent. Appropriate, somehow. Your father and mum have taught you well, but you are a less proficient butcher. I love you. Please live. K

Rocketing down the stairs of 161 Glenvale (I still had the keys, and Karen had loaned me her car for the afternoon), I saw a pile of binders from the annals of academic history piled in a corner. One or two were crammed with Holly's high school homework. Her familiar cursive in black spooled out on three-hole paper. As I flipped through the pages vigorously, nearly tearing some sheets from the rings, I stopped my rapid eye scan on "<u>Depression</u>" dated *September 23/90*, in Holly's loopy cursive:

The small stern face of my father is in the centre of, at times, a round, plump head with a receding hairline and neat, cropped hair. I remember Uncle Carl telling us how he always tried to film him from the stomach up, because of Dad's huge beer gut. Now his head sits beneath a dusty brown and grey coif. Mom said he's lost weight and that you can see it in his face too, from less beer ... She also said we stopped getting bronchitis every winter when Dad stopped smoking inside the house ...

In the basement, I tossed dozens of sports magazines and photocopied articles into a pile, destined for recycling. The inventory was growing— from my aging underwear to the remaining plastic guts of my remote-control car.

The front door did its familiar orchestra of sounds. I fiddled in my pockets with change or pills or whatever. Mom stared down at me from the top of the stairs.

"Did you go to your appointment today?"

"Yes, I got a lobotomy," I said, squinting into the late-afternoon sun coming in from the side-door window.

"We can always hope," Mom said, with her usual stiff expression, confident her sick comedy was going to win her an award some day.

*

Later that week I called, asking for Holly. I knew she was home for

Thanksgiving weekend. It was surreal phoning my own phone number.

"I didn't know anyone else liked George Michael," Holly said when she answered the phone.

"What?"

"Your friend Karen was listening to George when I called you a few hours ago."

I arrived at my home at six-thirty by way of the Eglinton 34 bus for Thanksgiving 1994. For all intents and purposes, *the last supper* I'd ever eat with my family in that house.

I played along with the last-supper storyline, the meal feeling like one big prop: Chinese Food for Thanksgiving.

According to Holly, Uncle Carl balked at the invite, saying his other niece had promised to bring him over some "lovely turkey sandwiches" and he was looking forward to enjoying those. "Mom went nuclear: she kept going on about how whatever her name is, her cousin, is always upstaging her now, and that Uncle Carl never calls..."

Twenty hours later: Thanksgiving 1994, version two, began with Chinese food fumes and my eyes adjusting to the pink living room, the candles glowering on the dining-room tablecloth and its familiar cornflower blue shadowed in parts. The house, this house, the house since March of 1981: the carpet burns, the time Holly sat on a glass and broke it and I pulled the shards out of her bum, the acerbic meat dishes, the napkin-crumpled Sunday afternoons with moods dumping, blood pumping through nervous veins, all coming to this last supper summit, the merlot-coloured candles lit, the tinfoil glint, the steam rising, aroma more hot than food-smelling, just a big vapour.

The glint of worn-down utensils I hadn't seen in weeks lay across the table in a metallic clump. "It's nice to see you, Nate," Dad said. "Hope school is going well."

Mom looked at me standing motionless in front of the silverware.

"Can you put these around?" I nodded and began to place the forks

and knives around everyone's plates.
"Did you take your pills?" I didn't
answer.

The spectral steam rose from the six
large Chinese food take-out containers,
lit by the warped merlot candles stuck
in the shabby brass holders.

"There's lots, so eat up," Mom said.

We sat around the dining-room table
for the first time in nearly twenty weeks.
The summer had been full of upheaval
and paperwork, reneging and negotiating. Holly was in her first year of
a master's program at Queen's and looked across the table at me in
what was muted horror. I just kept eating.

Dad served himself some fluffy white rice and steaming chow mein.
Holly poured herself a glass of juice.

"Now, this is Thanksgiving," Holly said, a spool of steam escaping
the rice as she opened an aluminum dish. "It's hot!"

The munching ensued. Nervous glances and the pharmacy keeping my
blinders in place. The grease on my fork travelled into my solar system.

Dad cleared his throat and set a dish of egg rolls down.

A nod, a deleted smirk, edited body language all around the table.

"So, Uncle Carl wants you to call him sometime," Mom said, snapping into an egg roll.

"I will."

"Want some tea and pie for dessert? We have apple?"

"Let's get through this crap first," Holly said.

Dad glared.

Twenty-three minutes of chewing and lay-away plans for indigestion
ensued with sips of intense-coloured juice and my refusal of seconds.
Nothing remained on my plate but fried-food dregs. The antidepres-

sant Zoloft had been newly administered by a psychiatrist who worked with Leslie, and it coursed through my body. Mom took the empty containers off the table. I was trying to explain that the side effects only occur when you stop taking Zoloft. My mom chimed in with, "Well, don't stop taking it!"

Holly leaned forward, and in a soft lob across the table, said, "We sold the house."

I was blank-faced. Dad took his plate into the kitchen.

"Nate, you want some coffee or tea? David?"

Holly stared at me; her lips flatlined into nothing.

As the kitchen filled with rushing water and clattering, I went to my room, immediately noticing a new paint coat on the walls and that my bed was made and appeared to have been slept in. Some of my school binders from last semester lay in a pile near the door.[22]

"Dad sleeps in here now," Holly said, standing in my doorway. "You want a ride home or something? Want to watch something in my room?"

The walls of my room were now a glaze of eggshell calm. The striped wallpaper Dad had installed in the summer of 1988 had been stripped, suffocated, murdered and erased, along with that dark majestic blue that filled the opposite walls.

The moral learned was money talks. Moulded after Gordon Gekko

---

22. I was ready to drop out of my second year of university, a coward on all fronts. During presentations, I would dry up, my mouth full of cotton. I could not, it seemed, interpret anything beyond myself. I could only hermit within an idea. I felt distracted and insane. Nor did I fully believe my efforts would lead to anything, and the anxiety of paying two or three thousand dollars to study virtually the same thing I studied in high school added to my anxiety. I was couch surfing, suicidal and about to see my home sold off to the highest bidder.

and Vince McMahon in the late 1980s, "The Million Dollar Man" Ted DiBiase once prophesized to his heroes like Hogan and Savage: "Everybody's got a price."

A few garbage bags sat like sandbags in one corner, and all this filled my paranoid mind full of debris and reruns. If I had to write a will, it would only fill a matchbox flap. But a self-involved snuff letter would occupy months of effort, filling thousands of Bristol board sheets on both sides: the meticulous marinating of my family's kamikaze descent.

*

Back at Karen's, I called Holly, who was up watching a movie on her old television set with headphones. "I'm in my room."

Over the last few years, whenever I went into her room, which was rare (I had no real reason to go to the second floor), the walls were always barren, simple outlines of old picture frames, band posters and, when she was younger, a few baseball pennants. She had started to clean out her room years ago, like slowly wiping down a crime scene, piece by piece.

"I … I know you've got your problems, issues and stuff; you're upset and freaking out all the time," Holly said, taking a minute to turn down the sound on the small television she had lugged from the basement, "but you know, we're all going through things."

Holly explained things to me. For the first time in months, someone directly let me in on something that was going on. She said something about the world expanding and that everything was changing. When I asked if she was high, she chewed me out a bit, calling me square and saying that I was missing the point. "Yes, I've been smoking pot. So what?"

"Just, asking. Fuck," I said. I was smoking a cigarette now, in the dark deep in the basement of Karen's house, through the half-open window. My stereo played quietly in the background until I heard the cassette gears click to a harsh metallic stop.

"In the summer you started moving in an unhealthy self-obsessed direction, and then you decided to act out your fantasy by cutting yourself. To show how you had become a monster. Quit manufacturing hate."

"I don't," I said, blowing smoke through the tiny mesh screen window. I turned on my own television. The word MUTE was green and wiggled in the corner.

That weird commercial about curing things with everyday household items came on. A preachy home-remedies infomercial that was revealed on a video or book you had to buy. Holly and I would listen for the voice-over part as the commercial faded. *Cure an earache with a hairdryer* was the funniest one, or *yogurt on a bee sting*. Sometimes we'd make up our own. *Stop a volcano's lava flow by rubbing your knees. Breathe underwater using a banana.*

I hated the taste of cigarettes in my mouth. I shut the window and brushed my teeth with loads of toothpaste. *Use mint toothpaste to extinguish your cigarette.*

I kept the phone to my ear, both mesmerized and repelled by my sister's trance-like speech, as if it was grand theatre. "Just don't unravel so much..."

"I might have to drop out of school. I'm fucked for money!"

"If you watch *Wall Street* with Charlie Sheen and Michael Douglas, it's all about that. Charlie becomes the little dog to the millionaire big dog, selling out his old-fashioned but individual father until he realizes the truth and saves his soul. Anyway, I think men find their identity when they become independent from the big father of the culture they are in which feeds off their naiveté and subservience. The wish to be one of the boys, like Mickey Rourke, who wanted to be a rebel but was ultimately living off Daddy's paycheque. He had no self and when he grew older he got some diamonds and a dog that according to his ex-girlfriend Carrie Otis, he carries around everywhere. Behind the caveman is just a little baby who at first is the master of his small world before he realizes how much bigger the world and the universe really are."

Seventy blocks away from one another, at times telling each other what channel was playing what, now together we watched most of an old John Candy film in near silence.[23]

---

23. On my very last visit home on November 15th to pick up some clothes and books, I got into a shouting match with Dad which led to me cutting my forearm with the steak knife. As the ambulance attendant held me down to check on me, I shouted at him, "You're not my doctor." Moments before cutting myself, I had leaned into my Dad's face and stared deeply into his eyes, grabbed his shoulder and with a pre-tear voice, told him " ... how fucked up it is you work for Andrew's father, considering what that piece of shit did to me ..." I can't recall verbatim.

16)

Touched by the Hand of God

Sunday, March 24th, 1996

Q: "So, you'd rather have a manslaughter conviction?" Conn asked.
A: "That's the only way I can go home," Erik answered.

———

Deputy Dist. Atty. David P. Conn spent most of his cross-examination suggesting Erik has had the last six years to design a sympathetic story that he was abused by his father for over a decade before turning a shotgun on his alleged abuser.

———

JUROR 12: Chinese American female, 42, of Akron. Real estate appraiser, born and raised in Hong Kong. Divorced mother of two. Is afraid of blood. Recalls seeing one of the brothers crying during first trial but wasn't concerned with it at the time. She believed one's childhood experiences can certainly carry some explanation to a person's behaviour. But at a later point in life, an individual must realize he or she is in charge of his or her own life.

The first trial in 1994 had ended in a mistrial. I followed the trial closely, clipping any reports or taping chance television spots, even two terribly acted and rushed television movies; plus I bought a fat paperback on the killings that revealed insight into Erik's fantasy world and described how he had been working on a screenplay about killing his parents.

"Looks like your guys are going to get the death penalty," Holly said on the phone, almost sounding sympathetic. That week I had caught the tail end of Erik's attorney, Leslie Abramson, using words like "apoplectic" in a statement to the media, which had me rushing to the dictionary for a definition.

The biggest question, of course, was, did their dad rape them in the fashion they described? Were the Menendez brothers tortured? The motivation for the murders was evident as they stood to inherit over 10 million dollars. Kitty was working on Erik's university application seconds before they gunned her down.

Once again I found myself lost in a semi-detached connection to celebrity; pondering my own sexual history, the Menendez trauma and the well-lit tears made me question what I had experienced with Andrew more than what had gone on with my family in terms of the casual fist fights and screaming matches.

I was not a killer; no one had died because of my actions, but I felt like a half-tone victim: afraid of expressing the truth, but also not truly knowing the truth either. The violence disturbed me, the end of their family coming at such a cost, such a public drama. My own family settled out of court with a few signatures and moved into their new digs while I became a living ghost, pumped with a rotating constellation of medication, in and out of a fuzzy self-obsession, with anger and general rottenness as a constant and reliable side effect.

The pills had stirred me into a particular focus, a numb, marbleized way of perceiving the small world around me. The Menendez trial was a familiar topic that pulled me in and out of my own static like a dark-blue suture every time they came up on any media signal.

Not much had changed in two years of deliberations: Erik insisted that he was not lying anymore but conceded that he did not want to spend the rest of his life in jail. When the verdict was handed down near the end of March, a journalist noted that Erik and Lyle did not react in any way, no tears, and that they did not look at each other at any point.

I was crashing on Dad's couch for the time being, trying to plan my next move. Over the last two years, I had played all my drama cards, and the house was sold, and I'd slept in spare rooms and couches. His couch was no different; the pills I was taking at the time cradled me in a silent funk, and my animosity turned into a numb feeling of rigor mortis and melancholy.

Fighting him seemed so far off, a distant time that only served to make me permanently homeless and insane: in my pharmacy-enhanced stupor, realizing there was no long-term home, couch or comfort, my battle turned inward. Why would I throw him down on the ground for another stomp when I'd already lost the war? I slurred a few words in repetitive whirlpool prophecy, until the pills and the counter all blurred into one big blob of pink or orange.

Holly moved in with Mom in a new two-bedroom condo-like co-op building near Mount Pleasant and Eglinton, and Dad moved into a one-bedroom apartment on top of a funeral home. For the past year, I had been getting medical notes and testimonials from the loom of my greatest mental health hits in order to somehow ensure a successful academic trip to Concordia. One semester in and I was panicking, dropping courses and trying to get out of another academic mess. It was as if I was building a case for how impossible going to school was for me. It ended up costing me more money in student loans, personal setbacks and undermined my confidence from day one of classes. I felt like I was a mythological character: left on the university doorstep at twenty-one with a bundle of preordained excuses and conditions, highly choreographed on medical stationary.[24]

---

24. "He also gives the impression of being under stress and lacks concentration. Parents have therefore requested a psychological assessment to determine Nate's present functioning and suitability of the French program for him. A screening for emotional factors was also included as part of the psychological assessment. This indicated that Nate may be generally dependent on others. Although he was able to make up positive resolutions to problem situations, often someone else took the major action to resolve the problem. There was also a significant number of expressions of anxiety in Nate's stories. On the sentence completion, Nate expressed communication difficulties between parents and himself, which may possibly be the source of some of his anxiousness and signs of stress seen at school. In the interview with Mrs. Moore following the assessment, his mother confirmed that there is difficulty at home around communication issues with Nate. Nate is a twelve-year-old boy in the French Immersion program who was found to have near high-average intellectual functioning on the WISC-R with strengths in abstract reasoning in visual-spatial skills. On standardized achievement tests, his scores were generally in the average range, although he needed extra time to complete the reading test. An emotional screening gave indication of possible dependency, anxiety and communication problems at home." (January 7, 1987, East York Board of Education, Dept. of Psychology)

Dad had just come back from the hospital after slipping at a beer store while returning some empties. After being hospitalized and having minor hip surgery, he said he was in the process of suing the store for damages. The whole thing had been caught on surveillance footage, and he had a lawyer who was reviewing his case. Dad had a pin inserted in his upper thigh. I visited him once at the hospital, but all he did was complain about not being able to smoke. He showed me his scar and talked about the procedure in gross detail, as if he had performed the surgery himself.

The semester at university in Montreal, my alleged academic comeback, had been nothing but drama, money wastage and sabotage. I had started doing the paperwork to salvage something, to stop the money drain, to make sense of it all, to cover my bases. If they gave out degrees based on how to get your marks erased because you were mentally ill, I'd have received two BAs by this point.

The head psychiatrist at the school's heath services summed it up in a medical letter mailed to Dad's apartment earlier in the week:

Nate has asked me to summarize the treatment he received at Heath Services while he was a student at Concordia. He has specifically requested that information be provided regarding the dates of his first and last visits, symptoms, diagnosis, treatment and behaviour/demeanor. Nate was first seen at Health Services on September 12, 1995. He last came on December 5, 1995. His symptoms included unusual psychomotor behaviour, thought disorganization, delusions, and auditory hallucinations that disrupted his sleep. These symptoms were consistent with a psychotic disorder and significantly impaired his academic functioning. He was prescribed Trilafon and Cogentin. He also continued to take lithium, which he had been prescribed in the past. He was briefly hospitalized in October 1995 and treated with Haldol. He did not return for follow-up after December, and it was later learned that he had returned to Toronto. Trusting this is satisfactory...

*

A week ago, our Aunt Amy (Dad's other sister) had rehashed a family-centric article in the *Toronto Star,* and the clipping was still crisp on Dad's coffee table, the same gruesome table that we had bounced each other of off at least three times. The newspaper story, spearheaded by my estranged Aunt Amy (herself now, like her father, an Anglican minister). My only recollections of her in the last ten years were her floating around sparse family gatherings all Holy, ghoulish and thunderbolts, bouncing theories off Grandfather about Jesus's intent or Joseph's fluorescent leather jacket, her chalky, tight, high-pitched voice arguing and slicing away at the gravy-filled air while the rest of us recoiled in itchy Sunday-best horror.

I watched Dad pace back and forth with a long great ash on his cigarette. The article brought forth what he had wanted so badly to forget from that dark-cloud year, 1968. In addition to new testimonials from the past, the article included several long passages from the original article, including the trial and news wires that ate up the controversial scandal.

"Want to watch something?" Dad asked me, moving in what I perceived as slow-motion across the hallway towards the small green phone he had plugged into a half-stripped wall. Dad loved renovating, continuously refurbishing a wall or piece of wood, always leaving bits of the places he lived in with a sense of vulnerability, of incompleteness.

Though I couldn't articulate the words because I was pilled, I tried mumbling something.

"I haven't felt this bad since my fiancée died," Dad told me, awkwardly pulling a tallboy from the refrigerator and plucking it open.

Dad walked past the stove, and I gazed at the kettle's slow resolve, its unhealthy sound as it came to a boil. How hollow and weak the metal sounded.

Up until a few days ago, he had been studying for a final exam to become a funeral director.

With those words, *"I haven't felt this bad..."* it became perhaps the first time I had ever heard him utter a sentence detailing an inward sentiment, devoid of physical or temporal properties or public inquiry into the location of shoes, socks, lawnmower, weed pick, coffee, person or condiment). *Where's my shoe, what's for dinner, where is Diane, where are my keys, the newspaper, the Visa bill, the car, the letter from Grandfather, your sister's postal code...*

Dad lit another cigarette.

"I can't take the test again; that was my last shot," he said, running his index figure along his cheek.

During my academic and mental uncertainty, Dad's apartment had become frequent destination for strong tea and long weak cigarettes; the two of us would eat together once a week, even grabbing a drink after one of his earlier dead man shifts once in a while.

I saw a vulnerable bicep deflating under his weak cotton arm, a set of unsettling eyebrows, unkempt for years, and his hair getting grey on fast-forward. A weakening man, caught in his own loquacious storm.

I was witnessing Dad's transportation to a time that predated my own mortal coil, that predated our own family's origins to this time before Diane Shaw dropped her last name, before Holly was born (1972) or Benji the cat reigned supreme (1970–1985), before any of us were ever photographed, imprisoned in celluloid glaze.

The array of pink pills I'd been popping all evening gave me a sick feeling all over. I staggered into the kitchen, wearing one of Dad's blazers and a paisley tie, a fuzzy toque, my hair curling out from the sides, the Epivals swimming hard in my blood, downed every few minutes with an anti-anxiety chaser. *Who was this fiancée, someone before Mom? Why hasn't he ever said anything about—Holly said something about an accident, before—*my face unshaven, raw, occasional pimples thwarted only by my itchy, uneven beard.

"I got too nervous," Dad said, summing up the reality. I made a wheezing noise. He continued. "I may be able to take it in a year's time, but I have to talk to the Dean to reapply."

"Shit," I said, my mouth a gauze of spit that felt foamy and at once dry, imaginary. He stubbed out his cigarette.

"That sucks."

"I'm going out for a minute. Want anything?"

I shook my head. "Naw." I had had more than enough. A strange buzzing sound filled my head now as I glanced into a tall jar of pasta, spaghetti, the translucent red jar, the same one from our house on Glenvale. "Be right back," Dad said, shuffling down the narrow stairwell into the guts of the funeral home.

I found three more pills and swallowed them, lit a cigarette and went outside onto Dad's balcony, noticing a neighbour walking up the metal stairwell. She was asking me some questions, when I realized I couldn't comprehend words. Into the charcoal night I broke through my silver breath, destroying the temporary poltergeist I made by breathing. I made my way back into the apartment, now fully controlled by my own chemical roulette.

I stood at the small kitchen sink, pawed at the dirty dishwater, witnessing plump noodles floating in the dirty soap suds. My tongue was animated, thick and heavy. The tips of my fingers tingled, seeking out more Epival, that sweet pink shrapnel. Two stray ones sparkled on the mauve carpet, and I downed them.

I moved my maelstrom towards the cluttered dining-room table, replete with text books and binders strewn across the pink tablecloth.

"Hello?" Dad said.

"Hi," I answered. I began to pour the pills out in a big pink train on the kitchen counter.

"I bought some chips if you'd like some," Dad said from the living room.

Twelve pills bright and pink. I spoke into my micro-recorder: "I'm

going to do it, I have to do it, I um, I gotta, I have to," my speech lubricated with drool and a veritable buffet of snarls and warbles, now
permanent on the tape.

I circled the dining-room table, covered in a sheet and full of paint
chips, and knocked several flash cards over in the process. As I
picked them up, my eyes fell on the alien terminology, as if a new
language had invaded us: *Adaptive Funeral Rite: a funeral rite that is
adjusted to the needs...4. Egalitarian: Male and female have equal
rights, duties...14. Enculturation (Socialization): The method by
which social values are internalized...5. Humanistic Funeral Rite: a
funeral rite that is in essence devoid...8. Neo-traditional Funeral Rite:
a funeral rite that deviates from the normal...18. Rite: any event
performed in a solemn and prescribed...9. Social Stratification:
categorization of people by money, prestige...Canopic jars used by the
Egyptians; four jars—*

My vision was now runny pink and clumpy, an uneven pie smear.
Objects were melting and reforming, and a raging black silhouette
was continually trying to blanket my turbulent peripheral.

The pills swam, and everything now had a thickness. My head was
ticking and I stopped hearing.

I imagined Mom at home, pacing with nervous agitation, her face poised
on the brink of tea or toast, sighing eternally, chewing on something while
speaking to Holly or Dad, her voice crumbling into the receiver.

I felt my stomach break in half, parts of me leaking, possibly soil-
ing myself. I let out a soft cry as if had God abandoned me forever.

I saw Mom waving her hands across an overheated bagel as it entered her mouth, the phone ringing, and her choking, not taking the
time to finish the chew before answering the third ring. With toasted
dough lodged in her molars, she would let out the newsfeed to Holly.

"I overdosed," she might have said, half-choking on her food. "I
mean, Nate overdosed," Mom switched gears, her coughing fit creating a temporary lull in tone.

"When?" Holly asked.

"Just now. Your father took him to the hospital," Mom might have said, her slippers scuffling along the tiles.

I half-imagined all this from my pink netherworld tomb. "Just now, he overdosed, he's asleep at the hospital."

My skull was clean against the ambulance slab, immovable; a gurney, and finally a bed: *Her only son, the only son of her nuclear family.* These were the molecules, the sounds, the aroma of a life vanishing, left unkempt, left to my own useless devices. A dash of autopsy ingredients, an obituary in rehearsal: my actions explained nothing, except that I was hopeless and autobiographical.

My nightly self-lust, self-destruct setting was enhanced by the chemical roulette: a swan song only I could hear.

God had died inside me.

I woke up strapped to the thin sliver of a hospital bed. The mattress was firm and a bit moist.

"You peed all over me," the nurse said, as I came into consciousness. I eyed the plastic straw.

"Sorry," I said, mouth swollen and dry.

"And you bit me," she said, blurring off in a shade of white I had never seen before.

Mom appeared at my side, dishevelled, raw and tired. "They say you can leave in an hour," she said, her mouth knotted in strange creases.

"Do you want something to drink?"

"No way."

"They have some questions for you."

"Department of Administrative, um, uh ... anxiety."

In what I thought was the final performance of my life, the playlist from hell had accompanied me into a pharmaceutical oblivion. The menacing songs on repeat, the pink bullets, the pharma-slugs in my stomach, I possessed a vampire's bloodlust, overplaying and pouring into my membranes; my central nervous system bankrupting into a histrionic nosedive; reddening pool of skin.

From the distance, one clean juice straw appeared on a table, just out of reach. I homed in on the wallow, inflating the agony.

This symphony ruled me, the twenty-seven pills they took from my stomach now dissolving in a sink, in a pipe, back into the water supply.

Nate, you listen to me, it's yourself talking at you: You forget about your tragic upbringing and you motor around, along, beside, inside, up and down, while your never worked a day in your life hands gently squeeze—the blood flowing through your rusty tributaries, the power and glory of it all and everything goes black and the cool mattress becomes transparent and you can see all the way to the earth's feeble cortex and as your vision goes deeper and you see further and further past anonymous shards of time, random earth debris and the molten synapses firing away, you see your Great Uncle Carl in a glossy black-and-white photo with serrated edges taken five years before your birth and he's wearing a squeaky clean business-class suit and a bib and his gimmicky bow tie, his smile is full tilt and the Japanese chefs are beside him, proud of their presentation until the photo gets snapped by a giant hot lobster claw and melts. Cut to infinite underwater bubbles. You see your sister at a cottage with friends; Elizabeth is there. You see your parents watching TV in separate rooms, the glow illuminating their eyes and nostrils and fidgeting digits. Despite this distance, you feel like your family is still booking your whole cocksucking life talking to each other like the corrupt sports agents they are, like the strangers-at-the-soup-kitchen type chatter they give you, like the let's-talk-about-the-weather-alienation-street treatment they are comfortable with, all the while getting you the cheapest and bestest suicide rate for your stupid unattended provincial funeral.

*

The next morning, I found myself recuperating on Mom's couch. I looked down at my feet, hidden under a thin blanket. "I'm going out for a while, Nate, so, just rest," she said. "I got you some ginger ale." I sat up slowly, looked around her empty apartment. When I coughed, I felt the sticky thing they used to monitor me was still on me, tangled in my chest hairs.

I walked with soft, uneven steps towards the answering machine in the hallway and pressed play.

It was last night: I heard my parents talking. Mom as usual hadn't reached the phone in time when Dad called, and the tape's brittle finesse captured my parents discussion as my body lay on Dad's stinking kitchen floor, as Mom paced on her own kitchen floor, as Dad's stomach grumbled, oozing coffee and spaghetti sauce, peering down at me, looking at my rib cage for movement.

Seeing the remaining pills lined up on the kitchen counter, the empty bottle on the floor beside me all crime scene and raw, Dad sounding residual, not certain whether I was in fact dead or poisoned.

As I listened, I wrapped the thin blue blanket around me tighter. The gargling answering machine tape played my parents' emergency exchange—as if the lines had been adlibbed by someone else with a tone of closure, exit wound and severity. There was no escape from hearing them, and understanding exactly what it was they were saying.

"Nate took some pills."

"He's supposed to take pills, David."

"Well, he took a lot. He's not moving."

"Is he breathing?"

"I don't know."

"Well, check."

"I think so."

"Call the hospital or somethi—"

The tape ended abruptly, cutting out and rewinding with a tight metallic whirl and belch. I tried to speak. I wanted to say something to disengage from the finality of the pre-millennial answering machine's cold facts that contained the secrets of the universe, but my throat hurt and my mouth felt extinct, as if words were impossible to emit. My head was full of spinning animation: little dots in heavy rotation floated past my eyes.

I slugged myself back to the couch, my out-of-work stomach turned in considerable pain, the smell of charcoal still strong and deeply tattooed in my nostrils.

PART III:

THE LAST SAVAGE

(1997–2011)

17)

Brutal

February 1997–December 2001

I n film, to demonstrate the passage of time, transitional montages
will culminate with textured shadows across a barren landscape—
glints of spastic sunshine on building sides, frost building up on
window panes, bricks and mortar becoming scuffed by sleet, and
wooden beams eroding and becoming brittle, while trees scuttling
through seasons are plumed with rain venting down, sun drying it up,
soil hardening and foliage muted with cold hints of early snow. This
passage of our family's post-Glenvale colour and friction was not
captured on film but was catalogued in cognitive recesses—*new and
selected*. The past settled.

The memories were so big in my head that even the dulling of the
drugs I was taking didn't wash them out completely. How could I gift
wrap a sister, Mom, Dad, dead Great Uncle, four dead grandparents,
various psychiatrists, bartenders and neighbours and Mom's strolls by
bread sticks jutting out of metal troughs decorating storefronts along
Mount Pleasant Avenue, south of Eglinton, several minutes by foot

from Canada Square Cinemas, Eglinton subway station, Orchard View Library and the new gaudy logo noise of Yonge and Eglinton version 2...order up!

Of all the things I kept with me on my odyssey, it was my RCA CC-432 VHS Analog Camcorder that acted as a strong phantom limb, a perennial, albeit cumbersome, necessity for my ever-changing wilderness. On one of many couch-surfing exits, forgetting I had stuck my camera in the bottom, I tossed my large duffle bag down a flight of stairs, cracking the camcorder's plastic body. Luckily, for a few months at the time, I was living with someone who said he knew a guy at his work who could fix it. And so the artificial life force that mimicked observation skills was extended. What had become a lonely broad-casting tradition (the sadcore video diary entries as midnight struck and one year dissolved digitally into the next) had grown into a weekly parody of life in an adult suit. I went insane when I thought about money, employment, society; others could escape the bleakness I championed, chartered and gargled with acuity.

During a particularly low stretch of months I could be seen at the height of fashion, combining Hawaiian shirts, blazers, my father's bowler hat and a thick black overcoat worn with army boots. My hair curled over my ears in a mangy frenzy, and my facial hair was trimmed into a goatee. My eyes were a deep set of stale chocolates, glazed over with an intense look of betrayal, detached from specific focus. My stomach was usually hot-wired in coffee, pizza, pasta or a gauntlet of carbohydrates home cooked by near strangers. In December 1996, I moved to Waterloo, a city an hour and a half outside of Toronto, to live with some friends for cheap and escaped each night into a deep, pilled-out sleep.

*

Mom now lived with banana bread and white furniture cleaned with

Windex, Lysol and J-Cloths, six or seven blocks from our first house at 61 Mann Avenue, across from the Dominion where I'd mispronounced the word truck often and at high decibels, and where the glass jar of mythological goose grease fell from my hands in the basement, February 5, 1976, and I fell on it, the broken glass and grease and cut my face and eye open from brow to right beside my right nostril, the pupil dangling by cords and wiring.

Dad's attempt at a stabilized career at the new funeral home was interrupted by the beer-store slip and his failure to get his funeral-director's licence, and by mid-1996, he had moved out of Toronto for good. Before disappearing into his rural pre-coffin life in Elgin, Ontario, he showed me the bottoms of his soles, how the treads had worn thin, and told me that he had never shown the shoes to his lawyer.

"They're going to settle for nineteen thousand bucks!" Dad laughed, as if he was getting away with something.

Within weeks of the settlement, he had fastened himself inside a permanent trailer, telling us later the land was cheap because it was built on a patch of degenerative swampland.

I had visited him that first Christmas, but left the next morning on a bus, unable to stomach the cigarette smoke and late-morning beer drinking.

And then a harsh laugh from Mom, oozing nervously on the phone, "Thank God we don't all live together!"

The beer store had set him free.

One weekend in February 1997, Holly took the bus and visited me during a blizzard. I made a short film of us making tea and shovelling snow. Holly did her best to cover her face from my tabloid ascents. We didn't really do anything but eat microwavable food and watch movies, and I do remember a yelling match one morning about the state of our family and Holly shouting at me about getting my shit together.

"Well it must be nice to live at home all your life with *mother margarine container* as your personal chef and laundry slave!"

"You sound so mad; why are you so angry? It's like you go to this whole other plateau of—"

"BECAUSE, HOL, JESUS! I feel trapped, cornered, a scalded dog, a dead slow-snake, a real monster, I dunno," I shouted in a booming action-film voice-over voice, "BECAUSE YOU only get three hundred opportunities to ruin your life forever!"

"Please."

"I don't hate any of you. We just seem to want nothing to do with each other at a gut level, you know, the deal is done."

Despite this glitch, things were OK, and we'd talk every few weeks after that on the phone. When Holly didn't return my calls for a month in late spring, I called Dad, who just said something disposable like Holly was working a lot and taking a night-school class.

In the summer, Holly finally visited again for the weekend. My friends wanted to go out for lunch, but Holly didn't want to spend the money, nor did I, so we wandered in the hot parking lots while my friends ate lunch.

Again, as had been the case in February, Holly moved her hands over her face whenever I tried to take a photograph or videotape her doing something like making food or reading the newspaper on the couch.

On a glossy postcard depicting Waterloo's bustling downtown core in winter on King Street between Weber and Jameson, I had scrawled the following:

Q: Nate, what was it like retiring from being a teenager?
A: YOU'RE TALKING ABOUT WALKING AWAY FROM SOMETHING YOU'RE REALLY GOOD AT, AT A VERY YOUNG AGE.

Thanks for throwing hot coffee on me as a teen pin-up boy waiting for his suicide shipments on the front porch. You scalded my self-esteem like a prince turning into a rodent covered in expired groceries ... it would have made a great Miracle Whip commercial, you Nazi.

Have a great boxing day
Nancy

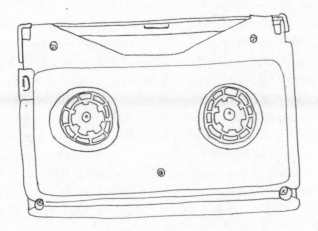

After inserting the tape into the fragile video-camera jaw and sliding my hand underneath the grip to hit the red REC button, I heard the gears inside the belly and moved in front of its tiny red eye. I waited patiently for the auto-focus to come to its senses. (The cassette was labeled "WATERLOO 1997.") The red light went on; the tape began chewing up real time.

The machine wheezed and gestated. I was at my kitchen table, head full of thumping pharmaceuticals as my early morning confessional began, sermon-like, an autopsy of my own living life. I turned the camera off and tidied up the evidence.

Dad, hello father, here, I am at Camp Granada! Hello Dad listen, listen up! I'm not accusing you of anything anymore. I know I did, but your appearance in my powder-keg nightmares is just syndication, nothing more, a nifty balm of worry, 100-proof vodka, a dreg of anxious breath afterbirth still raw as war, as in war in the air of my own premastered edition of myself. You are a worno, you have worn down your financial memory, down to a thin hobo shoe cud and I can revisit you pure, in un-Glenvaled Technicolor. In old library MICROFICHE, counting the years from the headlines, the grainy headlines with their chewed rat corners, rat-chewed corners before you met Mom...so here I am now, Nate in the time of Holly, post-stigmata, the Menendez home work-out videotape exploding and snapping in its own juicy gears and all we have is the segregated grocery bills and the solo consumption as if nothing EMOTIONAL ever happened. I will be your father figure put your tiny hands in mine I will be the one that loves you Davey until the end of time. Your sister Rebecca gives me a homeless man's shaving set last Christmas, so brief and cruel and glistening in a plastic cocoon of disposables—just like me, and your sister Becks saying "YOU'RE ALWAYS MOVING AROUND NATE, SO I THOUGHT IT'D BE PERFECT FOR YOU, YOU BUM!" and I'm not supposed to do anything but put down my ginger ale and ice and calmly start shaving while repeating THANK YOU AUNT BECS THANKS THANKS BECKY BABY all the while knowing she got it free with her REAL pharma purchases? Oh BECKY I'M YOUR LONG LOST DAUGHTER NANCY PROM QUEEN so be proud of me, I'm a doctor I'm a lawyer I'm doing my masters at HOOKER SCHOOL!

Every day congealed. Each morning when I woke from my pharmacy sleep, I awoke with a sliver of hope, as though this could be the day I made sense and everyone would understand what I said at the grocery store or over the phone and that somehow the abstract white noise filling my brain night and day would subside, like a bad techno song played on repeat, the cassette finally giving up, spooling out into a complex warranty suicide.

When the '90s finally folded, Holly took more classes to hone her business skills and become more desirable in the workforce. She travelled, snow boarded, started seeing a graphic designer and lived at "home" with Mom while I waffled in and out of contact with them both and became increasingly obscured through medication, missives and bouts of energy deprivation and acceleration. My weight yo-yoed, as did my appetite and overall economy.

Sometimes I would spend weekends in hospital. The pills would be re-assigned, the prescription stapled to my sleeve and I'd be sent back through the electronic door into the hollering city. The side effects would always turn me into a mute zombie or twitchy wretch. Once or twice, I woke up with the billowing screen door crashing back and forth, having fallen asleep unaware I'd temporarily expired for the night.

"They make me so nuts," I'd tell Mom live or over the phone. "I can't take them anymore, I feel these undulations, a pulsing wave in my arms and legs."

"Well, why don't you talk to your doctor about it?"

"He's an idiot."

Or to Holly from a payphone, "I hate those doctors...they just hand me prescriptions, expect me to remember every pill I've ever taken over the past six years, and to know my every mood for every single fucking minute of my life. Like I'm an expert on me. Fuck them. Darkness is cheaper."

I became elusive as the new millennium began, my bitterness rose to the surface in the form of callous Christmas cards: sardonic, as if penned by a bottom-hitting child star, unable to come to terms with reality, abject mail art that charmed no one, stylized in the form of psychotic family newsletters, which Holly, Mom and Dad all received separately, dismissed and recycled.

...You'll all have to kill me to be finished with me! I'm so sick of this I live in squalor, and no one does a goddamn thing about it, just take your fucked-up pills and live in garbage, live beside a funeral home and wait for an opening to come up and crawl inside a coffin and just die, die, die, that's what you want isn't it? There's just so much God damned injustice in this family and no one does a Goddamn thing about it! It just didn't start here you know, this goes back six or seven years when you all started to gang up on me, and put a price on my life. Which was zero dollars! I do apologize though to all my fans, those who watched me deliver my paper route, those who watched me chew gum and ride my bike, and tried my best to defend the honour of this family, those who witnessed me try to be the hero, try to do what is right, to take a coward like David and show him what he did, when I held the mirror up to him and knocked him down in the ground after he ran his mouth about how you Diane would NEVER get the house, what happens when we get back in town, after our little Kingston street fight? You all sympathize with him, and suddenly I'm a bad guy. It didn't just start right here. It didn't just start right now, this very second, me on medication all insane and angry, this goes back years! So to you, Diane, Holly and David, I apologize for nothing. So I thought I'd see what happened. I played it cool. Then, a few months later, David out of nowhere, attacks me for no reason. After I tried to clean up this family, he took it upon himself to strangle me and shove me all over the living room just hours before my first real girlfriend was on her way to spend the weekend. Then I have to make a decision about school, there is paperwork, loans and other things that I have to worry about all summer, I don't know if I can afford to return to university, and if I do, where I'll be living. But my insanity colours could not be tamed or washed out of the rinse cycle. Everything is so Goddam uncertain and suddenly old David is talking about how he has to go back to school to get his dead man diploma. And that I need to back off, to get a job. To concentrate on school. To keep busy. So I get a job, but it turns out to be

a scam. Then I get another job at Jumbo Video, part-time. Fine, I'm working. I come home one night after work and you guys are sitting around the table planning a vacation without me. Some sort of family time share. Fine, I say, count me out, that's great. I try to figure out what is going on, I'm staring at the OSAP forms, the line where you put your address, all that information about what your parents make, their income, where you'll be living, and the situation. I have no idea what is happening because no one is talking to me, you're all too busy conspiring behind my back for better deals with other organizations. A better man would have quit, but I stayed I stayed through the summer. I tried to understand what was happening to me, I saw my friend's therapist. You even gave me one of your antidepressants, my friends were like, "Those take weeks to work, Nate, one pill isn't going to do anything." *I don't understand what is happening to me . . . you see me as just a fucked up person . . . anyway I am in no position to speak, I have no votes. It's just me on this phone in these insane emails and whatever, all day 365 days a year . . .*

Persecuted manifesto sprung out in hostile blue-ink tributaries, garnering no acclaim from their readers, just exacerbating my toxic sense of betrayal. "Hey, Hol. I keep having the same dream. It's always the same exact time: a few weeks before we sold the house, and I'm in my room, looking at all my stuff and wondering what the fuck I'm going to do with it all, and like, where am I going to go, in a constant looping panic. All I know is that I have to move, then I wake up."

Holly replied: "Here's my last message, since you don't want a barrage, I understand, OK, Nate? I know that you have emotional pain and that you've tried lots of ways of dealing with it. I'll support the small steps that you take towards letting go of wounds, loving yourself, and relying upon yourself to not allow yourself or other people to victimize you. I'll support you because you're my brother."

I had mortgaged my youth, gnawed on pills and on depression and pushed everyone to the horrifying edge. I got drunk and photocopied a nightmare doctor's note, remixing the end with self-cruel parody.

You were initially seen in the mood disorder clinic by DR. R. GUSKOV in November 1994. Your initial diagnosis was bipolar disorder, depressed phase. Since that time you have been treated with lithium carbo I, approximately 1200 mg per day, augmented by either a low dose of antipsychotic agents or antidepressants. Mood swings, accompanied by occasional paranoid ideation, has impaired your social functioning and school performance. Your most recent medications are lithium, 1200 mg at bedtime, and desipramine, 100 mg at bedtime. *You will hopefully die soon.*
  Sincerely, Dr. Shane McMahon-Hemsley

*

You need sleep, Nate? How about you whip out your founding father of Emo Han Solo drag Polaroids? Or your savoury middle-class and white box-bedroom rebel-teen-cutter forearm scars, or your cool imitations of dead goaltender Jacques Plante, complete with a makeshift antique goalie mask and spackles of dirty Madison Square Garden blood? Do you think some girl, well, you know, that she'd like, go for that? You wonder all this now while you bask away in a manger, thinking of you and Andrew and his cousin playing the three wise man circa December 198_?, Northlea United Church for the Christmas pageant. You were Doctor Frankincense.

18)

Vanishing Point

March 2002–June 2003

My Tuesday night had been uneven, tossing and turning after a long close-shift at work—a Montreal phone centre entombed with hundreds of computerized phones similar to those used in any number of 1980s paranoia war movies. "The people we call can't see us," I explained to my supervisor, as I quizzed strangers nation-wide about their consumer habits on things like candles and the number of times they went on vacation, rented movies or played charades.

Wind kept coming through the window, mainly because I had to leave it open for Jimmy, the three-month-old kitten with (mostly) white and grey fur we adopted and who now lived and breathed with me, causing my roommates, who shared in his cost of living, to be jealous and suspicious I was bribing the animal with various procured meats. I couldn't imagine another year stockpiling morbid VHS footage of me and my life dregs. As I fell asleep that night, I dug and I plotted my ending: walking from a highway road, fifty feet deep in the forest, rocks and soil would be placed on a large plastic drop sheet. Then I'd dig a big hole large enough for me to lie in and then I'd just pull the sheet and be buried alive. This weekend was *Wrestlemania X8* in Toronto at SkyDome and I had my ticket. I was staying with Tabitha our first sleepover and our first real date.

I was now living in Montreal, having saved up enough money for a single semester of university in an attempt to see if I could do something from start to finish, even if it was only for four months.

"You are a brute," the soft voice said into the phone. "I'm wearing a pink dress my friend Jen made me." This was how it began with Tabitha, a voluptuous, dusty, vegan-muffin-baking stoner barista from England.

I mumbled a sound. "Jesus Christ! You're not about to make yourself vulnerable!"

I had no idea what Tabitha was talking about, but assumed it had something to do with who she *thought* I was. We had been talking on a daily basis for nearly two months now, ever since I moved to Montreal for school in January. We had an attraction to one another that we never discussed, dating back to a party she had taken me to in Toronto on New Year's Eve where I left after seeing people doing cocaine.

I was re-reading something she wrote me last month. The stoned speech is highlighted here:

You can think of homo porn, but girlies are mommies to be sugar-coated and fattened and baby-pictured up for your future home but boys are the Eros in your heart cruciform. You can't even dream of throwing me around the office unless I have a cock…Nate, did you know I was thinking about you and Roger Rabbit and Walt Whitman. I want to be your fag fairy, let me help you, like you help me. Maybe one day we'll live together and you'll be dating hot boys and so will I and we'll be sucking cock for art and baking vegan brownies at home. Anything is possible; it's all about differentiating your desire. Face it, Nate, you're not into girls. Go out and explore your sexuality now, don't trade passion for security because you don't want to be rejected by your mother. I think you're being lazy. I'll still be your friend; I'll be your bestest friend, but I want to be with someone who's into femmes. A gay boy can't objectify women even if he can have sex with them. Don't pretend that wanting a wife makes you straight; having a wife is, weirdly, a Christmas wish list numero uno for homos. Home alone, homos, it's all so Freudian.

Tabitha and I hadn't had sex yet, or kissed, though she did take my hand and place it on her lacy blouse one night in December and squeezed it next to her breasts. This back-and-forth filled our days apart, screaming at one another on the phone about desire and fantasy, only to end with laughter or confessions about degrading fantasies, mostly involving her. "I love it when you said you had that dream of me trying to get out of the pool on a ladder and you kept pushing me back under water," Tabitha gushed into the receiver. She called me that night at eight-thirty. "Nate, it's so cold tonight! I am wearing two sweaters."

I heard the faint beat of techno playing in the background. Tabitha had a stack of cassettes she'd play on an old crusty boom box in her bedroom that made warbled, hissing sounds.

"I know. I keep reheating this soup. It's so cold here too!"

"I was thinking about you today; if you accepted being more curvy, feminine and emotional, you'd feel less like it made you weak and you'd feel more like your real self."

"Yeah, that's true. I think a lot of it is in my head."

"Lots of people are blind or have heart troubles or asthma; that doesn't make them idiots. You do have to do some work on your self-realization and health, but in essence, I do not think you are a wimp."

"Thanks."

"It could be also that you are lonely and you aren't giving yourself the chance to feel good about being alone. But do you have any friends in Montreal? I can't believe you're coming here this weekend!"

"Sort of, from class, I guess. But it's hard. Yeah, I know, I'm so excited to see you."

"I'd love to be a woman you have over," Tabitha said. "And make out in your room."

I was silent. Tabitha continued, "You can be the dude-jock arche-type, and I'll be your adoring Barbie; we'll do performance art in the living room, where you talk bullshit for hours and I gaze up at you like a melting chocolate lab puppy."

She kept going, her voice making me see tinsel and soft pink sweaters and—

"We'll have really loud sex, and the next morning you can look busy and preoccupied while I sit on the couch all teary and dejected. That's what our relationship might turn into anyway."

"Maybe, if you're good," I said. "Maybe you're a psychic witch," I said.

"Oh yes. Do you know that you have a dark, sexy look that also goes a bit decadent, Rasputin, at times? As though you've been drink-ing absinthe in a brothel since you were four; except, when you really were four, you looked like, I don't know, a 1960s game-show host—you had this all-American-entertainment boy's club thing going on, like you could have been born with a cigar in your mouth and left the hospital to go fishing. Then you turned into this mercurial magician. You became very animated and you still knew show business, but you'd taken acid and you were now on a psychedelic, shaman journey, which is where you got your mask. It's cool, because I have two swords, and all the boys in Japanimation have masks and split identities. That's why I thought you'd like that Japanese novel *Confessions of a Mask*, though it was at a time I did truly think you were gay. But you don't have to cut your head off like he did. It must be some boy mythology mysticism, because just think of cowboys and the Lone Ranger and highwaymen and Batman. You said about Batman, 'He's the only superhero who is self-conscious.'"

I had time to put in a few hours towards my ongoing nuclear family feud:

"Look, Family-maniacs, it's unfortunate your parental coping skills are limited to one offspring, and it has always been this way, that is, the backing-away part in which you prolifically are akin to. Anyway, I'll be fine, I always am, it's unfortunate that I'm not allowed the same rights as my idiot sister whom I am better than. It's not like I killed people. At times of great struggle, I feel that things would be easier, you know, getting a job in Toronto, if I had a phone in Toronto, or a bed there right now or could actually fucking live there. I make shit money in Montreal and I can either concentrate on school or working just so I can live here. I just have it in my head that everyone on earth I know has been able to, at some point, move back home for a period of time, but I'm not allowed. I'm on this sick treadmill on and on and on like a wet Energizer Bunny no one wants to let inside. If Holly was in my shoes, you'd be driving hundreds of miles to save her and you know it! It's no fault of yours, just somewhere along the way you've all deemed me unworthy of ultimate concern, and it's become Biblical, the degree to which Holly is a priority; it's like the accepted standards and practices of this family. From that day forward Nate shall be as replaceable as the lamps he broke on season three of *This Shitty Life* sayeth the Lord. Do you know of any temp work or places that handle that in Toronto?"

Mom responded, and since I didn't have call waiting, she left a voice message:

"Hi Nate, got your phone message today and wondered what kind of temp work you were looking for? I really don't have any link to personnel agencies since I've always gone through the paper. And it's for the summer in Toronto? That's a few months off. I guess the *Toronto Star* want ads are the best. Just look every day and see if they offer some information. I'm so glad that you've found some relief for your frustration of making the move to Toronto. Perhaps you can continue to do some work using contacts. I've talked to Uncle Carl, but when I phoned on the weekend he was resting, so I said that I'd call again. If you want to phone him, and I know he would like to hear from you, try after 7:00 p.m. He likes to talk about current-events things in the news, so plan some things you can talk about so that you don't have to be talking about yourself all the time. Work continues in its own tedious way. Maybe we can take in a movie sometime or meet for coffee, so keep in touch."

Friday, March 15th, 2002

"Hello, Nate! My blood is boiling with you today. I hope you mean the romance you give, because I'm not lying around like a plate of French fries; I think about you rubbing your nose into me, burying your teeth and shifting the balance of weight against gravity in your body. You remind me, hot and sweaty, of a horse I used to ride. You take memories of my father and fuck me with them—"

"Hello?"

"Oh, you're home!"

"Just got home from class."

"When you get here, I can take you running outdoors in the park; it's fun and I'll kill you, then I'll make you do kung fu and yoga, which my ex-boyfriend George and I used to do. We were always working out together; it was the one thing, aside from cooking and pot-smoking we had in common."

"I'm just packing up and leaving in five minutes for the bus station," I said.

"Also, I got your tape in the mail late last night when I got back from trailer-trash bingo, which my friends Trixie and Beaver run. At one point, this cute Asian girl took her top off and stuck her fingers in her pants and smelt them. I thought of you … OK, I will see you soon."

Eight hours later, wearing maroon jogging pants, jogging shoes and a yellow windbreaker, Tabitha met me at Yonge and Bloor, standing next to her bike, just after one in the afternoon. Her light-brown hair was pulled back into two small, braided pig tails just below her ears. If God were to look back, she may argue that at times over that weekend I appeared rigid and anxious, but never dour or bleak. I was always eager.

At times, however, I felt completely overwhelmed in Tabitha's world of vegan soups, almond milk, vintage *Playboy* pin-ups and girl-sweat overalls.

Now, thrown into what she called "physical reality," Tabitha and I were weekend concubines of groceries and candles and her big queen-sized bed after a meal consisting of vegan sushi and fresh juice.

"Drink this," she said, her mouth already rimmed in juicy foam. "It's rigorous juice."

I carried the giant television into her room so we could watch *Ghost-busters*, while Tabitha went through a series of wardrobe changes. After the movie ended, we got under the blankets for real, finally collapsing into each other with long, eye-clenched kisses. She undulated on top of, beneath and in front of me, our bodies reacting to this new unleashed erotic situation we had created. On Sunday evening, I had to attend *Wrestlemania X8* at SkyDome.

"I have to go to the thing. I should be back by 11:30." When I returned for the final night of our sleepover, her roommates told me off for supporting a tourist capitalist venture like the WWF. I tried to explain how they had a food drive that day at SkyDome, but it was no use.

On Monday morning, I stood in Tabitha's cold apartment. The tooth-paste was like fresh mortar slapping along my gums, inviting a wall, suffocation, the end. Before my bus ride back to Montreal, I had an appointment with my general practitioner, who was standing in as my mental council as I was between psychiatrists. At the appointment, my doctor asked, *What triggered this? This need for you to feel like this is the end.*

And I was passionate about my ending, the white-light, end-of-the-tunnel cliché—not the journey. The journey never mattered. I told my GP, "I just feel like I'll run out of desire to live, like a fish out of water, and just throw myself at the mercy of whatever object is on a collision course to destruct." I would mutate into death; I'd make it happen.

Mom was semi-supportive, long distance and accessible. She was her own call centre now for my continued bouts of frenetic Unabomber-style payphone rants. My patronage to outdoor phone facilities spanned provinces. She phoned me when I arrived back in Montreal. "…Just think positively. Remember that I will always love you, but sometimes I back away because that's what seems to be the best thing at the time. I've also noticed how much you've improved in your problem-solving skills—that is, you find a way out of the dark side. Just remember: you will succeed if you keep in control and try not to see yourself as a victim, but as a person with a destiny…"

July–August 2002

The summer was a record-breaking, heated affair that included a papal visit from John Paul II in Toronto, prompting Tabitha and her friends to threaten to ride down his parade route naked on bikes. When we weren't visiting each other in Toronto or Montreal, I tried to beat the heat with Jimmy by rubbing ice cubes on his head and belly and covering up the windows with blankets. Some nights I would get a call from one of the waiters at Na Brasa, a Portuguese restaurant two blocks away, who would ask if I ever fed my cat.

"He is always begging for food out back," they said on the phone. "Yes, I feed him. Do you feed him?" For the next few weeks, I would joke with Jimmy, asking him if he was eating at home or going out for supper.

Tabitha and I managed to get away: a two-week train-and-car trip to PEI with Tabitha's middle sister, Laura. We took the lengthy train ride from Montreal, and Tabitha's refusal to buy cough drops of any kind proved to be a trip tone-setting move. She coughed for the fifteen-hour train ride, my only solace being the occasional dirty comment she made about the scantly dressed teens at the end of the car. Laura picked us up at the train station, and we car-camped for two days, which included the best seafood I've ever had, nude-sister swimming and roadside sex while Laura tented solo. The funniest beach memory was the two naked Kane sisters about thirty feet out in the ocean examining each other's bodies for some reason while two boys on land checked them out with binoculars.

I went deep-sea fishing on our last day in PEI en route to Tabitha's parent's giant country house in New Brunswick. When we arrived, I rested the bag containing the barely dead fish in it on their new deck, causing a big oily mark. Thankfully, they were about to have it stained, so I avoided scorn early. Tabitha's father was a short stout British man with a red face, as if he continuously held his breath in, ready to explode on cue.

At dinner that first night, Laura updated their mother on a close friend who was always having trouble meeting or keeping a boyfriend. Before this segment began, the meal unstitched into several pockets of discussion: our PEI trip, the train ride and the pope. Laura began her story, and her mother appeared poised at first but then overwhelmed by a visible display of curiosity. "So Maggie met this guy at a picnic we'd put together," Laura began. "Yes," their mother said, touching Laura's free hand. She took a bite of forked salad. "They agreed to meet the next day at the same park we were at." Laura delivered the backstory details of Maggie's make-up as a person with brevity and equanimity, creating a sort of mysterious intrigue. "So she went to the park the next day to meet him—"

"Where she was raped by ten bikers," their father chimed in, total deadpan and sourced from some reserve that Tabitha later told me was a typical type of parlance.

We spent the next ten days attempting to but not succeeding to go whale watching, taking the family dog on a terrible beach walk where he fell from a rock at a height of about ten feet and needed to be carried for a mile back to the house and taken to the vet. Tabitha thought this was an omen, as I carried the senile animal down the beach.

November 2002

My stability in school had evaporated once more, another unglorious reign ousted. Tabitha had spent the fall in Toronto fighting accusations of child neglect from her roommate in court over a misunderstanding concerning Emily's son and Tabitha's jogging. I tried to talk to Tabitha as often as she'd allow.

"You think I'm guilty!" she shouted over the phone, imperial in tone. Tabitha was asked to watch Emily's seven-year-old son, but when they went to the park together, he grew bored and wanted to go home. Tabitha wanted to finish her planned jog and asked if he could go home by himself, some two kilometers west along St. Clair West. The police found him walking alone and drove him home, where Emily was unpacking some groceries.

This infraction began to sting Emily, and soon the household was filled with a palpable tension and hostility. When Tabitha and I returned from a two-week trip to the East Coast, Emily was still raging, and kicked Tabitha out and pressed charges against her. The fumes from this ordeal were just now thinning out into resolve. Christmas would be a much-needed rest.

"She went ape-shit on me!" Tabitha continued, "And then you tell me to go to the police to see what I should do, and they arrested me!" For most of October and November, Tabitha lived with her ex-boyfriend in Toronto, and we exchanged communications as best we could.

*

"Hi Mom, thanks for taking me to your doctor. And offering me a pretzel-and-cracker toasted sandwich after. Doctor Brian did nothing to interpret these feelings and totally failed us. What we need is a team of doctors and trainers. I still say, you have far too much food, and I'm not criticizing, but you'd lose weight and save money if you ate what you had, or at least ate more raw food, and stopped drinking coffee twelve times a day. Your heart is like a Tim Hortons highway truck full of caffeinated fuel. Constantly eating that sort of food is bad for your stomach and for the environment. You have nine things of bread for one and a half people. That is beyond the pretzels and cereals. That is way too much food. We never had that much bread in the house. You should ration your food, and cut down on so much extravagant spending. Like crackers and garbage bags. Just throw the food out the window like they do in France. Also those fruit cups; those can't be healthy. That is food for people with no teeth or hope. They must rot your teeth; it's on the commercial. They are syrupy fruit, totally full of chemicals, and it's fake fruit, fruit made by children in Florida. That will upset your stomach. Tabitha says you need natural fats like butter and salt and that low-calorie food just makes you hungrier."

I called Mom again, and she finally picked up. Jimmy was asleep beside me on his back. I used to stretch him out that way to teach him how to sleep like a human.

"I'm really sorry about last night. I was really excited about how you seemed to have things organized about your courses, working etc., so I phoned your Dad, only to find out that he was drunk. I tried to get off the phone by saying, 'I think we should talk another time,' but he refused and called me back to say he had talked to you. Anyway, I think he wants to know your marks from January through April because he's not been informed or has forgotten. As for the past term, I think he feels like he has wasted his money and it will take longer for you to finish your degree—but I'm sure you feel guilty about it as well. I hope that this term will show what a gifted person you really are and that the marks will reflect the confidence you need to move on."

She began telling me how upset she got by speaking to Dad. "I had forgotten that part of my life with him and how we all suffered, but now we are free. I really think Holly has a lot of courage to go up there and face it all the time."

*

"Mom, it's your son, Norman Bates. Just for the record: I dropped two courses this semester because Jimmy was hit by a car, and I missed two weeks of classes because I had to work to pay his gigantic bill. I have been finding it hard to live with my new all-male roommate situation. Why I tell you this is because HOLLY DIDN'T HAVE TO DEAL WITH COCAINE ADDICTS OR ALCOHOLICS WHILST STUDYING FOR SCHOOL. SHE BASICALLY LIVED IN A FUNERAL HOME OF SILENCE WITH YOU! My roommates were COCAINE addicts and YES my eyes do hinder me from reading from time to time. My eyes are fucked and I can only read FROM ONE of them and it's not something you should hold against me and for the record I had job offers in late 2001 in Toronto but had nowhere to live in Toronto and was still in Waterloo and you knew this. You even bought me a T-shirt with TORONTO on it as some sort of unfit joke that you could get the

Order of Canada for. I expressed this clearly to you. Things are really hard for me now. I think you just don't want to think about how progressively unfair this is for me. And that Holly will have to deal with Tabitha and I at your place because we are coming on the 19th for a ten-hour blood-thirsting roast-beast cliché feast! WE'LL SEE YOU SOON AND HOLLY WILL OPEN HER SERPENT GIFT AND SAY THANK YOU BROTHER YOU ARE THE TRUE ICON AND I'M SORRY THAT I WORKED AT BUSINESS DEPOT AND WON THE GOLD MEDAL FOR SELLING REAMS OF PAPER LEADING ME TO BUSINESS SCHOOL DIPLOMA AFTER BUSINESS SCHOOL DIPLOMA. I'M SORRY THAT I HAVE HAD A STABLE LIFE FOR THE PAST TEN YEARS, HOME COOKED MEALS AND A PHONE WITH A 416 AREA CODE, CALL ANSWER, A CAR WHEN I NEED IT AND I'M SORRY THAT YOU HAVE HAD TO MAKE IT ON YOUR OWN FOR SO LONG AND HAVE NOT GOTTEN VERY FAR AND I'M SORRY THAT I HAVE AN EDUCATION AND YOU DON'T AND I HAVE A GOOD JOB. I'M SORRY. MERRY CHRIST-MAS, NATE, I LOVE YOU AND I'M SO GLAD MOM SUGGESTED WE SPEND THIS TIME TOGETHER AFTER 65 YEARS OF NOT SPEAKING TO ONE ANOTHER! AFTER ALL, WHO AM I TO OWN CHRISTMAS? RIGHT? THIS CHRISTMAS, THE STUFFING, THE TOOTHPASTE..."

"Nate, it's your mom. I certainly do have a lot of compassion for you; it breaks my heart and makes me cry to think of your situation. I just want to try and help you get on with your life. I'm hoping that by talking with Brian, you might find out reasons for not being able to get a job. What has to happen in order for you to become independent and have good self-esteem. I don't really want to go back to the way things were and I don't want to dwell on the things that went on in our family. To me, that's not healthy. But we have to take this opportunity to try and heal and go forward. You will have to accept someday, Nate, that I did the best that I could at the time and nothing we say or do can change that. I just want to see you heal and feel good about yourself and that's why I want to keep on going. Not every time is going to be good, but it's all that we have right now and I want to keep giving it a try."

*

"I had a dream we were with your family for Christmas in the 1980s, and they were like Arnold and the Wonder Years. Your mother made spaghetti sauce with hard boiled eggs in it."

Tuesday, May 13th, 2003

"I'm not a mist! I exist; you denied my reality for a year!" Tabitha shouted, slamming the door and sprint-walking out of view, down Uncle Carl's splitting driveway.

Tabitha and I had broken up in late March, and I moved back Toronto and had nowhere to go, so I stayed with my uncle, who was spending more and more time at the hospital. He was on his last hundred hours of life when I arrived. The fumes of the break-up still occupied the odd, late hours travelling to midtown (Yonge and Eglinton) to take a couple of shifts at the tele-survey call centre, as the Toronto branch said I could transfer from Montreal without any difficulties.

Moments before my scheduled drive to Toronto from Montreal, Jimmy took it upon himself to kamikaze suicide off the balcony. I guess he thought I was abandoning him, noticing the boxes, the strangers helping me move, the general upheaval.

With my uncle Carl in and out of the hospital, Tabitha came to visit once or twice for morbid post-break-up torture sleepovers. She would sit on the couch naked, walking by the large front window, drapes gapingly wide open. I shook my head in partial terror, but mostly just smiled like a pervert.

"Sometimes I cry when I think about the type of food you eat," she said over the phone, frustrated with my general silence. "You waste my time and energy, Nathaniel!" Tabitha said, "And you deny everything!"

I had told Tabitha very casually that Mom told me that Andrew had gotten married. It was the way Mom said it, just the blunt sound bite.

I never knew how to properly explain my bouts with nervous energy to Tabitha. Everything I said to her was put under a giant microscope. Even relaying something about my mom telling me Andrew was now married made Tabitha suspect I was not being honest with her about my feelings. To me, it was no different than any number of tales I'd conjure up for her from the mid- to late-'90s. She explained her desire for different experiences of sexuality, like playing the part of the short-skirted nurse bending over to wipe the drool off of a bald man in a wheelchair, who keeps trying to pinch her butt while eating from a bowl of popcorn.

Tabitha continued, "I forget we can't discuss a certain subject, watch a film or walk down a street because of 1998!" She'd shake her head in frustration. Then, recovering from her caustic lashing, she'd begin to drone out a Goth-like refrain, "1998," and shook her head miserably. Despite the intent of her cruel focus group, it made me laugh.

"I don't believe Andrew abused you, you are such a whining coward. You totally participated in it and you were sad when he married. When we played badminton, you admitted you had been in love with him—it was an abuse you very much enjoyed—enough to try to repeat it with me—you said he would suck you last, because you fell asleep after you came. He dumped you for another boy, right? Fuck, Nate, pick up the phone! Maybe you really don't know how shallow and selfish you are; I try to show you by telling you exactly what my feelings are; I feel quite a lot of disgust for shallowness. It's also extremely frustrating, considering all the time I believed I might have been talking to a real person but I realize now I was not. I hope your family listens to this message. I guess I prefer men of other cultures; maybe I am just not attracted to North American men. In any case, I don't see you as a real man but a masturbating boy. I know eventually you'll grow out of this ugly phase, but I'm not sacrificing myself to help you grow. I am trying to wake you up. But I also never think about you. It's not that I haven't tried, Nate. It's just that your routine has gotten boring and I am numb to your histrionics."

A few days later, Uncle Carl had come home from the hospital, only to be persuaded back the next morning in a dramatic intervention. The second cousin, Doug, had come by to take me for what ended up being our final visit. We had to dress in our SARS aprons and stood looking pensive as the nurses led us into the next stage of antiseptic visitation. Uncle Carl handed me his wallet and his watch. He was in considerable pain; the doctor later told us his stomach had grown so weak that his lungs were resting on top of it, now collapsing from the inside, making it impossible to digest any food.

All those times he refused to stay for dinner, the meals, pieces of cake were symptoms of a finality that would take him away from all of us prematurely, even if it was just by a few years.

I was waiting to hear when the memorial for Uncle Carl would take place, since he had not left any instructions for his funeral arrangements other than he was to be cremated and no plot, no gravesite, nothing really. Mom's voice was up first on the answering machine, and it was official: Uncle Carl's staged-wake tombstone-less, barely-catered memorial service would be this coming Sunday at noon with our second cousins and their heir-apparent family.

I phoned Mom back.

"Got your message. So is Holly going to fucking speak to me at this thing?"

Tabitha phoned to tell me she was in love with someone named Ronnie from Holland whom she had never met and wanted me to be happy for her. I was exhausted. Her voice chewed into my skull, my chest, and made me feel queasy as she went through an abject itinerary of how I had failed her during our 372 days of hell, fire and brimstone—and then some.

"I remember watching a video of you when you were young; I remember feeling startled at how much I disliked you. Even though you were only a little boy and totally innocent, I saw this shallow arrogance and jealous domination of your sister and the weird fetish of sexual repression and control you had with your mother—will you ever grow out of it? This mode of introverted sexuality made you the stud you are today needing blow jobs and unable to touch me, a denial of femininity and sensitivity in yourself. A kind of masochist self-worship, you just fuck yourself; you don't need me. You just use me to reflect you and masturbate you. I have never met such a lazy man... maybe it is your bloated pomposity."

Tabitha carried on, but every one of those insights she had were tweaked and manipulated in this hyperbolic sermon. I didn't know what the point of it was other than a big break-up PowerPoint presentation: gratuitous and shaming.

"I guess how you behaved is just a reflection of everything else. I used to wonder what some girls put up with from boyfriends whose behaviour I found gross. Now I know why my friends were worried. It's not like you are the only stupid boy I've dated for this period of time. But I, too, am trying to improve my life. I think I am doing the healthiest thing by submitting to the attractions of more worthy and at least more exciting people and spending more time with my friends."

The unravelling boycott was cardio for her, a big dump, a press conference for one, where she could lower my stock value and fuck with my self-confidence. The details she went into to cut me down and hold up a dystopian portrait has since gone unmatched.

I drew a bath, tried to clear my mind of my whole life. Shutting the bathroom door behind me, I undressed. The less opportunity to open portals to the past, the better. I moved the suction grip-pad and filled up the unfamiliar tub.

It was a challenge not to think of Andrew in our glorious VHS reels, the ones, hidden in their plastic black rectangular video time capsules. I couldn't hide anything, even alone with the door locked, the lights off, where you can only see your fingertips, tree-lines of time that circle the rubbery skin—a constant confession.

Sunday, May 25th, 2003

From the videotape marked: **"UNCLE DEATH '03"**

I started up my old camcorder and heard the familiar gear gurgle. 2003 was barely half done and already so much terrible garbage had transpired. I took this deep breath and spoke, staring into its unblinking red eye:

It's eight days before Uncle Carl's 83rd birthday, and I am watching their feet walk towards the house . . . oh, are they knocking? They'll figure it out.

I saw the feet of my estranged second cousins, my sister and Mom enter the airless bungalow. I continued:

Holly hasn't said shit to me and barely spoke to Carol or anyone like she doesn't want me to hear her fucking voice or something like I'm going to impersonate her. Mom says she's getting married in August; I'm like, remembering my top Uncle C-Note memories were not shared with these bizarro family members. The pink-haired warrior surviving my father's ridicule, his 8mm film collection, the song "Lucky Star" blaring on the radio in '85 or '86, and us nearly getting into a car accident

because I insisted we turn the volume up and Uncle Carl was accom-
modating me (THANKS A LOT MADONNA!), the year 2001 turning
over and Uncle Carl asking me if 2000 even took place or did it jump
from 1999 to 2001? "There was no year 2000, right?" The Playboys
and cherry chocolates under the couch. Our insane behaviour led Uncie
Carlos to reconsider the frequency of his visits, always a sliver of brittle
cake and a gulp of tea, a few photographs, then his car tires squealing
east back to his anorexia camp! Oh yeah! Aunt Wildabeats probably
even named her daughter Carol in some homage to our beloved gang-
ster pharmacist Uncle Carl. I'm wearing his socks to mark this sad oc-
casion. I think it's show time. Here we go—

The plastic affair began as planned at noon. I had to take the phone
off the hook because Tabitha kept calling me to tell me off. Officially
in attendance were my mom's cousin Carol and her husband Doug the
bloated water-colour painter, plus their two sons, who we last saw in
January 1987 at Grampy's funeral. I remember vividly that Holly had
shaken me in the cloakroom, "Why aren't you crying?" and I was ten
or eleven, standing in shock as our family's estranged sides showed up
and shook our little hands and asked if we knew who they were.

I hadn't spoken to Holly for more than ten seconds straight in over
three years. She walked up the stairs from the side door, her hair now
cut shorter than I remembered it, resting neatly on her shoulders. She
was wearing a subtle black shirt with dress pants, while following behind her was Mom, wearing a deflated smile.

Without a formal ceremony in place (no priest, no lawyer, no outside friends in attendance save for the across-the-street neighbour,
aged nineteen years, who just kept saying, "I can't believe he's gone,"
over and over again before sobbing and asking us to forgive her for
her emotional display), I decided to say a few words. My head pulsed
with confusion; the cheap wine was rotten or high in acidic resin, coat-
ing my tongue in a harsh, unnecessary way.

Later, Mom would go on to explain that she knew what was at hand: for over a decade now Great Aunt Bethany wanted to position her daughter as the heir apparent over Mom, and it would be a competition to see who would win out and ultimately get their name on the will. This was a stunt wake if there ever was one.

These tidbits and facts had been carefully released from Mom's coveted war room of intelligence.

"There you are," Mom said, her grimace on pause, followed by a long sigh and gum-chew combo. She scanned the living room. "Should we get more chairs?" She sniffed the air, "Gonna open a window." Mom wore a variety of items ranging in pattern (stripes, floral and leopard print scarf) and texture variables too (silk, poly blend and plastic).

Mom drowned in the terrain of Uncle Carl's furniture (the very couch where, just a week before, I had held his ticking remains, taking breaks to run downstairs and cry in the basement over Tabitha over Jimmy over life and facing death head-on with my uncle in a gruesome summer showdown; "Where are you?" he shouted, then asked me mercilessly to insert a laxative rectal shit capsule, wash him, light him a cigarette, make him some soup, pour him an Ensure drink ...) and sat back with a plate of food, only to drop the contents (several grapes, finger sandwiches, piece of marble cheese) onto the carpet. Holly and I caught each other's brown eyes, and in a Moment, we shared a smile.

In the kitchen, Mom and I briefly squabbled over the sequence of carbohydrates.

"Maybe I'm losing my mind," Mom said. Holly stared straight ahead, not yet adjusted to the abject core the afternoon offered all of us.

The food kept coming in trays, courtesy of our second cousins, the heirs apparent. As she undid the dips and vegetables and sandwiches,

I remembered my great uncle Carl bragging how Carol didn't ever have time to cook food because she was so busy as a real estate agent. Then I saw Mom with her action-figure accessory—a loaf of home-made banana bread. Her earnest baked signifier sat on a paper-plate slab, high on an emotional altitude. Mom pontificated about the unique ingredients and how recently she made it for this occasion.

"I was up late last night," Mom said. We sat drinking terrible wine, and the neighbour came over and began to cry on the couch beside me. "I'm sorry," she said. "He was so nice." We were silent.

"I don't have time to bake, Diane," Carol snorted.

I read from a folded piece of paper with nothing on it but waving lines and a sparse grocery list:

"There's a fire in life that burns," I said, pretending to read from a note.

These phrasings came to me; I forgot them immediately, like wiping the database. I improvised another line, "We're lost in a beach-shell memory, a photographic paradise," closing with ". . . and you always said the right things to me."

I figured someone should say something, beyond the stock phrases. *He liked to travel; he came to my hockey game; he was a fan of country music; he was the youngest of four brothers; he liked going to Mexico . . . He liked* Playboy *and chocolate, kept them in proximity.*

Unable to discuss the reality, the will and money, the fight over his estate, the obvious divide, the strain—we were all improvising. "Gonna just take these dishes to the kitchen," Mom said.

We passed a tiny black-and-white photo of the four brothers from Saskatoon with Uncle Carl being the youngest, sitting on a chair next to his brothers—a faint image of a blonde boy awaiting his mother's joy, the ultimate momma's boy. They lived together here from 1953 until her death in January 1976.

This was a collage of a family, masking-taped together for an after-noon in Saran Wrap prestige, one last visit in the iconic bungalow, a solid twenty-minute walk from Eglinton and Brimley in what I called early Scarborough.

Tears streamed purple down Mom's face as she braced herself in the stairwell. Her deep buckshot sobs soared down the basement into forgotten pockets. "That's all we have now, our memories; we knew him the best," Mom howled, mouth now webbed in saliva and ruin. Holly took the remaining bits of food and a small box of photographs into the car. I threw my body on the bed that night in my uncle's spare bedroom, wearing his clothes, endeavouring a sensation of ghostly presence as I fell into deep slumber.

I don't know if my uncle was a well-read or emotional person, though some Moments I have recalled with great depth in the shrapnel of his rattling voice a shade of regret.

"My friend Eddie didn't like the idea of having a boyfriend." Eddie was a friend he had met while working in East General Hospital in the '60s and '70s, who worked in labour. They would hang out over an occasional cup of coffee. Uncle Carl's sentence about Eddie's reluctance for his friendship always resonated with me. I don't think I ever met Eddie, but remember him being some fat plumber in a Polaroid.

I was disturbed by the most detailed dream of Jimmy. He was sitting on the lap of a large brown bear in a junkyard. I wanted so badly to wake up next to his sleeping face, tiny nostrils breezing at me. I awoke to the harsh tone of Uncle Carl's rotary and pulse-tone phones simultaneously going off.

In the morning, what I believed was an outline of my uncle Carl's skeleton passed right by me, thrown in the raging morning sunlight. My eyes were sore and raw. The dust in the house was thicker than a century, sprawled out in an outline of a large recumbent hand.

19)

Special

Late November 2009

Steps from Dundas south of Ossington, the waitress at the Burger Shack was explaining to me how the long glossy banquet tables were made from old bowling alley lanes. Holly spotted me. We had been hanging out again on a regular basis for about six months when we decided to take Mom out for a lunch and then back to her place to sort through some of her belongings in an effort to downsize her wardrobe, books and carbohydrates.

I was now working three days a week for a sports-media website (*Shooting Star Wrestling Review*) that had a focus on vintage and contemporary pro wrestling. I was one of five people who gathered material from archives or recently recorded "shoot interviews," which were usually by retired or semi-retired wrestlers pontificating on their careers, inside gossip and any other assorted details fans might want to delve into.

"It's a fucking zoo out there," Holly said, shoving her big leather purse under the table. "Sarah says she wants you to come over and play monster."

"Tell Sarah to take a number," I said. Sarah was an energetic three-and-a-half-year-old, capable of long deliberations and inquisitions, frantic doodles and misplaced vowels, bowls of cereal and talking stuffed animals. She was my estranged niece, and at this point, I'd met her only three times.

"Burgers are a neutral food," I said, my tone as sincere as I could manufacture, adding "and besides, the city is obsessed with them—gourmet burgers, onion rings on top, bacon, seaweed; they're everywhere, Hol."

"Yeah, I guess so," Holly said, "good to keep Mom abreast of all civically ordained glow trends." The waitress was filling up some ketchup bottles and glanced over. "I always end up asking the waitress to tell me what to eat."

"So what's new?"

"Nothing much. I woke up this morning."

"That's a good start," Holly said.

"How is life with your husband and only child?"

Holly mouthed a thank you to the waitress who brought us both large glasses of water. "You sound like an ESL student," she said. "So, any girl in the picture?"

"I like this one person named Sherri. She's a bit slippery."

"Where's she from?"

"Earth. Not too long ago, actually," I said. "We're not dating. I just like her and try to talk to her. I see her at work, and we worked this conference together for, like, a weekend, but I think she has a boyfriend."

"What is she like?"

"She's twenty-three and looks like Katharine Ross from *The Graduate*, minus the wedding veil and with thinner lips, cleaner hair and she wears pompous berets sometimes. Comes into work hung-over a lot."

"*Coo-coo catchew*," Holly said, glancing over the menu.

"She also played the shrink in *Donnie Darko*."

"Your office teen crush?"

"No—*Katharine*."

I didn't want to explain all the details of Sherri to Holly but I let her listen to the messages. The first was about her hair being curly today and buying too many grapefruits.

(The gorgeous details: supersize horizon-greedy blue eyes, a pinkie of perfume behind her mouse ears, lips pursed together, taking in air and time, almond-toned skin, ski-slope nose, curves along the cheekbones and a brutal bomb of hair hidden in soft light-brown piles under a tartly red felt beret. Our first few encounters, in which I fumbled my way into an after-work drink, I'd felt anxious, like I was being tipped over on a carnival ride. I said something weird, like she was *the caramel apple of her father's eye,* which led to absolutely no reaction on her part; denying comprehension, sympathy, presence. A few weeks later, we worked a conference together for two days straight, which led to a showdown of misguided proportions: her staying over one night, watching old VHS movies and taking a shower at three a.m. to cool off.)

The second message was softer, quieter, and at first, didn't even sound like her at all. She described her wrecked evening: "I guess you are out [pause, exhale]. I was in a car accident tonight. I spun out and hit the guardrail, smashed my side of the hood and door. I was so scared of what it would feel like to come up against the rail and how close I came to flipping over it and drowning in the lake. It happened so fast. Now I'm in bed and I just want to curl up into you and never feel scared again. I want you to draw me up into your arms and call me a warm bagel and stroke back my salty tears. Goodnight, sweet prince of darkness."

"She sounds sincere. A bit weird, but when was this?"

"Three days ago."

"I'm starving. Where's Mom?"

"Oh, I was reading on PHYSURG.COM, and they have this article about scarred women and men and how hot they are. Like girls would only want me for a short-term deal. It says, though, that men don't care; they'll keep a girl forever if she's scarred. So there you go, Hol."

The waitress sauntered up, black apron with burger-bun dust on it.

"Can I get you guys something to drink to start?"

"We're waiting for someone," Holly said. "Our mother, actually."

"Oh, that's nice," the waitress said.

"We're hoping for the best," I said. "In the meantime, I'll have a ginger ale."

"I'll have a tea, please," Holly said.

"Sure," the waitress smiled, pausing before her departure.

*

When Mom arrived, she had windy tears in her eyes. She was decked out in a hefty beige winter coat, and her walk resembled that of a near-blind sports-team mascot.

"I wasn't sure which place it was," she said, sitting down beside me.

As a waft of burger fume came forth in a cloud of sweat, I recalled Mom's infamous Sisyphean patty-slapping ordeal in Technicolor, and Dad's insanity joke.

"I got *Growing Pains* on DVD. I liked Mike, D-student, always trying to cover up broken lamps with glue and parental distractions."

"You never tried hiding your destruction," Mom interjected, as another cloud of food smell floated by, all tender and toying. "Remember the time you threw fabric softener all over the basement walls?"

I didn't play the "remember" game back: *remember the porch coffee, tossed as I passed by on my bike, like I was a rodent you were trying to fumigate with caffeine.*

It was a pure war; part of me was summoned from hell to battle through. Those were the clothes I wore, the weapons I used.

"So how is Sadie?" I asked. "Still in school?"

"What do you think is *in* the burgers?" Holly said. "She's like a leading monster in a horror-film franchise," Holly said. "She can't be killed."

"She's twenty next week," Mom said shuffling within her large beige winter jacket, which now sported a fresh glob of mayonnaise, with just a hint of it on her cheek. I watched the coat glob glisten as I passed her a napkin. "We could sell tickets to see Toronto's only two-hundred-year-old cat," Holly suggested.

"Yes, Pay-per-view funerals are getting expensive."

"Anyway," Mom said, her face glazed now in a near-frown, "How's work?"

"Still working for that media company, writing stuff for their site," I said, adding, "Cut and paste and JPEG shuffling."

"What media?"

"That's classified."

"It's wresting, Mom," Holly said, her voice a shorter fuse now, anxious, insistent as if partially defensive, suggesting not to doubt me.

"Oh," she said. "Do they pay you?"

"Yes, just me; everyone else works for free. Including my boss."

"Oh, stop it," Mom said. "So what do I feel like eating for lunch?"

Holly turned to me; I saw her eyes get all bright and direct. "Hey, do you have a blog?"

"Why?"

"I Googled you and it came up."

"No. I mean, I don't know how to delete it," I said. "Shall we rent a movie?"

The winter sun was relentless now. Mom adapted with a pair of amber-tinted sunglasses. She was wearing a mauve blouse and a bank-robber neckerchief.

"I still remember the time you made us watch *Cape Fear* for that first Christmas without Grammy."

"I didn't make *Cape Fear,* Mom. There were other rooms in the house too. You didn't have to watch it."

Holly shook her hand in front of me. "The blog? What's it called?"

"Shapes and gardens are fun," I responded.

"No, seriously, what was it again?"

<< *TheGlenvaleWarDidNotTakePlace.blogspot.com* >>

"I fell *five* times last year," Mom said. "Just got to be careful."

The statement billowed into a daydream: a sensational sports-stat graphic, suitable for the back of a baseball card. *Diane, 66, fell 5 times in 2008. 2 head colds. 3 migraines. 4 cavities.*

"I was rushing for a bus one time; the other time I fell off the bus, getting out at my stop at Mount Pleasant."

Neither Holly nor I had ever witnessed these falls, but Mom's partial recreation on a loop busied us in delirious late-night bonding sessions. Mom's sporadic tumbles made her more human. We wanted to know why she was falling.

The burgers and fries were consumed in under an hour, but the caravan of family excess spilled into late afternoon.

Holly had mentioned to me that Sadie was sick and she was thinking of taking our antique cat from Mom for a while. Sadie was known for her low-mirth disposition since her arrival in mid-1989, replacing Benji, who had died four years earlier, having arrived a year before Holly was even born and three before me.

"Knee deep in banana bread, as usual," I said, bringing a box of books from the hall closet into the living room.

Holly was washing a cup for a drink of water.

"Mom, why do you put Sadie's food in the kitchen sink? It stinks. My God, open the window," Holly said, her face clenched.

"It's cat food; it's supposed to smell that way. Jesus," Mom replied.

"Real cat," I said.

"Yeah," Holly said. "She's all cat."

Mom told us about work: Slocombe & Michaels, an investment firm where she worked part-time, had started trimming the fat.

"They're laying people off left, right and centre," she said, holding the fold-out instructions over the cadaver of wood I held in my hands. Holly cut up an apple.

Mom was watching a car park in the driveway across the street while a small pot of tomato soup bubbled over the right rear element. Our lives were not at all comparable, each of us on Earth unique and special, as special and unique as the next set of circumstances, DNA and pulse. We, the amoebas from the memory pond, go belly-up from time to time.

"Michelle is fighting to keep me on board, but I just have this awful feeling."

Holly was standing beside three boxes of books.

"So we can put some of these away?"

"Sure."

"Then we'll put the bookcase in the spare room. That's the plan right?" Holly said, now taking charge of all things.

"Yes," Mom replied, now aware she was chewing on her fingernails. I toiled with screws and tacks, looking at the peg holes along the planks carefully. Sadie sauntered into the room where the construction was taking place.

I pressed two pieces of wood together successfully, standing half the structure upright, flipping the rectangle shell of wood when required, studying the line-drawing instructions, mimicking the man's position with the pieces of wood with acuity.

"Your father has been secure for years off his investments from the house, you know. I don't have any rich relatives who can leave me anything."

"That's true; you don't," I said.

Mom's economic weakness was news to me, as I had, up to this point, believed Mom was a mythological pioneer of survival. She had somehow managed to cultivate an ongoing existence: partial excess, part restraint, in order to facilitate life for herself and Sadie.

"So, we'll see," Mom said, disappearing down the hallway.

Sadie was like a main organ in Mom's world, an occasional vocal signal post that measured her own mortal coil. She curled up on the empty cardboard box the bookshelf came in. "And Sadie is sick. The doctor doesn't know exactly what's wrong with her."

I looked at Sadie, pawing at the empty plastic bags the screws came in, regressing into kitten-like behaviour a decade and half too late. From the kitchen mom's stereo blared classical music.

"It's like an institute in here," Holly sniggered.

"Be careful, Nate," Mom said, hands on her hips, a piece of muffin shrapnel lodged in her mouth. She studied her new bookshelves.

"So I've been talking with Susan," Mom said, twisting a plastic bag of freshly baked muffins with a big knot and swollen air inside, "and she thinks it's a great idea to move down for a bit."

Susan was another Kodak apparition, late-1970s, my only recollection being a photograph of three blonde kids on our couch on Mann Avenue, some in pirate newspaper hats, and one, Tracy, too cool for their childish leanings, sat bored, her pirate hat beside her, never worn.

By the time the first row of hardcover mystery novels made their way onto the bookshelf, Mom had unfurled a massive get-away plan, a relocation program that would, as she put it, "solve all of my problems, you know?"

"It's far away, Mom."

"It's my safety net, I guess, for now. I can rent this place out."

"And you'd live with Susan?"

"She works at one of the local colleges, says she might be able to make some calls for me, get me a job on campus," Mom said.

"Why do you have all these football clippings, Mom?" Holly asked.

"Just a scrapbook I'm making for my class."

"Sports class?"

"No, it's a general interest course on broadcasting, different kinds, you know?

The phone rang. It was Dad. "Nate's here, yes, he sent you his things for taxes. Well, you'll probably get it tomorrow. I have to go."

She returned to the small table where we were drinking tea, talking, shuffling and sniffing. "Your father is in his usual mood," Mom said.

"Taxes are sometimes late. Big deal," I said.

"I know what you mean; I think that your father is just impatient sometimes."

Her walk, now a physical stutter, was combined with an irritated cough, a trickle of arthritic pain, and the slow sashay of her silver-haired Vader-helmet-shaped bob with each step as she observed my IKEA trance.

"So you have a passport?" I asked, "deportation forms?"

"Yes."

"Why do you have twenty coats? You can get rid of some. Keep two, and we'll take this to Goodwill," Holly suggested.

"That's *my* decision."

"And these books, you can't ship a thousand books to Dallas."

"I can't think about that now," Mom said.

"Better to get rid of the stuff now," Holly said, trying to be both sensitive and diplomatic.

"I don't know!"

"OK, you decide. I'll go and get some more garbage bags."

I shuffled some papers. "These continuing education courses sound like astronaut school."

"I'm halfway through my course on famous trials."

The pantry was full of ants. "It's 'cause you carbo-load," I said. "It's in the Bible, they just—"

Mom interrupted, "OK, just help me move the things out of there so I can clean up a bit."

In the storage room, I found Holly. "Remember these?"

"Not really. The '90s are a blur for me, thankfully," I said.

Holly put *The Doors* T-shirts back into the garbage bag. "We have a lot of crap in here," Holly said. "What's this? A *Cape Fear* colouring book?"

"I wish," I said. "Are you hungry?"

"A bit. But I don't want to eat here," Holly said, dragging a garbage bag towards the exit.

*

Now recovering from the bookcase ordeal, I collapsed down on the beige-striped sofa, with all its foreignness.

Enter Mom.

"How you doing?"

"I feel fine and I feel good," I said. "Feeling like I never should."

Occasionally, when there was nowhere else to go, to be, I'd find myself washed up on the shores of this small co-op apartment Mom owned for an awkward meal or tea over harsh lighting, and she would update me on the state of the community, blasé names dropped as if she were reading off a predictable list, a grocery store extra, a former babysitter or area hood, the boy who broke into Northlea United church to vandalize it is now a radio host in Oshawa, things like that. The throwaway characters from those stretches of years who rode their bikes, who screamed obscenities, who appeared on swings with girls and then disappeared, who were early smart bombs of divorce, relocated into an anecdotal trough.

"What's this?" Holly asked, holding an old black-and-white photo up.

Mom squinted. "That's our basement on Elmer Avenue, just after we moved in. The army offered to pay for a down payment on a house, and the navy gave Uncle Carl his college education as a pharmacist. That was the deal I think the government made when you got out of the war. Mom and Dad bought the house at 46 Elmer Ave. I don't know the year they moved in, but I do remember starting kindergarten at Kew Beach Public School, which was at the bottom of the street. That's why I always liked taking you guys to the Beaches when you were younger, because I grew up there," Mom said, opening a recycled plastic bottle full of tap water—dribbling some down her chin.

"And now you're moving to the desert."

"I've known Sue my whole life; it seems surreal. She got me my first job at the CBC, because Grampy wanted me to work for the government when Sue and I finished Weller Business College, so I did for about six months then decided to join Sue and got a job in the TV Drama Department, which was located up above a restaurant at Gerard and Yonge. Sue was in the Radio Department nearby, and I worked in the Children's Department for about three years as the secretary to the supervising producer.

"And you met Mr. Dressup and Mr. Rogers?"

"Not Mr. Rogers, which was an American production, but yes, Mr. Dressup and the Friendly Giant."

"And that's when you met Dad?"

"No. I got my job at the University of Toronto in September after I came back from Ottawa and I met your Dad around the beginning of October 1969, and we were married in September the next year."

"And that's when you had Benji, our first cat, and he got trapped on the ledge?"

"He was just a kitten . . . your dad, you know that picture of him inside of your dad's coat, right?"

"Yeah," Holly said. "I love that picture."

"Oh yes, it was terrifying for me because the windows would blow open and sometimes close, and one time he was out on the ledge and it blew closed and he was pawing at the window, and I had to get him to move away from the part of the glass that I was trying to open, or he'd get pushed right off, so I had to trick him and get him to walk the other way by shaking his Yummies so he would want to come in, and he walked back across the window ledge, and then I was able to open the window, and once he'd pass, was able to close it and then open it again."

"Benji was way cooler than Sadie."

"I remember when we were going to the cottage we hit a whiteout on the 400. Your dad had to drive really slowly, hoping to be able to see the red tail lights of the car in front of us, and Benji sat right up on the dashboard so he could see where we were going—fascinated, I guess, by all the snow. He was never upset about going in the car because I guess he knew he was going on holiday with us."

"When we actually went on holidays," Holly said, flipping through photographs.

"Why did we go to a cottage in a blizzard?" I asked.

"Because it was available, and cheaper I guess."

"Seems insane," I said, adding, "like *The Shining*."

"There are tons of photos, Mom," Holly said, plowing through the Kodak tomb.

"He always wanted to be with us. He loved us. He used to sleep with you when you were sick."

"There's a bunch of photos," Holly said, handing me a glossy stack. "They're mostly of you dressed like Han Solo and Jacques Plante, holding the wooden trophies you made and awarded yourself."

"I earned every one of those trophies."

"Then Dad threw them in the fireplace."

"Sounds like a wicked commercial for self-esteem," I said, taking a few seconds to relish in the deleted scene of Dad taking the time to remove my name plate (a plastic Coke-bottle cap liner) from each piece of wood before throwing it into the flames.

"I remember when I saw your trophies in a stack of wood by the fireplace," Holly laughed. "It was funny."

"Do you want to keep this sweater?" Mom asked Holly.

"No, that's OK. It's too seasick green for me."

"Didn't I get it for you?"

"I don't think so."

"I think I got it for you for Christmas one year."

"You aren't the only arbiter of clothing, Mom," Holly said. "Want some pizza, Mom?"

"Where would we order it from?" Mom asked, walking out of the boxy living room to the tiny hallway connecting the rest of her apartment.

I clamped my hand over my face and ran it slowly down to my neck. "I'm going to make some tea."

Holly scoured through a selection of hulking video cassettes. She lifted up one colourful VHS case, her eyes now bright and alive.

I put the videotape into the aging VCR and hit "play," and was confronted with a VHS flashback of a hand-cut margarine container being fashioned over Sadie's head.

"What is this?"

"It's the first weekend in December of 1991, when I rented the school video camera and I think this is our historic trip to the convenience store, filmed in the back seat, 7:16 p.m on a Saturday night, or as I call them, our family vacations. It was a month before Uncle Carl bought me the video camera and changed the course of our family's history for—"

"Why are you watching it?"

"'cause it's on TV."

"Only because you put it in. Are you leaving?"

"Not sure."

"Well, if we stay, let's watch something normal," Holly said, noticing the video now showed Sadie with a makeshift space helmet on at the controls of a homemade *Millennium Falcon* cockpit.

In those videos, I gave Sadie feelings and intelligence, threw lines to her as I sat beside her in the homemade sci-fi cockpits of my loneliness, my innovations, fatherless and motherless, loveless. Sadie struggled to perform and find her place in human society. It became an ongoing video metaphor; the cat and I didn't belong in our contemporary forms. We were attempting to right this situation by leaving the planet. We were both struggling with the most fundamental questions of identity and personal history, and together we suffered from the loneliness of never seeing anyone resembling ourselves.

"I just wanted to see what was on it."

As I played the tape, I heard Sherri's soft-sleep voice speak, now a ten-month-old audio fossil from the previous summer. With its brevity and sheen, I tried not to picture her face as she said, "That video camera was like your best friend."

The footage of my lost youth that Sherri wanted to see, that I had promised to bring for our next fumbling sleepover at her house; somehow it comforted her and made her beam in a way she never gave off in any other setting I'd seen her in.

My crisp youthful likeness appeared in VHS glory. She pulled me in, my face wincing as the inane activity spooled out on the screen. Sherri's special feature commentary, live and meteoric: "I would have fucked you right on that couch," she said, and this warmed me all over, knowing she was squirming almost naked under her thick sand-coloured duvet. I heard my own voice on the tape but watched and lived in Sherri's blue-lagoon eyes. Her broken-rose mouth was raw from kissing, and little puffy bags hung under enormous eyes. And then, with the tape ending, dinner starting and the night fading black, Sherri shook her head, her smile flatlining, herself nearly dissolving until the day she did and our unspecific short-term program was officially over. And that was the last time I ever spent any real time with her, Holly, but I can't tell you, I don't want to tell you, I don't want to say her name and relive it aloud.

Holly shook a tape, "Let's watch *Flashdance!*"

"The artwork in the video store always made me uncomfortable, and the poster you had too, so sex-say," I said. "It's like the *Coal Miner's Daughter* version of *Dirty Dancing.*"

Mom was a mirage of cotton in the early evening glow; she stood in the hallway looking into her bedroom, perhaps at the pile of clothing and a plethora of itemized self-memorabilia. Her expression was dazed; a glaze of uncertainty. Yet still, she remained determined. This was all really happening.

I ejected my former VHS likeness. I pushed myself through the living room into the boiled waters of reality.

Thieves Like Us

Summer 2010

The office was hot. In my dress clothes and the too-tight black pants and sitting down all day long cooking, I couldn't stop refilling my water glass. Ice cubes were ready as I had made a point to both clean out the little ice-cube tray and make a fresh batch for the day.

The little office with its deficiencies in supplies (sparse elastics, folders, labels, coffee pots and wrestling magazines piled a mile high) was a form of assurance, that I did, in fact, belong somewhere on the planet, that all my studying had, in fact, paid off.

Kamala (*born James Harris, May 28, 1950*) had been on my mind all morning. It was my goal to have pilfered sound bites from Brutus Beefcake, Danny Davis, Jimmy Jack Funk all the way to Kamala this week, ready for mass consumption by ex-pimple-poppers worldwide, and, by default, to systematically frame my life in a steady work ethic, a sense of dutiful routine, one that would help harbour that particular crescent smile I would find myself wearing during commercials and grocery-store trench strolls, wearing it unforced, the muscles forming with intestinal fortitude, overcoming that disastrous emotional glacier known as my face. I had been working here now for a year and a half.

Mom's photographs came in an email attached with electronic TIFF hooks and portrayed her version of the American dream: newfound familial bounty, daring wardrobe choices (lots of sand-coloured silk blouses, white cotton pants and a large-brimmed straw hat) and multi-teethed dinner-table portraits overloaded my screen. *Now she was laughing and riding on the back of a red motorcycle. Now she was standing in front of a mountain squinting. Now she was eating at a restaurant with a group of grey-haired friends.* All these digital images clung to a JPEG netherworld in archived permanence.

I stared deeply into Mom's foreign smile. Her spinoff life was working, and a new cast had finally been assembled after our own nuclear family's epic meltdown had cooled off for good.

Our chat on Skype beaded with a sitcom's morbid routine; our back and forth was, of course, all in fun.

"I just want to see the will," I said jokingly.

"I changed it," Mom beamed. "I'm giving it all to Zsa Zsa Gabor!"

"Whatever. You and Dad will outlive me by twenty years. Holly and Sadie will get everything."

"You're funny."

"I book the prop skull all over the world and get a percentage of the total gate," I said. "I'm a Hamlet skull-prop secretary. I make millions of dollars."

Mom never offered more than terms like "sweltering" and "dry" and spicy." I'd often read the *Dallas Star* online to figure out what was really happening to the city that now consumed her and provided her with rich sunlight and dry winds from the north and west, with air pollution that petered out from a hazardous-materials incineration plant in Midlothian. I looked up grocery stores and museums and zoos. I wanted to imagine her world beyond the war-room censors.

"Haven't heard from you in a while."

"Isn't that our family motto?" I said. "Seriously, though, not to get all *Origin of Species* on you, but do you remember the skipping-rope thing? They stole it? The reason I ask, is, I have these mythologies about everyone, myself included, and I remember the skipping rope and then for some reason, when I was at day camp and they stole my chocolate drink, you yelled at the kids, and I always thought you were taking revenge on your rope thieves that day at my camp. Like those '3M: A Part of Our Heritage' commercials when Canada invented the wheel, pyramid, Superman, basketball…"

"I was under five, I'm sure, and living with Granny."

"Granny?"

"Your Grampy's mom," Mom said.

"Didn't know we were calling her that."

"*Anyway*, I was in an apartment and playing with some kids, and told them I had to go in for supper when I was called to come inside. Then later, I couldn't find it, and when my Granny asked where it was, I told her I left it outside and then when I went to get it, of course, someone had taken it. My Granny went around and found the person who took it, but when I did it again, she told me it was my own fault. Dad had been back from the war for about six years, so it was probably 1950."

"OK. Holly just emailed me and said Uncle Carl's guitar is from the early '80s and that he bought it at the Twelve Fret on Danforth. There goes my eBay gem! So another thing: there are photostats of your birth certificate, and it says you were born in Montreal. Is that true? How come you don't speak French or ever do anything French? I mean, we had that orange French dressing—"

"Yes, I was born in Montreal, and then when I was two, we moved to Toronto, but my Dad was overseas in the army. He came back when

I was three, according to my mother, sometime near Christmas of 1945."

"Right. That's when you saw him for the first time."

"I certainly don't remember the time, but my mom told me that all the families were down at the CNE and they gave out presents for the kids because it was near Christmas and I got a teddy bear and what I said was 'I got a new Tubby,' Tubby being my old teddy bear."

"Is that why you like teddy bears so much? You have twenty."

"I never really thought of that. I guess so."

"You should put up a profile photo on your Skype thing, Mom."

"Oh, I found your Macho Man jacket mixed in with my things when I unpacked. Do you want me to give it to Goodwill or do you want to keep it?"

"What for? A job interview?"

"That's funny," Mom said. "So you're going to see your dad for Christmas?"

"That appears to be the plan."

I stared at Mom's pots and pans that I had arranged on a wall in my kitchen. Sparse photos, paperwork and winter coats were strewn across my apartment, as if a crate of props had softly exploded.

After completing my sound-bite purging project, I tackled an abject "wrestlers who got fired" list. Then I compiled a moribund list of wrestlers who had overdosed or committed suicide, which was going to be sent over to the graphics department for some depressing design job.

Eddie Gilbert — 33

The Renegade — 33

Chris Candido — 33

Test — 33

Gary Albright — 34

Bobby Duncum Jr. — 34

Big Dick Dudley — 34

Brian Pillman — 35
Marianna Komlos — 35
Umaga — 36
Eddie Guerrero — 38
John Kronus — 38
Davey Boy Smith — 39
Johnny Grunge — 39
Chris Kanyon — 40
Billy Joe Travis — 40
Chris Benoit — 40
Rick Rude — 41

*

I mailed a postcard to my old house on Glenvale, and a reply came from a man (the homeowner, also named David, like my Dad) via email, as I had provided them with contact information should they require it. He, his wife and child had been there since early 1995. In his email was a brief greeting, and he expressed a curiosity as to why exactly I had sent a postcard to his house. I said it was part of a historical project. He was cordial, and also informed me that when cleaning the downstairs bathroom door for eventual renovations and repainting, his wife had discovered the words LET'S KILL DAD written on the top of the door. Clearly this was by me, of course, but to whom? I think I was cribbing the title from the film *Let's Kill Uncle*, which I've never seen. The new owners work in computer electronics.

I'm glad the mail was not seen as entirely insane, and my postcard was a non-hostile gesture. I wanted to contact the house, in its most current form. Also, I'm a ghost. Below is the basic trajectory of our four emails back and forth:

Our home in Leaside (161 Glenvale Blvd) just received a postcard in the mail yesterday. One side is your new book. The other side says

"Leaside! Novel! The historical house! 161! Best, John." Any idea what this is all about?

I used to live there! In the 1980s. Just a one-time postcard mailout to places of significance, celebrating the book's completion. It's with my agent now. Just felt it was fitting to send the "home" a card. Nothing more. Hope you are well, and I apologize if you were in any way disturbed by the mail. Not my intention.

Thanks for the info. No, I was not disturbed. Just intrigued. By the way, we purchased the home in 1995, so I guess we purchased it from your parents. One thing that did surprise us about the home is that two years after we moved in, my wife was painting the main-floor bathroom door. When she got to the top of the door, there was printing saying, "Let's murder Dad." I hope that was just a teenager getting frustrated. Good luck with your book. David.

Yes probably just teenage frustration. I can't honestly recall which one of us wrote those words. And our father is alive. Yes, we lived there 81–94.

*

One Sunday at Holly's house, she pulled out what she believed at the time to be our mom's cookbook—with what she perceived to be Mom's notes in the back. She read aloud from it while we started prepping for homemade pizza, her kitchen table now a talcum forest of flour and oil and tiny cans of dough and olives. Only after I consulted these ancient texts on my own did I realize it was, in fact, Grammy's handwriting and not Mom's. I recognized Grammy's elegant hand, which to a degree, Mom possessed; however, Grammy's handwriting was a tighter, more italicized cursive. I guess you could say her handwriting looked as though it wanted to take flight off the page, while Mom's was insistent on remaining there in cold true blue. In my preteen years, Grammy would write me letters with clippings from the trashy tabloid magazines she liked to read, sending me everything from "news" on Stevie Wonder's blindness (November 1985) to an article on wrestlers' salaries (July 1986). Grammy had noted that David enjoyed orange-flavoured cake icing in June of 1977. This made sense to me because I did recall a series of cakes that had an orange rind afterlife. The cookbook was around 500 pages, resembled a book you'd see in a church pew, and was dated by Grammy in 1947, when Mom was four.

Unlike most of our family newswire topics, Mom's relocation to Dallas was front and centre, emblematic and summer-fresh. By late June, Mom had unpacked the last of her winter coats, slacks (as she called them), blouses, sweaters, four teddy bears, thirty heavy books and other assorted memorabilia in Susan's guest room. Now 2,310.8 kilometers from Toronto, where she had lived since she was two years old, Mom's Skype talks were otherworldly.

"Oh, so, did you hear? Mom's working part-time for a football team!" Holly said, with vibrant animation.

"The Cowboys?"

"No, some college team, as a receptionist. Her friend Sue works there, too, like at the college, and got her a job. She charters their buses, handles any home-game matters. That's what she calls it: home-game matters."

"So she's like a part-time travelling secretary?"

"I don't think she travels with the team."

"Strange."

"She wants me to bring Sarah down for the holidays on July 4th and Thanksgiving."

Campy desert-themed cutaways suddenly bristled towards me in crisp, lightning-real flashes: the rocking chair, tumbleweed blowing by, the harsh, jagged additions to the classic southern meals in a sunny breakfast room Mom would perhaps insist on, or bringing out her hyper-coloured fruit salad with cottage cheese onto the banquet-sized tables—the way she would cut the vegetables in choking shapes as if trying to fit the pieces into specific dimensions: that quaint tunnel of space known as the throat, placed like a seal over the windpipe. Her use of watery broths and, according to Holly, temperamental treatment of meat, always somehow undercooked, underwhelmed, as if distracted by a higher purpose during culinary segments.

"On Glenvale, the oven used to cook things one hundred degrees too hot, so Mom got used to lowering the oven's temperature by a hundred degrees, and when we moved to Corinth Gardens, despite the fact it was a completely different oven, she kept cooking things on a lowered setting!"

Holly turned up the radio; a show on pigeons' mating habits blurted out in surround sound.

"This is nonsense. How do they prove any of this stuff?" I said.

"Science?"

"It's so fake and impossible to prove any of that is real. Pigeons think this and can count and can see the colour blue. Nonsense."

"You're just like Jesus Christ Kirk Cameron, your buddy from *Growing Pains*. You can go and read *the book* together on *Larry King*."

"Right," I said softly, noticing Holly had Uncle Carl's guitar in her living room.

"Do you know, I heard, if you strum it just right, the ghost of Uncle Carl comes out and tells you 'That sounds fine,' and turns down another slice of banana bread or to stay for dinner."

After an hour of pizza prep and clean up, we picked up Sarah from her friend's house and went to the park.

"I'm watching every move you make, Sarah," Holly said, adjusting her position on the driveway to observe a grandmother with two kids walk by, heads lowered, focused on the sidewalk squares, not noticing the silky soda drying on the lid of a discarded 7-Eleven cup along the grey desert of terrain.

"I'm a fairy!" Sarah said, her hands gesturing in twinkly moves.

"Oh, I don't know why people lie," I said.

"I was in the waiting room with her the other day and read this article saying kids born later in the year, like November and December, are given unnecessary medication more often than kids born earlier in the calendar year. Sounds like they couldn't sell ad space and just had this random drug piece put in instead of an ad for a Jeep," Holly said.

"Maybe it was a drug ad," I said.

"Like all drugs, right, have some risks of side effects; it's so vague, like the guy who wrote it just went to Wikipedia or interviewed a Tim Hortons drive-thru supervisor. This gender-journalism gem! Fuck him! Boys are always treated more often than girls but the Nov/Dec thing affects both... such inconclusive Pulitzer Prize material!"

"Is Sarah named after Sarah Connor?" I asked.

"Yup. That's why we only use two-million sun block."

"We should watch that tonight."

"What? *Terminator 2*?"

"Yeah. It's my favourite documentary."

"I like my sci-fi with a twist of mental-health subtext."

21)

Run

August–September 2010

The ex-wrestlers all thought they were unfairly paid and should have main-evented more. They all worked in laborious trenches now, loved their families and occasionally went to wrestling conferences to sign autographs. They all say wrestling has changed. They all gave off the same level of vulnerability. They were action figures...once...

A pile of eight-by-ten–inch glossies were now strewn across my desk with pink stick-it notes for each: *<FEATURE, FINISHING MOVES, BEST MATCHES, WARDROBE MALFUNCTIONS, FALL PREVIEWS? FOR FALL>*

This new editor moved with erratic steps through the office, on his cell doing play-by-play of his own actions. His gusty narratives were impossible to block out. "No, I'm here 'til four today, ate lunch already, about to check on that, the site was down this morning for twenty minutes, it's fine now, X-Pac is next week, we're confirming the location today, maybe Road Dogg too, I'm doing that now, I'm doing that this afternoon, those are supposed to be coming in any minute now, I didn't get those yet... Doink the Clown, Paul E. Dangerously too. I know! So cool."

Outside, the rain baptized the blind-covered windows as a dull thunder percolated in mystery.

As I waited for the usual tributary of exclusive video clips to download, I typed a formal-looking letter to Dad, signing off with:

THANKS FOR THE BIRTHDAY CARD AND CHEQUE. WHAT WAS THE OUTHOUSE ANECDOTE AGAIN? THE ONE WHERE YOU WERE A PYRO? SORRY MY WHOLE LIFE IS ONE QUESTION AFTER ANOTHER THESE DAYS. I WAS JUST GOING TO GOOGLE IT BUT I REALIZED I DON'T HAVE A CLUE WHEN IT WAS OR WHERE IT WAS OR IF YOU WENT BY A DIFFERENT NAME BACK THEN.

MUCH LOVE, NATE "THE FRANCHISE"

From what Holly told me, Dad was now made of straw and soot, barely 100 pounds and 5' 8" (he had shrunk a bit since his raging prime), still smoking and cooking all day long. His was a fire that never went out, the cigarette always an ember of death's orange-eye glow, the same as his favourite popsicle flavour, and how these tiny alien eyes guided us to my room, on his back, and the cigarette smoke and the lively follicles in his evil mustache all dancing around my face while hours later I would dream I was Randy "Macho Man" Savage and tear my father's moustache off in one swift move, bringing balance back to the galaxy.

September 1, 2010

What a friendly, communicative letter I just received from you, Nate. It motivated me to start writing, right away. Since you stressed that I write "neatly," I thought better to start by using this lined paper. To rhyme with paper, you want to know about my caper, with the outhouse. Let us back up a bit so that I may give you the background, as we didn't need an outhouse, and details speak volumes of the way your grandfather was treated by these particular country people, and the efforts he needed to go through to take care of his family.

As I said, we didn't need the outhouse. We lived in a very square, central-hall plan, cinder-block house in Dunnville. It was ill-heated— the furnace seldom worked, and we heated with a Quebec heater, which was turned on before we left our unheated bedrooms. We all gravitated to the tiny bathroom in the house to strip, wash, clothe and do other necessaries. I believe there was a wash stand with the traditional bowl and ewer. There was a bathtub, I believe, connected to pipes. There was however, no water.

Now, an aside if you don't mind. In order to have a bath, water had to be pumped from a cistern (not a well), heated and carried upstairs. To which a bucket of cold water might be added, after which we three could mindlessly enjoy the pleasure of a bath.

This is a long aside, on a rather long saga, I believe. One day Dad slipped on the back steps, I think. (We had one set of stairs going up, one set of stairs going down or vice-versa). He was scalded badly. In pain, he ordered Mother to put butter on the wounds. She complied and was later reprimanded by a wonderful doctor we had, but who had a terrible bedside manner. He said something like, "You foolish woman! Do you realize that I must scrape off all of that butter before he can heal?" (Another aside about the doctor: when he realized Mother was not a good producer of milk, in spite of her ample breasts, he explained that some cattle are good for beef, others are good for milk—your grandmother was not impressed and certainly not pleased.)

Back to the bathroom: There was one other fixture of note. Did you miss it? I don't think so. It is the "throne" of course. It consisted of a frame with a pool in it and a toilet seat on top. It had to be emptied at least once a week.

Another diversion or aside: To empty the can, Dad had to cross a road, transverse a neighbour's property, and dump the awful in the river, (sorry I can't remember the name; it passes Dunnville, Ontario) right across from the intake for the water we drank and cooked with daily. Needless to say, we had water that was very tasty, even without the tea bag. (We always loved trips to the grandparents in Hamilton and Toronto, where we could drink terrific water.)

From the foregoing, you will ascertain that we did not require an outhouse. We had a perfectly wonderful system in place to take its place. We could walk to the privy in the dark and never get wet (perhaps a bit cold).

I believe when Dad and Mom moved in, the outhouse was on its side—not erect. Dad, being conscientious, got it erect, probably with help from others. The next Halloween, it was on its side again, and some seven, eight years later, still on its side.

I don't know where the door was—probably on the bottom. My entrance was the opening over which the toilet seat would have been. In other words, what Newfies, the newly "have" province, would call the entrance to "The Long Drop." (There is a longer two levels of dropping positions. I don't know how it works but I'm pretty sure nobody on the lower level gets dropped upon.)

I hope you don't feel less of me if I tell you that at the age of about six, I used the "entrance" with an older young lady to play a form of doctor. I'm not sure what she was interested in, as she wouldn't have got much from me, but I was interested in poop and passing it. I met her three to four years later, but we didn't converse about it, to be sure.

Now you have the history of the poop-house. You now want to know about its demise.

Here we go: Dad now had three children and a pitiful, perhaps by then $1,200/year salary. (Perhaps he started under $1,000.) He had to take care of us. There was no effort to improve accommodations (at least until he had left, as they couldn't find another sucker to live there unless *they did.) Dad achieved a wonderful appointment at St. Matthias Church in Toronto. Dad talked to me, and no doubt Rebecca, trying his best to make it our decision to move to the big city where he was born, raised and schooled.*

"The big lie": The lies parents tell. I had a dog. Dad has always had a dog—he got one for me but said "He's the stupidest dog on the planet" (more or less). He knew the dog could not survive in the city and so told me that he took him to a farm. No doubt he did, but not to live there, but to die there. I didn't figure it out for at least ten years. Don't get me wrong: Dad did the right thing, no doubt. Santa Clause was, of course, another one, but Dad wasn't strong on the Easter Bunny.

You're now waiting with bated breath—when am I going to get to the story in question? Well, it follows: Dad wanted to leave everything in our home hunky-dory. There was an accumulation of newspaper in our country kitchen. (This is an area outside the kitchen, unheated, and useful for storing wood, some produce and whatever.)

He contracted a young lad, perhaps a bit older than I, and me, to take the paper out to the field behind the house and set it afire. Remember that I'm not yet seven years old. My birthday was within two weeks of arriving in Toronto, and I'm really not as smart as I look at this time.

We get the papers out to the field and try to light them. No go! It's too windy. The matches keep getting extinguished. I get this BRILLIANT idea. Why not put the papers in the outhouse? The wind won't be a problem. As it turns out, I was right. The papers started burning immediately.

It was smoky inside, so I went out. (By the way, this is fifty-year-old unpainted pine.) I remember deciding to get on the "roof" of the outhouse and pacing back and forth. Then I noticed smoke coming through the cracks, and soon flames. I thought better of staying on the roof "side" and got down.

In seconds it was all aflame. My neighbour went running to hide in the cellar of his home across the street. (The one Dad passed every week to get rid of the "crap.") I, on the other hand, ran to the house, through the country kitchen, into the kitchen, and cried "Mommy, give me water, lots of water, now! GIVE ME WATER!"

Mother tried to calm me, wondering what was going on. She finally looked outside to see the "shit house" afire and flames spreading towards the house.

Mother called the neighbour. His dad was home, probably worked shift work. She called the fire department, hoping they would respond. (I don't believe they had to as we were rural.)

The neighbour collected some water to spread on the grass and stop the spread of flames. I don't know what my mother said at all—I really don't think that she had a lot of cuss words, as I never remember one from her.

As for Dad, he heard the siren on one of his trips to minister, and he prayed for anyone who might be endangered by the fire. Little did he know that it was his "precious" outhouse that was the centre of the problem.

I made the papers the next day, perhaps for the first time, just days before leaving Byng (our county).

The Caption in the local paper: **"Little House to the rear of the Rectory burns to the ground"**

22)

Mesh

Monday, October 4th, 2010

I n the years of my assorted youth, (1986–1993), news of a wrestler's contract being terminated was never something I had access to, in any great detail. In fact, as I scrolled through a series of historical missives about wrestler's firings, I could scarcely recall a WWF contract being nullified before the era of wrestling dirt sheets (roughly 1996–1997). By then, the first wave of online tabloid culture had given rise to wrestling's rumour mills, full of hearsay and legit "industry" news. Up to that point, firings would be absorbed on air in a matter-of-fact way, incorporated into a storyline, or wrestlers would be "suspended indefinitely" until a new contract was negotiated. Many times, wrestlers' names were never brought up again; into the ether. My assignment this week was to gather material for a section called "SUSPENDED INDEFINITLEY."

In fact-finding quarantine, I gently Googled while listening to an extended remix of George Michael's 1996 song "Fastlove." I Googled that too. Reading the minutia about the song, finally, after years of wondering, I discovered what song George had gutted to add to the remix's multi-faceted hook: "*Sending you forget-me-nots, I want you to remember...*" from the song "Forget Me Nots," the 1982 hit recording by Patrice Rushen.

In a secret file on my desktop, I had made a growing list of long-winded questions, written in a one-way interview with Randy Savage, who I knew *never* gave interviews.

I left the file open, pushed my uneven wheeled chair back and headed out into the blissful wind. I crossed the street and went inside a quiet Italian café. I wanted a gin and soda, and squeeze of lime.

I studied the late afternoon water hole: a couple hunched in the early stages of unravel, red in the face, as one of them asked a question to the oddly toothed waitress with the shaved head, and the balding manager, counting French fries in the freezer, reminding whoever was in earshot to cut limes and put them in a clean pitcher when it's slow.

I exhaled violently, letting out a sigh that teetered on threat. On her cell, the bartender laughed, then shook her head.

"Totally," she said into her cell. I wanted to be drunk now. "It's odd to have secrets at an early age," she added, wrenching her neck away from me, still on her phone, disappearing partially behind a tray of dirty bottles and glasses.

PreliminaryQuestionsForRandySavage.DOC

QUESTION 1: Thanks for taking the time to talk with me. My name is Nate, and I have a lot of issues, I mean, questions for you. To start off, I've seen you live a few times at wrestling shows: Maple Leaf Gardens versus Ricky Steamboat with my sister and dad when you were Intercontinental champ in the summer of 1986, then at *Wrestlemania VI* in 1990, then again at Maple Leaf Gardens two more times, once against Razor Ramon, once against Shawn Michaels, in the early 1990s. I think around 1992. *Wrestlemania VI* was disappointing because it was like $65, and I had the worst seats. You were no longer the main event, and wrestled somewhere in the middle of the card. I think eighth. Strange because the last three Manias, you were top dog. I saved up the money from my job at Dominion, and during an intermission or something, I ran into some classmates who were watching from their dad's SkyBox. I pretended to be there with my cousin, which I wasn't. When I was seventeen (1992), my uncle bought me a video camera for Christmas, and it had these dubbing functions on it so I could make video dubs and do voiceovers. I made one video with you crawling back to the ring at SummerSlam 1992 in a match against the Ultimate Warrior, where Mr. Perfect and Ric Flair attacked you. The song I chose was "Ordinary World" by Duran Duran. You losing the match went with the thesis I was trying to prove, that the times had changed. I also made a montage with you and Hogan in it with John Lennon's "Jealous Guy." Then I'd edit clips of me playing road hockey or whatever. I guess I was dealing with "our" collective place in the world: no longer relevant or worthy of attention, no matter how colourful our attire was. Sorry, but that's how you made me feel. Your hyper-colours were like, so desperate. Things were better a few years before. I identified with your best-friend status with Hulk Hogan in 1987–1988 intensely. I had a best friend then, too. We were the Mega Powers, too, you know. When you and Hogan split in early 1989, Andrew and I bet two dollars on the outcome of your match against Hogan at *Wrestlemania V*. I bet on you, and you lost. I still believed in you though. Andrew kept saying, "I told you." That summer, you teamed with Zeus, that large muscular black guy, and I started working at Dominion and was trained by a black boy named Matthew. Andrew and I still hung out, here and there, but I wasn't invited up to his cottage, and he was more popular than I was from the previous year. So I'm skipping all over the place here in my first question to you because I'm a bit nervous. It's crazy, I mean, you were such a huge part of my life, and we both had best friends who were

more popular than we were, who were blonde and well, we both know how those two separate relationships turned out. I mean, in 2002 you wrote a whole rap album about how much you hate that guy, didn't you? In 1986, I built a toy-wrestling ring with a fruit crate and some bungee cords. One afternoon my father got mad at me for something and stomped his foot through the centre of the ring! I had to rebuild the ring with thicker wood that I deemed "foot-proof." I made a purple cape for your action figure out of material my mom had in her sewing box. Did you and your Dad always get along?

QUESTION 2: In the winter of 1986, Andrew came over along with my other friend, Eric. We made a tape-recording of us wrestling. I told Andrew I was Macho Man and Roddy Piper put together, and he started singing, "Put together as one, there are people dying… " imitating the song "We Are the World." I cracked up so hard. We took turns doing play-by-play as we wrestled. Andrew said, "Oh my God, he's juggling with a saw blade. They seem to be calling wrestlers in from all over the world to try and stop this… They say they'll be here tomorrow morning?! *What the heck, where are these people*!?" Years later, I used sound bites from the tape for the friendship memorial VHS I made for Andrew called "The Death of the Mega Powers."

On this same VHS tribute, I made another montage with a George Harrison song, "All Those Years Ago" that had clips of me and Andrew playing hockey in our driveway and the Mega Powers (you and Hulk) kicking ass in the ring. Also around this time, Dad started working at Andrew's father's funeral home; I think it sort of made Andrew think our family was desperate, or that we were beneath not only his family, but virtually every family in the community. My father became The Undertaker, grew pale and smelled of deadly chemicals. I wrote a lot of strange notes to my good friend Andrew at this time issuing challenges and questioning loyalty. No one really understood what I was going on about. Andrew was avoiding me at all costs, started playing squash all the time with his new best friend Alex from California.

I felt that Andrew and I had been friends for so long that the end of our friendship had to be at some sort of blowout *pay-per-view* spectacular. Towards the end, whenever I spoke to him, he would shake his head. He would shoot down every idea I had for us: going to a movie, playing road hockey, going shopping and going to the park on our bikes. Around that time, I also turned my jean jacket into a Macho Man Randy Savage ring jacket. I added bright colours along the arms, wrote out "Macho Man" in glittery paint on the back, and from the arms added long streams of bright material (yellow, orange and pink). I was going to wear it to school for Halloween along with a cowboy hat I'd spray painted orange but chickened out at the last minute. I didn't have a beard or sunglasses; mainly, I was afraid of being ridiculed. How did you feel wearing that stuff at the time? Did you ever wear it out in public? Outside of wrestling? It's not very practical attire.

QUESTION 3: Going back to 1994, you were working for the WWF but not wrestling, doing play-by-play. It was near Thanksgiving. On this night, I locked my mouth up with fork and gristle for the last time at the twentieth annual Thanksgiving dinner. That's when I found out our home was being sold and that I would have to find my own place to live. It's a shame that things happened the way they did, but in the end, I think people have always respected me for being someone who always stood behind his beliefs and stood up for himself. In the closing Moments of the meal, it was revealed that there was no plan on using me in a domestic sense any longer. Though I never surrendered a tear during the meal, history was made and a new era began. Confusion, anger, betrayal, embarrassment, disgrace, disgust—all compounded and formed a kind of squall in my pharmacy belly.

Leading up to Thanksgiving, I had attempted suicide twice, I mean not officially, how do you really define an officially licensed suicide attempt? Have your parents treated your personality like it was a dead corpse? For how long now? I cut myself with a steak knife. There were a lot of elements that worked during that period, a lot of political jealousies and rivalries... for years I didn't forgive anybody involved in that—from Dad to Holly to Mom... even our cat. But at the same time, I realize that life's too short to carry around hard feelings on an everyday basis.

Aware of my freshly inked contract with GOING INSANE AT TWENTY, my family devised a plan to call for the signed real estate deal to drop on the family table just as dessert was served. However, as despicable of a scheme as it was, many argue that it was a necessary act for them to concoct. I take issue with anyone who ever suggests that there was no other choice. But, Diane was under a fair bit of pressure financially back then. I can feel for her a little. I think Diane has told me herself—and I believe her—that she wishes things had been done differently and has regrets about it. In one evening, my family screwed me not only out of family status, but also my childhood bed and my dresser. Around this time, you left the WWF for WCW for a $400,000 contract. There's a rumour you called up Vince McMahon drunk the night you signed with WCW to tell him you were leaving him. Is that true?

QUESTION 4: I've edited about forty wrestler interviews since I started working here. Mostly guys who were mid-carders for a while in the late '80s or early '90s. But since a lot of them had key matches with bigger stars, we can attract visitors because they talk about these types of matches with bigger stars, and people are interested. But you would be a dream interview because you haven't made any public appearances or gone on the record since you released your rap album Be a Man. I feel like I'm drunk dialing you; anyway, the first year I knew you, that Christmas I asked for a set of workout weights and I studied photos of you and your forearms, the way your muscles formed along your triceps and biceps, even your leg muscles. I figured somehow I could resemble you in one way or another, I even thought of buying a small swimsuit and getting the stars and "Macho Man" on the back like you had, but the only colour they seemed to have at the local Eaton's was this bright baby blue, a colour you never wore in the ring.

In late June 1988, I christened my Spanish-Canadian classmate Juan Miranda the Juan Man Gang, after your opponent at the time, One Man Gang. After weeks of build-up, we had a cage match during the last week of school that consisted of us wrestling beside a linked fence, and the first person to reach the top of the fence won. Macho Madness was at its peak. I lost when Juan's friend, acting as his manager, held onto my leg, preventing me from climbing the fence. After the match, people said, "That's it?" I guess we could have thought of a way to make the match more interesting. About a month before, at an inter-school track meet, Juan had been throwing me around on the lawn, when Andrew kicked the fence and told Juan to stop it. And Juan did. It was just like when Hogan saved your ass all the time.

QUESTION 5: The story I am about to tell you is of historical fact that took place in Leaside between the years 1981 and 1992. I arrived in Leaside after moving from North Toronto. It was in Leaside where I first met Andrew Murray Beverly. He was a funny guy with a wit for insults and jokes.

During the early '80s, I became good friends with Andrew.

We went to the same church, located conveniently across the street from his house. He'd invite me over after church sometimes, and before you knew it, we'd become close friends. But not best friends.

A few years later, I found myself on a bus every morning going into East York to my new school, Cosburn.

I soon learned that Andrew was attending a school in the SAME area as I, and we frequently met up on the bus. One time I recall, on our way home from school, we decided we'd stay on the bus and go to Broadview Station. It was a very cold day, slowly turning into a blizzard. We made it onto the Bloor subway line, where we waited for twenty minutes in a delay of some kind.

Finally we made it to Eglinton Station, where we hopped on a bus heading for Laird. We got as far as just past Mount Pleasant when we decided the bus was taking too long. We walked in the snow through the high school field and saw people that were smart enough to actually get off the bus instead of doing our shortcut, tobogganing.

The next year was the commencement of our final year of public school. After the September strike, of which almost every day was spent with Andrew, I slowly began to take command of my status in my school, and by October, I had my first girlfriend (Corry). Andrew knew this, and whether he liked it or not I will never know, but what I did know was for the first time I saw the true nature of evil power that he so proudly possessed. Andrew went out of his way to make certain that my relationship with Corry would end in ruin. He managed to talk to one of my friends who also knew Corry, and whatever he said did something, because she dumped me like battery acid.

I did not talk to Andrew for a month.

The night he did this was just before Halloween. Andrew and I were preparing for Halloween, Friday, October 30th, 1987. At a party in another part of Leaside, I was losing my first girlfriend. Ninety percent because of Andrew, ten percent because of this guy named J.P.

I had a few other girlfriends that year but I never told Andrew about them.

Although at this time in our friendship, I did not particularly like him, Andrew and I realized we were best friends.

Spring 1988: A track-and-field meet at East York Collegiate for all East York public schools. I was sitting on the hill with some people from my class when my friend Juan (The Juan Man Gang) began to throw me around like a rag doll. My friends begged Juan to stop. He wouldn't. Crash. One giant kick from my 6' 2" friend on the nearby cage ended Juan's onslaught. Did you think you needed Hogan during that big run on top in 1988?

QUESTION 6: I'm jumping all over the place here! It's all coming out in a gushing wave. Around *Wrestlemania II*, March 1986, at school all the Greek boys were wearing your classic purple Macho Man T-shirt. Our school wasn't really full of Hulkamaniacs; it was a bit of an alternative school anyway. Later on, it reminded me of Roch Carrier's "The Hockey Sweater," which is a story about a boy who loves Maurice "Rocket" Richard, and his Montreal Canadiens sweater gets worn out, so his mother orders a new one from Eaton's, and when it arrives in the mail, it's the wrong jersey, it's a Toronto Maple Leafs jersey, and all his friends ridicule him, and he's so ashamed and has problems during a game of hockey with his friends, and the ref tells him to go to the church and pray for forgiveness, so he goes and prays that moths will come and destroy his Maple Leafs jersey. The image of all the boys wearing the Montreal Canadiens jersey reminded me of the hallways of my middle school, which, as far as I can recall, were full of Macho Man T-shirts, and not the yellow-and-red Hulkamania shirts. That summer, I watched you wrestle live for my birthday at Maple Leaf Gardens along with my sister and my dad. There were these boys that sat in front of us who were huge fans of yours. I was rooting for Steamboat, but these guys insisted that you would win. Over the next few months, I studied your matches more closely. When you crushed Ricky's throat with the timekeeper's bell, I just started thinking that you were the greatest. I admired you; I thought you got the job done. I thought you were likable even if you were doing bad things. I wanted to see more, highly anticipating your next moment of controversy.

QUESTION 7: In the beginning of 1996, that's where I'm next on the journey of our entwined lives, um, I had been on medication for nearly eighteen months, and after dropping out of university once again, began couch surfing, mainly at my dad's place which was on top of a funeral home where he worked. The funeral home was not Andrew's father's company, though my father still worked there from time to time. Holly was in her last year of university. My mother lived alone. My father was studying to become a funeral director, and I helped him every once and a while deliver bodies to the morgue or pick up flowers for a service. I'd tune in to see you on Monday Nitro feuding with Ric Flair over the WCW world title, but my biggest memory from this period was definitely the pharmaceuticals. It was March 1996, a cold evening.

My father had the night off or was on call, and I was joining him for a drink or something when I decided I would take all my Epivals. It was one of three pills I was on. So while he was on the couch in his living room, I lined them all up on his kitchen table. I had a tape recorder with me and was slurring as I did a running commentary of my actions. I just kept saying, "I'm going to do it," or "I've got to do it." The next thing I remember was being strapped to a table in the emergency room, a nurse telling me I threw up on her and the taste of charcoal in my mouth. My mom picked me up from the hospital, and I stayed with her for two days. This began the wilderness years. Ten years after first seeing you on television, there I lay, recovering from an overdose, the television screen off, the world stopped dead in its tracks. February 1986–March 1996: a decade of watching your Technicolor peacock meltdown, your voice gravelling away, colours fountaining out of you and that was it, 12–22, the complete seasons of my life, our life our various haircuts, mine moving from Hitler (like my Dad's) to Elvis or George Michael and yours with a dark dye tint, Photoshopping the grey out with a glossy brush of glistening chemicals.

Atmosphere

Within the confines of early half-sleep, I saw Mom's coal eyes up close as she prepared the salad for her new family. In her eyes, I saw the Reich eagle's wings spread wide and slow, as Mom glanced down to watch a carrot being chopped. But it was Christmas, and how quickly the satanic bird-Mom mirage changed its tune to a Christmas choir, Christmas foil, sleigh bells and endless belly laughter: ho-ho-ho. I couldn't get back to sleep. My restlessness was a long-playing vinyl groove, thick and succinct as a Gordon Lightfoot CD played on repeat, his voice ghosting on about heroes, Lake Ontario, highways, faces, longing and briny lost love.

I thought of Mom in Dallas. Time difference was an hour earlier. I'd call her later, before dinner, my corduroy pants silent, store-fresh, my sweater in its pre-gravy-stain virginity, my hair without grease, a nice light-brown sheen, and Mom would be elbows deep in mashed potato triumph. Today Holly and I were heading to her in-laws: the plan was to visit them, Dad, and whoever else we ran into on the short road trip.

It was now nine a.m. I had shaved, showered, watered plants, taken out garbage, put the remaining laundry away, packed up two-days' worth of clean underwear, socks, shirts and a suit jacket. A frantic urge besieged me to read my interview previews online at *Shooting Star Wrestling Review*.

Four interviews had been carefully prepared to go "live" online January 3rd.

I yawned hard, hand through hair, opened my eyes and they watered. A fat cloud greeted me outside. It began to fall apart.

The sun broke it open.

The phone rang. It was Holly.

"Holy shit," she said into the phone. I imagined Holly's nostrils working like well-timed pistons and gears redistributing moisture. She raised her red face and blurted out—"Liz was in a car accident last night... she's dead."

"What?"

"It's so fucking sad; we just started to talk about visiting each other, like maybe me going to BC."

"What happened?"

"She flipped over in her car and broke her neck on the highway, like midnight or something last night, on the way to her parents' place."

"That's awful."

"I just called to wish her a Merry Christmas, and Jake answered, he said he called me at home but I guess—"

"That is horrible."

"On top of all that, the rental property tenants or whatever are complaining there is no heat or water, so I have to go back to Toronto. Do you want to come or stay with Dad? I can come get you later, it's not that bad driving. I'll take Sarah to her friend's place for tonight."

"Whatever is easiest."

"Plus, you have to call Mom, she thinks we're on the hook for some sort of Texas Chainsaw New Year's Eve party. Forget it, too much is going on. I feel like I'm losing my mind."

"Yeah, she said something about that last week."

"Dad's gonna pick you up, at the train station as planned. I can't go though, OK?"

"Yeah."

By two in the afternoon, I was in Dad's Elgin, Ontario, trailer clutching my backpack full of clean underwear and gifts. Having travelled over three hundred kilometres, I was overheated, half asleep and not exactly ready for the drastic change in air quality.

"Dinner will be ready at five," Dad said, immediately returning to what appeared to be an overzealous all-day cooking marathon for two people.

"So you heard about Holly's friend then, I guess. Liz?"

"Yes. Very sad news."

I walked into the living room to see the same sad pink couches, aged eleven years from the last time I logged any serious time on them, statues of a once seemingly arranged life: these are the couches we'll put in our house; this is where we'll sit and read *The Globe & Mail* and drink coffee before we go to work in the morning—

Along a small wooden shelf, I saw a doll on a mantel, and my crummy acrylic lithium-based art, with a baby-blue and sand coloured-décor that looked ghastly like a small child's memorial bedroom.

Christmas Day passed like a warm Polaroid in crinkles: presents with rips fixed up, family-driven holiday movies on television complete with banter, snow being brushed off of shoulders, a wacky uncle careening into a snow bank, a gluttonous shellacking of Christmas stock footage, sopped up off the cutting room floor and remixed one more time.

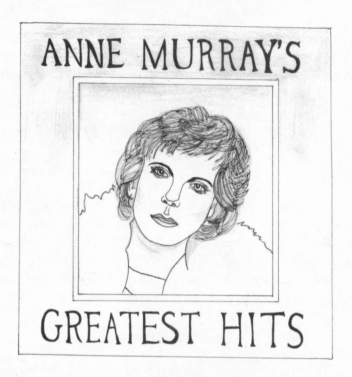

"Things are busy, lots of activity in town today," Dad said, lighting a cigarette.

"Oh yeah, which town is this?" I asked

I put on an Anne Murray CD and listened to "You Are My Sunshine." A tickle of pain crept into my stomach, so I focused on every dusty particle in the room.

The kitchen table was full of clutter and paper-route evidence, confirming my father's peasant status in this makeshift village.

"Fuck off, coffee," I said, blowing over the steam billowing from my cup. "Dad this coffee is crazy hot. I'll let it cool 'til St. Patrick's Day." I always spilled coffee when I first woke up, walked down the street or wobbled with a cup through subway traffic. Now sitting completely still could be added to that magical list.

I hadn't been in Dad's bunker in eleven years. Inside this cocoon of discolouring, a nicotine film of brown had formed along the ceiling and walls.

This yellowing behaviour.

Dad was now outside with his dog, Jazz, a stray he picked up one morning on his route two years ago, and who had some growth dangling from her chin that resembled a cancerous testicle.

The trailer was compact, smelled of rust and bristled with modulated carbs.

I looked down the hallway at the open bedroom door and crept into Dad's room; the smell of dog hair had reached a state of alchemic stagnation. My dresser and bed (1981–1994, bought at the Art Shoppe on Yonge and Davisville) lay dormant and snug in the eight-by-twelve bedroom. On the dresser's surface, a series of progressive photographs were garnished in theatrical dust in chronological order: his childhood on a couch with his siblings (1952), the love-locket-sized picture of Katie Flint (1965) and the classic (1982) family portrait of Mom, Holly, Dad and I taken for Northlea United Church. The final photograph came in the form of my father's living and breathing form asleep between eight at night and three in the morning, when he'd wake to do his paper route, snapped by God himself.

The coffee table was in a tool shed out back, as if it now served as a prop closet for some later re-enactment. Dad and I locking horns in the living room, his body going stiff, the low table getting the worst of it. *Why did you always turn your head and back, it's not self-defense and I'm not going for your head, and you watched boxing, so I don't get the positioning; it's like your body is pretending you are not being aggressive, when you are, it's frustrating. You're a dream, one I've conquered, now you're just static in the hallway Christmas morning, Boxing Day, April Fool's, St. Patrick's, and Halloween and back again—my father the boomerang.*

As I stared at Dad, all I could see was this extremely deflated version of the husky dinnertime character. He must weigh 114 pounds now, I thought, glancing at him sitting on the dusty-rose couch, as if he were preparing to tell the story of his life for the first time, like a stage actor delivers a monologue: the Sunday feasts, thick gravy, the family growing up in black and white on a farm house in Dunnville, moving to the big city, getting a big paper route, picking up the bundles from a drug store at Dundas and Ossington, at a store he would later work at as a delivery boy in 1953 when his brother Patrick, the last of five children, was born. Dad fiddled with an opal pushpin brooch, which he placed in a small dish, looked over a brochure and moved some plastic wrap from the kitchen table to the indoor stove. *No one would ever pay twenty-five cents to stand in the rooms he grew up in.*

"I'll be back in a minute and fix us something to eat," Dad said, disappearing down the hallway. For a millisecond, I imagined body slamming Dad through his floorboards. *Ohhhh yeeeeaaaahhhh! History beckons the Macho Man!*

Elizabeth's death was a fresh psychic scar that gouged the day. There were the mid-summer appearances at our dinner table after sprinkler prances, the three times Holly and Elizabeth locked me out of the house and laughed until my tears somehow lubricated the locks and they let me in, the time she kissed my cheek in my room and then vanished.

Dad's brow was knotted in a perplexed state. "Sound is off," he said, playing with the remote. "Did you turn it down?"

Holly said she and Elizabeth had met up a few times over the last few years. The early hours of Elizabeth's death and the vague details reminded me of Dad and his tragic pre-Mom life. *There was an accident.* That was the way it was laid out for me. *Someone* had died. Over time, Mom's reticence to speak on the matter rescinded, but she warned me that she had fought tooth and nail with Grandfather and my aunts never to speak of that time in front of her children. "I told them,

'I won't stand for it!'" she had once re-enacted for me with fierce facial struts.

"No," I answered. "Gonna take a shower."

*

This is how I pieced it together in my head in a tableau of near memory:

As Dad smoked outside of Old City Hall's large unfriendly doors, the image of his own father, (Grandfather) and his candle-illumined face moving towards him is inescapable. Grandfather slapped Dad hard in the chest with the ceremonial oil. "Remember David," Grandfather began, "those who receive unworthily do not actually receive Christ but rather their own condemnation," he said, pulling his shirt completely off...

It's the morning of the inquest: Dad feels the nicotine and sincere toxins on his lips.

Two nights earlier, the group had circled Katie's body at the morgue, a prayer and a chant and her body on the slab, no motion from her closed eyes. The stillness of her cold brown hair and tiny mischief nose. Dad stared at her form, blurring his eyes. Beauty and love and Katie extinguished. He felt militant in the morning, not refreshed. He combed his hair a hundred times. The calls from her parents and from Allan, her older brother. He downed his orange juice and in the bathroom, wiped his mouth on a facecloth.

The communal belief, equally digested, was that Katie had let the Devil inside her, so cult members spanked her to force her to push the devil out.

Satanic midwives.

Inside, Rachel Weir, a cheaply dressed, chirpy, gum-chewing twenty-year-old with bright eyes, scanned the entire courtroom, never settling on anyone, and took the stand at quarter-past nine. She rose when her name was called, and whispers scratched the courtroom floor. Rachel claimed the real leader of the group was Marilyn Williams. "She was the real leader. Whenever something went off in the dynamic of the group, like with one of the priests or something, they'd run to her ... the weirdest thing was, or troubling, that is, was the more sad you were, the more attention you got, like it was a badge of honour to come from a broken home or to have been abused somehow."

At five past ten, Dad (Katie's fiancé, twenty-six years old), who the press said could possibly be a clergyman himself someday, took the stand. Dour and strait-laced, Dad stated the facts with an icy speech. Some snickered and snapped their tongues in teeth sockets. Shocked at what can only be called a callous recollection of Katie's final days.

"On Tuesday, I paddled her a couple of times."

"Why?"

"It was childish behaviour." Gasps in the audience. His narrow face, wolf-eyes were a mask.

"Did you see Katie the morning of her death?"

"I cannot recall if I had gone into her [Katie's] room and spoke with her that morning."

He spoke in cold, formal language. Facial posturing and breath were carefully expressed, exacting, as if meticulously extracted from a guarded vault.

The doctors began to testify at 11:15 a.m. Katie Flint died in brutal pain. *An abscess in the brain stemming from a recurring ear infection broke, swelling into meningitis—killing her. The abscess was caused by inflammation and collection of infected material coming from the ear infection.*

The newspapers all had the same chilling vibe: a cult horror in a church rectory... Grandfather using bizarre rituals and brainwashing to control parishioners was no joke. *Katie Flint died an agonizing death and was not given proper medical attention when she needed it. When the paramedics found her, Katie was naked except for underpants. The Anglican Church continued to see exorcism as legitimate practice.*

Early the next morning the inquest continued with Grandfather walking boldly to the stand, his hair raven black, his voice chalky, boomed in parts, adding *hmmms?* to the ends of speeches. His answers were slow, puzzling and evasive, while his mouth remained at half-mast, false, never veering off into the jubilant or souring to droopy, faithless frown. He denied spanking Katie. Two days before her death, Katie complained of stomach aches and did not eat anything after breakfast Monday. She had a plate of crackers later that night and did not join the group for evening prayers. Tuesday was more shrieking and moaning. The day of Katie's death (Wednesday), Grandfather described her beaming smile as he entered her bedroom, how she was full of life, trying to get better from whatever was ailing her.

"She wanted to beat this," he said. "She threw her arms around me, and I prayed for her with all my heart with all I had. And she went quiet and sobbed a little." He denied virtually all allegations, scanned the courtroom to lock eyes with Rachel. As he got off the stand, she hissed at him, "You're supposed to be a Christian, not a damned liar!"

After a break for lunch, more witnesses took the stand. The city's coroner was called to make testimony. Dad felt his temple pulsing. Katie's older brother, Allan, wrung his hands over his knees. When asked the cause of death, the coroner stated, "Improper, well, non-existent medical care, actually."

Later in the day, when Grandmother took the stand, she dodged nothing, replying in negatives to the question. No, it didn't occur to her to run a bath, call the doctor, check for fever, or take Katie's temperature. Yes, she knew Katie had vomited, one of the girls on her floor mentioned it, and there had been buckets deployed and mops and the girls taking turns checking on her. No, she had no knowledge of Katie's meals that week—if she had missed meals, consumed them, kept them down. No, she had definitely not slapped Katie, and that noise was probably Katie hitting herself, something, Grandmother said, she was known to do. The intensified cries continued into the next morning (Wednesday). Katie's health had changed. Piercing shrieks, softened by walls. As they washed dishes, as they set the table as they folded bed sheets. Yes, they all could hear agonizing octaves. Not constant. Sometimes she would sleep.

By noon the day of Katie's death, Grandmother was fed up with the girl's tantrums, and called Mrs. Williams's home, where she asked her to get Grandfather to the rectory to visit Katie immediately and perform an exorcism to rid her of the devil once and for all. Two hours later, Katie was dead.

One ex-member testified, saying they were not faith healing. "They were unsettling to be around. Something felt wrong. I couldn't enjoy even the simplest Moment of a day without having to listen to some protect-me-from-the-devil speech."

The last day of testimonies dragged on until Ms. Julia McCullough came forward, ending the queue. "I was at St. Joseph's Hospital about a year ago. I was awaiting surgery for cancer, when a friend told me about this faith-healing group and thought I should like to meet with them [Grandfather]. I agreed and immediately regretted it. After only minutes, he insisted my lifestyle was seducing Satan." Grandfather visited Julia the night before her operation, reciting an odd prayer he told her was designed to chase out the devil from her insides. "Something about how hell's atmosphere had been breached, and I must have faith to seal and repel it, that I had to repair the hole I had left open for Satan to find me... that I was possessed and had I come to see him earlier in the year, I wouldn't have cancer, intimating my disease was caused by my false way of living, and when I told him to please leave, he looked at me, gripping my leg, and said, 'You will one day need me still,' and told me he'd pray for that day each morning until I came to him."

After ninety minutes, the jury agreed my grandparents were negligent in Katie's death. Dad's grey eyes in a small newspaper photograph, the caption underneath read: "Planned to Marry Dead Girl."

Dad's hollow-looking face, caught in the flashbulb, was part of a mysterious family tableau, one he would never walk away from completely. Less than two years later, he married Mom. Two years after that, Holly was born.

*

The exactly named No Frills items, labelled in yellow, were all over the trailer like a bomb-shelter exhibit. Dad dwelled over the kitchen counter, no method to his pattern as he tweaked the heat levels on the elements, perhaps deciphering, dreaming part of his life was no longer numb, that he could access a reality chamber devoted to certain periods, certain individuals or entities.

He was a real-life spectre. Dad took plates down from the cupboard and placed the four potatoes on them, salting each one heavily. He moved like paper in the kitchen, tightly belted pants and a black skull-and-cross-bones T-shirt I had given him for Christmas, his cigarette smoke a shadow tailing him in a blend of fuzz and dust, while his antique runaway dog, Jazz, scratched and itched away, never walked, never groomed, but loved. Still attached to the chain from outside, it followed her wherever she walked.

A large swarm of birds fluttered past the trailer's main window. It looked like a school of fish in some well-timed aquatic outtake. "Want to go outside?" Dad opened the screen door, letting Jazz and the chain ramble in the winter blitz.

"Your reception is out. I'll go look at the antenna, might be a branch in the way, the wind maybe."

The screen door banged open with a ruckus, and Jazz walked in, crooked, snorting like a filthy stray horse. As she shook and her metallic collar and tags clobbered into one another, David looked down at her quizzically. She snorted at his feet.

"Who hath dared to wound thee?" Dad said, looking at his weary dog.

"Hmmm? You have a burr on the side of your paw? Let me get some tweezers," he said, returning the dog's paw to its bashful state where the two burrs clung.

"I think she has them on her back legs too, Dad," I said.

Dad moved hastily through from the washroom with tweezers and ointment, "Here you go, my darling," he said, down on his knees. As he repaired the wounds and extracted the burrs, the adjacent roads were filled with a chorus of car honks and well-wishers. Car lights went on and off as blobs of coat collars went from one vehicle to another.

"There you go," Dad said, rubbing Jazz's head.

"Some birds," Dad said, adjusting his footing, "have been attacking my roof the past week or so."

"I think I saw some activity on the roof when I took Jazz for her swamp run," I said, moving towards the door. "I'll grab a saw just in case we have to cut down the antennae."

Dad shook his head as if admitting he understood I was joking, and even possibly found the line entertaining. It was harsh and bright outside in the afternoon with the day-old snow and ancient sun collaborating away.

He sauntered after me, head lowered, focusing on the ground's imperfections, the soft spots. I climbed the tree until I could peek over the roof.

"So?" Dad asked.

"The wind has blown the branch into the antenna a bit," I said, looking down at Dad.

I began to saw the branch. Dad walked towards Jazz, nodded at her and looked up at the activity in the tree.

"Watch out," I said, "it's going to come down." I pulled the saw from the cut. The branch hung on, about to snap clean off. I climbed down, watching clumps of snow fall first from the tips of the cold green buds. The branch was heavier than expected and was hell-bent on hitting Dad.

On the ground, I moved towards him. "Watch it!" I said, and pulled him back several steps gently, the top of the fallen branch brushing his feet.

"Perfect," I said. "We can eat that branch for lunch."

Dad laughed. "I'll fix us a tuna fish *sandweedge*," he said. I looked at Dad's dog with the dangling testicle on her chin, and the fallen branch, dragging both towards the trailer. Leaving the branch by the woodpile and ax, I took Jazz towards the small dirt road surrounding the lot of trailers. "Let's go for a walk, dog mutant." She galloped, pulling me in quizzical directions.

When I entered the shack I saw two sandwiches were made and sitting on plates, beside which an open bag of potato chips glistened in the light.

Wreaths of smoke and steam rose from another pot and the dusty sheen of the trailer's innards greeted me in a daytime constellation. I found my father lying asleep under a fraying blanket covered in a pattern of white blossoms.

After dinner (roast beef and potatoes with thick gravy, turnip and green beans), we polished off a bottle of red wine while watching an old Bruce Willis film.

"See you in the morning," Dad said, turning into a blur of soot and grey sweater down the hallway to his bedroom.

24)

Sooner Than You Think

Friday, May 20th, 2011

The morning was bright yellow and loud with traffic on Lansdowne and started out with a rental van, tons of empty garbage bags and Holly ordering herself a large tea and me a regular coffee from the Tim Hortons.

"Sure you don't want anything else?"

"I'm good."

At her rental property, we dealt with flood damage, cleaning and wiping up along the floorboards, replacing them in some cases, as we repainted and stain guarded, moved clumps of wet and dead drywall into plastic bags, then into the truck.

The heat from the sun outside began to fill the basement. There was a bad, heavy stink.

"The city will be here in an hour," Holly said. "They think it's because the pipe is clay, or part of it is clay, anyway, so they have to rebuild it from scratch or something. We also need to go to the apartment where I moved the tenants and move some stuff out to make room for them."

"Sounds like an adventure."

"How's *whatshername?*" Holly asked, while we cleaned and sprayed, re-painted, and garbage-bagged the flood mucus.

"Who? Oh, Sherri?" I said, taping a wall we were about to paint. "She's good. She told me about this time at a convention last week when this old man tried to pick her up who was, like, sixty, and it turned out to be Ted DiBiase, who was there signing autographs!"

"Who was he again?"

"The Million Dollar Man. She said he was old and he insisted he was important, and asked her up to his hotel room."

"Gross," Holly said.

"Yeah and he's like a born-again Christian or something, like a minister."

After four hours of basement autopsying, recovery and scrubbing out the dirt and funk, my fingers were pruned in a mulch of varying chemicals.

"I'm going to get a coffee at the corner. You want one?"

"No. We'll grab something to eat in an hour. There's a Portuguese café just down the street."

As I emerged from the basement, the smell of bleach followed me; I felt baked in a toxic crust and could only imagine what it was doing to my sneaker treads. I grabbed a coffee from the store next door, and as I sipped from the Styrofoam, I spotted a tiny library branch. I sat down at a fifteen-minute express Internet terminal, complete with a crusty mouse and antiquated tower-styled computer, even a slot for floppy discs.

The floppy-disc slot reminded me of countless wait-times for the slowest loading 8-bit video games with their minimalist music and square-pixel heads, noisy disc-drive stutters and countless hours holding onto the joysticks, praying the program wouldn't crash and we'd have to reset.

My face twitched from the coffee and its formaldehyde effects.

On Yahoo's homepage a thumbnail photo of Randy Savage appeared with a headline full of doomsday terminologies: "fatal," "accident," "crash" all entered my peripheral like bits of sand and grit in senseless wind. My breathing accelerated.

Clicking on the link revealed the story of the crash. My heart palpitated and my throat felt dense with interference. The words on the screen structurally were off-putting, false and cruel.

On edge, I checked Twitter, CNN and CBC to confirm the page's content was of sound mind:

A source tells Fox News the ex-wrestler "suffered a heart attack while driving and hit a tree." Florida Highway Patrol said Savage, 58, leapt a concrete median, veered into oncoming traffic and smashed into a tree head-on. He died from his injuries at Largo Medical Center. Savage, whose real name is Randy Poffo, had just celebrated his first wedding anniversary with his wife Lynn. It was his second marriage.

I logged off and pushed my chair out, leaving the library with mulched socks from the flood repairs and a sting in my chest.

Savage's death appeared to you at eleven in the morning at a west-end library Internet terminal, his head swathed in bandanas, cowboy hats or the rare glimpse of him with ratty brown hair strewn in sweat and post-battle honesty. This May afternoon, 2011, just like the day the world came to know the name Randall Poffo (a.k.a. Randy Macho Man Savage) feels off, corkscrewed, nudged; as if you were targeted to absorb and reflect such late-breaking news. His odd face, hidden in sunglass gimmickry, multiplied by the Internet presses, world newswires, flooded the earth and the whole world to the tiniest mentions, cribbed links, general searches; the world grazed on the news all day and night, his body (in highlight clips with complimentary voice-overs praising his success and lasting impression on a generation of now adult men and women) jumped and leapt and breathed in a series of manicured

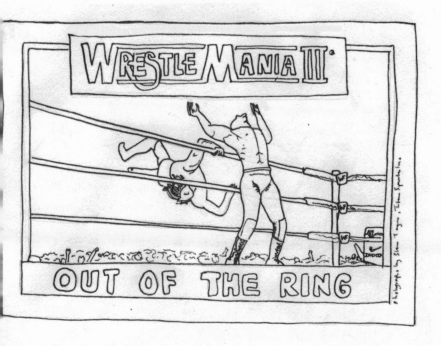

action-packed Moments, while his body lay in a Florida morgue await-
ing autopsy, no longer with Momentum...

Back at the rental property, my face must have appeared lifeless,
perhaps animated with vehement contemplation, because Holly asked
me what was wrong right away.

"Macho Man died. I just read online, at the library... just down the
street."

"What?" Holly's face was paused, the heat and smoldering mechanics
of swamp repair temporarily suspended around her.

"He crashed his car this morning in Florida."

The plan was to work through the weekend completing the temporary apartment switch for Holly's tenants while repairing water damage as the city workers replaced what turned out to be an ancient 1960s clay pipe from inside the house.

Saturday and Sunday were more shifts teeming with moving and sorting and sanding and patching up. In all of this labour, I hadn't checked a newspaper for any clippings. I was so beat, and despite the Internet's boundless fortune of replica and press releases, I wanted the texture only found in newsprint.

As I approached my apartment, Mom's ID appeared on my cell. "Yeah, no, I got your message, was just charging my phone for a bit this afternoon, didn't plug it in, yeah, Macho died, yesterday morning, no, Friday morning, yeah, no, I haven't really thought about it, you did, you got the paper? What do you mean? It's a paper, who cares? That would have been so cool from the *Dallas Sun* you should have kept it. No, I'm not at Holly's, I'm out… yeah, I think the house is all fixed, you'd have to ask her—yeah, sure, talk to you later."

I pawed for keys and pushed myself up the three steps. I fiddled with the keys, tap water, shoes off. I was now home.

Monday, May 23rd, 2011

At ten thirty in the evening, WWF's flagship television program, *Raw,* aired a short montage tribute to the passing of Randy Savage. As the announcers set up the clip, I Skyped Mom and told her to flip around and find *Raw.* Combining clips with a voice-over and a song by Coldplay, the production was slick and colourfully vibrant.

When it ended, my mom turned her gaze back to me and said, "I liked the shots of the children smiling in the crowd."

The children's pale arms with fist pumping and throats cheering, eyes excited and alit in sugary delight, was as memorable as anything in the montage. Those cheers, twenty-three, twenty-four years old, were preserved in their anonymous and raw honesty.

"It was sweet," Mom surmised.

"Gotta big day tomorrow. I should get to bed."

"OK, sweet dreams."

"You too."

SUGGESTED DISCUSSION QUESTIONS FOR BOOK CLUBS

1. Chapter 1 is titled "Bizarre Love Triangle." What connections can you see in Nate's relationships and friendships to the song title?

2. Does Holly have a positive influence on Nate and his anxiety around most people? She is inclusive with her friendships around Nate, but do you think this causes him to withdraw from other chances of making friends?

3. The polarity between Nate and his father's brash and stubborn nature cause their conflicts to remain unresolved. Do you think Nate's submissive nature changed as he grew weary of his father?

4. In regard to the chapter titled "True Faith," do you think Nate holds a sort of faith in his friendship with Andrew? Is it a false faith that is perhaps not reciprocated?

5. Why do you think Nate so readily accepts Andrew's aggressive assertion and, at times, what seems like bullying?

6. How do you think Philip and Sandra's homophobic insults influence Andrew and Nate? Do you think it offends them or makes them more paranoid?

7. Do you think Nate feels like he has to be protective of his mother when his father gets violent, or does he look to her as a protective maternal figure?

8. Do you think Nate's mother called in the therapist because of a genuine concern for her son, or was Nate right to feel victimized?

9. What does the poem that follows "Round & Round" (Chapter 4), titled "The Phantom Cousin" reveal about Nate?

10. Why do you think Nate felt "somehow relieved" when leaving Andrew's place after their big fight?

11. Describe Holly and Nate's relationship dynamic as siblings and then as friends.

12. Does Nate's seemingly purposeful self-alienation in his school life and home life make him a more likeable or sympathetic character?

13. Nate seems to place Andrew on a pedestal, and it's definitely not reciprocated. Is there something you can predict about the friendship?

14. Why was Nate so set on attempting to pursue university against the wishes of his family and therapists?

15. Why does Nate fixate on the Menendez case? How does his description of the murder case and trial relate to his own family drama?

16. What does Nate's attachment to his analog camcorder say about his aptitude for communication? What does the accidental breaking of the camcorder represent?

17. Why do you think that Andrew has such a profound effect on Nate for so much of his life? What could have happened if their relationship had continued?

18. Why do you think Nate accepts disrespect from the people he meets in life?

19. Later on in the novel, in Part III, what does Nate's and his mother's game of phone tag represent in their relationship?

20. Does the fact that Nate manages to find a job in Toronto help his hopeless view on life, family and careers?

21. Does the family dynamic get better or worse, and in what way, when Nate's mother and father live separately?

22. Why do you think Holly could remain so level-headed among the family drama, while Nate has a harder time balancing his relationships? Is it disruptive to how the sibling dynamic played out?

23. Describe what Elizabeth's death represented for both Holly and Nate.

24. What changes in Nate when he finds out that Randy Savage has passed away?

25. How does Toronto as a setting add to or detract from the story? Does it make is more "real"? Can you feel the main character's connection to the city?

IMAGE: Dad & Nate

About the Author

Nathaniel G. Moore is the author of five books, including *Wrong Bar*, nominated for the 2010 ReLit Award for best novel, and *Let's Pretend We Never Met*, which the *Georgia Straight* called "breathtaking." His fiction has appeared in *subTerrain*, *Joyland*, *Taddle Creek* and *Verbicide Magazine*, and he's written for Bravo TV in the short film *Sahara Sahara*. A frequent contributor to *Open Book: Toronto*, the *The Globe & Mail* and *This Magazine*, Moore lives in Toronto.